THE LAST BEAUTIFUL GIRL

The Last Beautiful Girl

NINA LAURIN

sourcebooks
fire

Published by Sourcebooks Fire, an imprint of Sourcebooks
P.O. Box 4410, Naperville, Illinois 60567-4410
(630) 961-3900
sourcebooks.com

Library of Congress Cataloging-in-Publication Data
Names: Laurin, Nina, author.
Title: The last beautiful girl / Nina Laurin.
Description: Naperville, Illinois : Sourcebooks Fire, [2021] | Audience:
  Ages 14. | Audience: Grades 10-12. | Summary: Isa Brixton and her new
  friend Alexa, who is a skilled photographer, start an Instagram account
  featuring portraits of Isa in the crumbling mansion she now calls home,
  and soon the rising numbers of Isa's followers online and at school
  match the growing darkness in her personality.
Identifiers: LCCN 2021014776 (print) | LCCN 2021014777 (ebook)
Subjects: CYAC: Social media--Fiction. | Popularity--Fiction. |
  Mansions--Fiction. | Spirit possession--Fiction. | Horror stories.
Classification: LCC PZ7.1.L38233 Las 2021 (print) | LCC PZ7.1.L38233
  (ebook) | DDC [Fic]--dc23
LC record available at https://lccn.loc.gov/2021014776
LC ebook record available at https://lccn.loc.gov/2021014777

Printed and bound in Canada.
MBP 10 9 8 7 6 5 4 3 2 1

THE LAST BEAUTIFUL GIRL

PROLOGUE

LIKE THE ONES BEFORE HER AND THE ONES AFTER, IT'S THE
glow that draws her in.

Amory, Massachusetts, is a college town, and, among college
students shuffling across campus in sweats and ripped jeans, Desiree
knows she won't stand out too much. She ditched her phone—even if
it's switched off, she has a superstitious fear of being tracked through
it—and she's never owned a watch. Who the hell wears a watch anymore?
But now she wishes she did because she has no idea what time it is, and
she worries she might be late. It's already getting dark, and she can only
guess what's happening elsewhere. She can see it in her mind's eye: the
old building that used to be a church but is now a theater, all lit up,
the backstage abuzz with activity, people running back and forth, wired

from usual pre-show jitters. She loves this. Her costume, she knows, is already waiting for her on one of the mobile racks with their creaky wheels. The exquisite dress is sheathed in plastic, and a piece of tape with her name scribbled in Sharpie marks it as hers. Desiree, the star.

The house stands a way off from the road, grass and open space around it marking it as different. Special. It's a beauty, shockingly well-preserved. The only giveaways are the boarded-up windows that now look merely dark, an inky abyss without the reflective gleam of glass.

It doesn't occur to Desiree how she can see all this when there are no streetlights anywhere near, no lights from within the house itself. The sky is cloudy, a heavy indigo mass devoid of moon or stars. But there's a glow about the place. The house is waiting for her. Welcoming her. Like it's hungry for her presence.

Just like all the other times, she has no trouble getting in. The front door is solidly gated off, but the doors near the back are unlocked, and she slips in with barely a creak of hinges. Lighting her way with a trusty flashlight, she goes in.

The first time she came here—only weeks ago, although it feels like months—she was surprised by how clean it all was. Especially since no one seemed to guard the place or take care of it. Like the house hadn't quite given up on itself.

Downstairs is all emptied out, save for a chandelier wrapped in many layers of tarp and cobwebs. Upstairs is where all the furniture is stored, also wrapped to protect against dirt and time.

But the most astonishing things, by far, are the paintings. They're all of the same woman: pale face, auburn hair down past her waist. The costumes and poses and styles vary, but it's definitely her.

Desiree continues all the way to the fourth floor. Catching her breath—the climb left her more winded than she expected—she looks around: the hallway is blocked by some old wooden planks haphazardly nailed together. There are even bits of old, discolored warning tape. Just like last time, she ducks under it without effort.

At the end of the hallway, the door stands out, its unusual ornamentation unlike anything else in the house. The beam of her flashlight reflects in the smooth, shiny lacquer of its surface; she can see the ghostly outline of her own face. When she grasps the handle, the door opens smoothly.

There are paintings of the same woman everywhere. The smallest one would probably reach just above her waist, the gilt of its frame glinting dully. She's overcome with the sensation of being watched, like the paintings' eyes move, ever so subtly, to follow her every movement. Except, before, she used to find it comforting rather than eerie.

"I'm sorry I took that dress," she says out loud, not sure who she's talking to. "But we needed it for the play, do you understand?"

At the same time, she knows, deep down, she's being dishonest. *She* needed it for the play. But, earlier today, she realized she couldn't go on stage in it as it was. Something was missing, the costume incomplete.

She feels along the wall: in the corner, cleverly camouflaged with the same drab wallpaper that covers the walls, is another door.

It gives a soft click and opens to reveal a storage space. The lid of the trunk lifts without resistance. The ray of light from Desiree's flashlight roams the trunk's dusty insides, but, except for some fabric at the bottom, it's empty.

An unpleasant jolt travels up her spine. It was here—the jewelry box. It has to be here. This is where she left it last time, she's certain. No one else has been here since. Right? She never told a soul that she came here.

But the jewelry box is nowhere to be found, just like the stunning necklace and earrings inside it. She dreamed of it at night. She saw herself in the costume, with the earrings and necklace glimmering along her jawline. That's why she's risking it all to be here.

She grabs one piece of the fabric at the bottom and pulls it out, gingerly shaking out the dust. It's a dress, one she hasn't seen before, and she has to admit it's pretty. And well-preserved, given how old it probably is. A gown of dark-red velvet. A thought flits through her mind: *if I wore this to prom, everyone would die.* And, so, curiosity wins: she steps into the dress and eases it up her torso. It's not a bad fit, truth be told.

At the other end of the room, she notices another door.

Desiree has to duck to pass through, but, forgetting all caution, that's exactly what she does.

At first she thinks this new room is filled with windows. The light of her flashlight bounces like mad back and forth. Then she realizes that it's all mirrors, over a dozen standing mirrors, nearly floor-to-ceiling.

Mesmerized, Desiree looks around. From every surface, her own face stares back at her.

The darkness behind her seems to be stirring.

In a rush of panic, she spins around, only to realize she was seeing the mirror's reflection in the mirror opposite. Face-to-face, the mirrors create the unsettling effect of a dark, endless tunnel into nothingness.

With a sigh of relief, Desiree turns back to her reflection.

Only it's not there. Nothing's there.

And then, just as quickly, there is something. It takes Desiree a beat to figure out what—or whom—she's looking at. Auburn hair still snakes around a face in wild curls.

But the face is gone. In its place, a smeared wax mask with black holes where its nose should be. Exposed teeth jut out of gray gums. Only the eyes are alive. Locking onto her own.

Choking on a shriek, Desiree stumbles back, away and away until she trips over the hem of her pilfered velvet gown and topples to the floor. She doesn't hear the house creak and groan like a waking beast. She can only look and look and look, her gaze forever fixated on the mirror.

The floor beneath her creaks too. Dust—or ash?—rises up in small black puffs.

Floorboards crackle and splinter, giving way beneath her weight.

Like the ones before her, and the ones after, Desiree never sees it coming.

PART ONE

ONE

THE FIRST FULL REHEARSAL IS ROUGH IN THAT WONDERFUL way. Starting a new work of art always is. And, in theater, it's even more so: an actress is both the medium and the message. I'm not just writing a story or painting a picture and then ditching it—I *am* the story, I *am* the picture, I'm all of it at once, with my body and face and soul.

But, of course, a great costume never hurts either.

I twirl in front of the full-length mirror in the costume room. The dress is over the top on purpose. Heavy burgundy velvet with gold brocade and giant rhinestones, the dress is fresh off the rack, but it fits me like a glove. I do an exaggeratedly clumsy curtsy, flipping the hem of the skirt up over my knees like my character would have done. I look a little ridiculous but also, maybe, kind of hot.

Because this role is daring. This role is not for the girl who wants to play the princess and the ingenue. Sure, Yvonne is a princess, but…a different princess. This role is for a girl who's not afraid of looking ugly or having people laugh at her.

Our drama teacher had doubts when we started casting. I think even my best friend Eve thought, deep down, that I couldn't do it. Not going to lie—I had butterflies in my stomach before my turn. But, at the audition, I killed it. I left everything I had on the stage. Even before the cast list was posted, I knew the part was mine.

Eve sticks her head through the door of the costume room. "There you are! Are you coming? We're about to start."

Eve is dressed in her normal clothes: high-waisted jeans, a crop top, and those flats her mom brought her from Milan that the whole school envies. She looks me up and down, gown and all. "It's not a dress rehearsal, Isa."

"I know. I think I'll wear it anyway. It's what Yvonne would do, right?"

"You're way too pretty to be Yvonne," Eve teases.

"Yvonne isn't meant to be ugly," I say. "The other characters just hate her because she doesn't fit in. Besides, I think that's kind of the point, isn't it? That looks aren't everything."

Eve rolls her eyes and taps one of those fancy flats. I'm one of the few at our Brooklyn private academy whose parents aren't uber-rich—and, believe me, no one at this place ever lets me forget it. Most of their parents are bankers and CEOs and the like while my mom is a photographer and my dad does something with school administration and rich people. Eve's shoes from Milan cost more than my entire wardrobe, and, if I want to keep up, I better get creative. Even then, every so often some mean girl will quip about how much she loves my "daring choice of an H&M skirt" or something like that.

It all changed when I joined the theater club. They began to respect me, grudgingly. And this role will take me to a new level. At the end-of-term play, everyone knows there are college admissions people in the audience, looking for talented students. Not that I'll ever tell anyone, except maybe Eve, but I could really use a scholarship.

"You've got this, Isa," Eve says. "You'll act the hell out that role. And, if they're too stupid to give you a full ride to every college in the universe, then it's their loss."

I steal one last glance in the mirror, and a dark thought eclipses my joy like a cloud.

As if picking up on it, Eve asks, in a lowered voice, "And your parents? Any news?"

"They haven't decided yet. They're up there now, touring stuff, I guess," I answer carefully. I don't want her writing me off yet.

Eve comes over and gives me a hug, making the skirt of the velvet gown rustle. "It'll be no," she whispers. "And even if it's yes, my offer still stands. My mom is on board. It'll be fine."

"It'll be fine," I repeat, willing it to be true.

"Now go and knock them dead."

I give her the thumbs-up. Velvet dress swishing around my ankles,

I leave the costume room and head toward the stage entrance. There's a gasp from my classmates. Wearing the dress was the right choice.

If my parents go through with this—if they actually make me move and leave all this behind—I might literally knock them dead.

TWO

"I'M NOT MOVING UPSTATE WITH TWO YEARS OF SCHOOL left, Mom."

I'd thought about this at length and decided to play it rational. If I want to convince my parents that I'm mature enough to be on my own in Brooklyn, having a shit fit won't help the cause.

"Think about it. It's ridiculous. I'll have to go to a new high school, which probably doesn't even have a theater program. Everything I've worked for will be for nothing!"

"It won't be for nothing," my mom says. "You're being dramatic, Izzy."

"Mom, *dramatic* is just a sexist word to describe a woman who's passionate about what she does. And I'm not being dramatic."

Only now I realize she used my childhood nickname. Not a good sign. Only second-worst to my full name, *Isabella*.

"We thought of everything. The high school in Amory is great. One of the best in the country..."

"So is my actual high school," I point out. "And I don't have to start over from zero."

"...and they have a theater program. I checked. Theater, dance, arts. And they do at the university too."

"What does it matter?"

"You'll have a leg up in admissions, for one thing. And it'll be free, for another."

"There's so much wrong with that, I don't know where to even start." I fold my arms over my chest. "Taking away someone's well-deserved spot in the program because my parents work there? You're always the first one to speak out against this stuff."

But, for some mysterious reason, my mom's social consciousness seems to have vaporized. *Of course.* We don't need it anymore, now that it's inconvenient, do we? This whole new development is so out of character that it's like someone swapped my once-cool mom for a complete stranger. My mom, Taylor Brixton, the edgy photographer, a celebrity almost. Well...she used to be.

"I even showed the dean your Instagram," she says. "He thinks you'd be an ideal candidate."

"You showed my photos to some strange guy? Those are private!"

"Well, you did post them for the entire internet to see," Taylor points out. Which is…not wrong, I guess. But still.

"Eve's parents will move into Eve's old room and give us the big one. We'll each have our own desk. It'll be fine. Don't you trust me?"

"I'm not going to impose on Eve's parents like that." Taylor—I've called her that for forever, except when I'm mad at her or when she does things like, you know, turn my entire life upside down (I think it makes her feel like a Cool Mom, so she doesn't object)—shakes her head. "Izzy, you can't live with someone else's family for two-plus years like some languishing exchange student."

"Mom. We've been over this. Izzy is a little girl's name. I'm almost seventeen."

Mom sighs. "*Isabella*, I've always done my best to do things that are in your best interest. I've always encouraged you to march to the beat of your own drum, haven't I? I always wanted you to be an individual, to express yourself and find your voice. Haven't I?"

I nod. "And now you're cashing in."

That might have been harsh, however deserved. My mother's fair skin grows pink, and I almost regret what I said. Almost.

She's not wrong. My whole life, she's always been as much a friend as a mom. Except friends don't rip your life out by its roots for a bigger paycheck. I mean, there have to be other teaching jobs out there, a bit closer to home. And why on earth did that college in the middle of nowhere choose *my* parents to court, of all people?

Taylor sighs. "Isa, I don't think you realize universities don't just hand out coveted teaching positions with possibility of tenure. We were extremely lucky—"

"I beg to differ."

"We were extremely lucky," she repeats stubbornly, "to even be considered. Not to mention lucky to live in that house. When I saw it across that lawn, it's like—like it was glowing. Like it was calling to me—"

"That's not luck," I sneer. "That's a quest in a video game."

"That's not fair," Taylor says. "All I want is for you to at least consider how there might be a silver lining. I mean, you'll be surrounded by history and culture..." She's oblivious to my simmering fury. "We'll live in a historic mansion that once belonged to a famous artist's model, not to mention your namesake—"

"Isabella Granger," I cut in. "Yeah, yeah, I can google, big whoop."

"And you don't find that the least bit interesting?"

"First, she's not just an *artist's model*. She was a great philanthropist of her times, a patron of the arts. How crass of you to remember her as that chick who posed for paintings."

"Isa, I love you, but this is somewhat in bad faith."

"Well, I find the whole thing crass. It's like living at the Louvre. And wiping your ass every day in front of the Mona Lisa."

I can practically hear Taylor grit her teeth: *crick-squeak*. I know I'm only digging my own grave, but I can't help it. My hands are shaking, and my body is hot all over, and, suddenly, all my strategy is out the window. "I can't believe you're doing this. I—I'm the star of the school play, for god's sake! How could you?"

And now I've done it. Mom's face hardens. Definitely no longer Taylor the mom-friend. Taylor is full parent. Something I've only seen a handful of times, and it never ended well.

"You surprise me, Isabella. That's not how I raised you. There's more to the world than Brooklyn, and you're coming with us. I think it'll be an enriching experience, something for you to write about in your college applications...to places that aren't Amory University, if you must."

I let my mom think I'm sulking in my room, but there's no time for sulking. I better find a way to fix this.

I pick up my phone and text Eve.

> Sorry. Still no. :/

> This can't be it!!! We'll think of something.

My stomach knots. She doesn't understand, or pretends she doesn't understand to make me feel better, but it's a waste of effort. We won't think of anything. It won't work.

I put my phone down. My worst fears are unfolding in front of me: I'm on my way to being forgotten. Like that turn-of-the-century chick whose house we'll be squatting in. Faded out, her name meaningless.

I sit down at my computer and look up Isabella Granger once again.

For someone who lived out in the sticks, Isabella Granger sure had an impressive life. She rubbed shoulders with famous novelists, posed for the most daring artists of her era, and hosted glamorous parties at that mansion of hers, with painters and musicians and writers. She had a prodigious art collection. It seems almost unfair that so much awesomeness was heaped upon just one person. Can you even have a life like that anymore? I've never related to those annoying people who whine that they were born in the wrong era—I like my phone and social media and, well, modern medicine just fine, thank you. But I gotta admit, reading about Isabella Granger's life makes me feel a bit...insignificant. So, I have an Instagram with a couple thousand followers—so does everyone else. So, I went to the music festival last summer—so did everyone else. Especially in Brooklyn, where you can run into "down to earth" celebs while getting your fourteen-dollar vegan burrito for lunch.

I do an image search, and the screen fills with iterations of Isabella Granger by every famous artist of the era, in every conceivable style: here she is in an imitation-pre-Raphaelite painting, looking like a natural with that auburn hair, and there she is in a Klimt-like art nouveau portrait, wearing a low-cut sheath dress that must have been scandalous at the time. Imagine, causing a stir just by showing a knee. I don't know what you have to do these days to get a reaction.

There's no denying that Isabella was beautiful. If anything, it's she who was born in the wrong era, not me.

Sprinkled among the paintings are some images clearly taken by an intrusive photographer. In them, she looks a lot less impressive. That sylphlike beauty, pale and thin-lipped, doesn't translate to 2019. And, in black-and-white, her hair looks plain, her face ashen. I click on the link and read:

> Although Isabella Granger was a passionate supporter of the burgeoning art of photography, few photographs of her survive. The majority of those were taken by her husband, artist and photographer Samuel Granger (1861–19??).

Clicking on his name, I find myself on a Wikipedia page.

> Samuel Granger was a turn-of-the-century artist who later abandoned painting to focus on the emerging art of photography. Known as one of modern photography's pioneers, he refined the technique of...

Blah blah blah. I scroll to the end.

> Samuel Granger died in the early twentieth century. The exact date and the cause of death remain unknown.

THREE

"THAT SUCKS, ISA."

Eve is looking good and not terribly broken up about it. Is that the new Kat Von D lipstick? I'm a little bit resentful. Okay, a lot resentful.

I'm calling her on Skype from my room—or what was once my room, but not for much longer. In the background, I bet Eve can see the bare walls, since all my stuff is already packed. The whole house has been packed up over two and a half agonizing weeks. I never realized we had so much junk—things no one's used in ages but somehow never thrown away.

"I tried everything. Taylor says I need to 'expand my horizons.'"

"Most people move *to* Brooklyn to expand their horizons. Not out of it."

I scowl. To think Eve always said she was jealous of having Taylor for a mom. "I told her that."

"What are we going to do without you at the theater?"

What, indeed. Someone else will have to pick up the starring role in the production of *Yvonne, Princess of Burgundy*. Someone whose name starts with an *e*, maybe, and ends with another *e* and has a *v* in the middle.

Sensing the touchiness of the subject, Eve clears her throat. "I'll come down to visit you. I'm passing my driver's license test in, like, a month. I'll drive down."

"Will your mom let you?"

Eve grimaces. "I'll find a way."

In the Skype window, I can see Eve's sewing machine in the background and, draped over it, a burgundy velvet dress that looks familiar.

I don't want to ask, I really don't, but the question escapes anyway. "What is that?"

Eve turns around. Her cheeks turn pink, and her gaze keeps darting away from mine.

"Oh, they gave it to me. There were some holes in the lining. And I figured I'll fix it faster than if they have to send it out somewhere… you know?"

Oh, I do know. I also know that Eve just happens to be a bit on the short side, and the skirts of most period costumes need to be hemmed so she doesn't trip.

I can't blame Eve, though. I'd have done the same. Not because of some stupid rivalry—girls should lift each other up, not compete with each other—but because the show must go on. The play always comes first, no matter what. If anything, I hope she does great in her new role.

Still, there's a lump in my throat, and I worry that, when I speak, she'll hear the strain in my voice.

"At least you get to have a whole mansion to yourself," Eve says.

I grimace. I've seen pictures of the house. Looks like an absolute dump. I shudder inwardly.

Still—anything is good enough to change the subject. "Yeah," I say. "It's this big historical place they've restored for us. This artist's model used to live there." I catch myself using the same qualifier I'd snipped at Taylor for using. "Apparently, she was a big deal at the turn of the century."

"That's so cool," Eve says, but I get the feeling this is more out of pity than anything else. So I cut the conversation short, knowing full well we might not see each other before I leave Brooklyn.

I try to tell myself this isn't a big deal.

The final move takes place on a stifling morning in mid-September. A giant, grimy truck transports our boxes of stuff, overseen by my dad, and Taylor and I follow right on its heels in the new family SUV. I spend most of the trip staring into my phone, and, for once, Taylor seems relieved that I don't try to talk. What's there to talk about, anyway? What could I possibly say to make Taylor feel as bad as she deserves?

Dejected, I open the front-facing camera on my phone, then practice making a face until the result is goofy yet still cute. I snap some photos and fire the best one off on Instagram.

I watch listlessly as the photo uploads (taking forever, by the way—only two bars of signal out here) and then as the usual parade of likes and comments begins, hearts flying in all directions.

Everyone secretly feels sorry for me. Bitterness rises to the hollow of my throat. Tears fill my eyes, and I reach for the glove compartment, take out my sunglasses, and put them on so that Taylor, who's given up trying to cheer me up, doesn't see the wet tracks beneath my eyes. Then I open the front-facing camera again and take another photo, sunglasses on this time.

The truck bounces along the bumpy road that runs around the limits of the university campus, right until it pulls up in the shadowy spot near a corner of the house to what probably used to be the servants' entrance. The paved road leading to the front doors looks brand-new, but there's a fence blocking it off, so the SUV has no choice but to follow the truck.

At the side entrance, the head of facilities is waiting, looking smug. Before Taylor has a chance to stop the engine, I'm already getting out.

"Hold on," Taylor is saying, but I'm already slamming the door behind me. I race around the house to the front so I can see. My almost-new ballet flats sink into the damp grass, but I hardly notice.

I take off my sunglasses.

This place is huge.

The few pictures I hustled up online didn't do it justice. It's four stories—what does one person even do with a four-story house?—in a sprawling U-shape. And it's wide, built in a time when every square foot was not counted as stringently. Sunlight caresses the facade with its giant arched windows and long columns, like something teleported here from Renaissance Italy. The brick has faded, and the carved stone of the decoration above the door is eroding, as are the stairs and railings. But it makes the house look distinguished, not deteriorated.

"Sweetie," Taylor's breathless voice takes me by surprise. My mom and dad, along with the university guy, have caught up to me and are hovering on the periphery. "Wait up. It's not safe."

"The pavement is new," says the man. Redundantly, because I can see that myself. "And please be careful inside. There are some problems in a few of the rooms. With the floor. But we're working on it."

"Thank you so much," Taylor gushes, and I don't understand why she bothers with this pompous, annoying man. "I know it was such short notice."

"We finally have someone dedicated and trustworthy taking care of the Isabella Granger house," he says. "So it's a win-win situation."

In Brooklyn, this house would have been bought by a redevelopment company ages ago, broken up into eighty studio apartments, and rented out for six grand a month a piece. Here, in the middle of nowhere, it's all going to be ours. I try to wrap my mind around it. Failing that, I raise my phone and take a picture. Then I think of a better idea. I turn around and take a selfie, my arm outstretched until my shoulder threatens to pop so that enough of the house is visible behind me. I start to scroll through filters, but realize quickly that they're unnecessary.

The colors and light are just perfect. I'll do everything in my power to show everyone back home that this place is *just awesome* and I'm as happy as can be. The photo goes straight to Instagram.

"Can't this wait for five minutes?" Taylor speaks up.

I barely hear her. Phone aloft, I head for the entrance, my ballet flats leaving muddy tracks on the granite stairs. I take a picture of the crumbling carving above the door, which depicts some scene from mythology I can't make out because of the damage. The door itself is missing, and the empty doorway is blocked off with a single plywood panel.

"You have to go around," that guy—the head of something or other—calls out, but I'm already on it. The back door is unlocked, and, with nary a whisper from the newly oiled hinges, the house lets me in.

Despite the stifling heat outside, in here the air is beautifully cool and crisp. The slanting sunlight that falls through the windows is luminous but not hot. Its rays bounce across the crystals of the giant chandelier hanging over the main staircase, like something out of a Disney movie. I picture myself at the top of these stairs, my elegant, gloved hand resting lightly on the carved banister as I overlook my guests below, all waiting for me to make my grand entrance. Fanfare announces it at last, and everyone turns to look at me and gasps.

The vaulted ceiling is painted with other scenes from mythology: Aphrodite, the goddess of love, if I know anything of Greek myths.

Unlike the plump, pink, and fair-haired depictions in Renaissance art, this Aphrodite has heavy auburn locks in the pre-Raphaelite tradition. The more I look, the more I realize it's not the only difference. The lines of her face are so clean that they must have been restored—I don't see how they could have survived like this for more than a hundred years—and something about her face strikes me as odd. It looks…different, not like you'd expect on such a fresco. Modern-looking, not softly rounded with a tiny bow-mouth, but sharp and shrewd. Her piercing green eyes gaze straight at me, defiant. Challenging me. *Mirror, mirror on the wall*—

A heavy hand lands on my shoulder. The echo of my yelp races through the room.

"Mom!" I snap, embarrassed.

Taylor is beaming. "It's nice, isn't it?"

"It's interesting."

"You must be wondering about the ceiling. The woman who stands in for Aphrodite is Isabella Granger herself. Every woman in every painting in the house is Isabella, and the frescoes are no exception."

I look up once again. It makes sense: once I peer closer, the face does look like the one in the paintings and photographs I've seen online. But maybe the light has changed, a thin cloud has covered the sun outside, because now it looks different. Still very much Isabella, but no longer alive. The green eyes are flat, just paint on plaster—well-applied paint, sure, but nothing more than that.

"How do you know all that?" I ask Mom. "I spent half a night googling, and—"

"Not everything can be found on the internet, Isa. There's still such a thing as libraries."

"For now," I say, grinning, egging Taylor on. She returns the grin, and, for a moment, it's like the good times, before this whole mess with the move.

"Let's go pick out your room," says Taylor.

"I can have any room I want?"

"Yeah. Heck, you can have more than one—we'll never be able to fill them all. Well, except in the wing that's shut down on the fourth floor. It hasn't been renovated yet. Apparently, the ceiling had collapsed in places, the floor is damaged, and it's still a little unsafe."

Taylor starts up the stairs, but I fall behind. I snap a picture of the frescoes, another one of the chandelier, one of the grand staircase itself. But, before I post them, I send them to Eve.

Except, instead of the normal whistling chime that means the photos have arrived safely on Eve's phone, there's nothing. An annoying loading icon.

"Mom?" I call out. "There's no—"

"Oh, yeah," comes Taylor's distracted voice from the second floor. "There's no Wi-Fi for now. But don't worry. The company is coming to install the satellite in a few days."

"A few days?!"

"Is it such a big deal? Use your data. There's enough on the plan to last the week."

"There's *no signal*," I fume and give the phone an impatient shake.

Indeed, there's only one bar of signal, and even that keeps flickering out. "The walls are too thick or something. Nothing gets through."

"Even better—look up from that phone of yours for a change. And there's a café on campus, not too far from here, that I'm sure has Wi-Fi. You'll get to know your new town a little more. Now, are you coming to choose your room or not?"

I curse under my breath. If this is how it's going to be, I might as well be in the 1920s myself. Soon I'll be writing mournful letters to my friends back home with a quill on parchment, like the heroine of some second-rate Victorian Gothic. Seeing that the lone signal bar reappeared, I tap the screen—only for the red alert of death to pop up.

Unable to send photo—check internet connection.

Rage surges within me. It's unlike anything I've ever felt, a feeling cold and hollow like this house. I raise my hand, which feels like someone else is moving my muscles for me—and, the next thing I know, the phone is tracing a large arc in the air as it sails down the stairs.

All the breath leaves my body. *What the hell have I just done,* I have time to think before the phone lands on the floor facedown with an angry, sharp crack.

Echoing my thoughts, the lights on the entire floor crackle, hiss, and flicker out.

FOUR

THE LAST TIME I HAD THE DUBIOUS HONOR OF BEING THE
new girl was in elementary school. But that's not why I'm feeling lousy
this morning. Being the new girl isn't some sort of horrible ordeal like
you see in teen movies—I'll win everyone over if I have to. The problem
is I don't want to. I've known most of my friends in Brooklyn since we
were all learning to read. Trying to replace that just seems pointless.

The morning of my first day of school, I wake up before the
alarm, and, at first, I can't remember where I am. The ceiling is high
and unfamiliar, and the strange, musty, *old* smell in the air is different
from what I'm used to. Then it all comes back, settling in like a weight
on my chest, and, in a vain attempt to shake it off, I get up and go open
the curtains.

I chose this room because, at first glance, it looked homey. Unlike many of the other rooms, which had been stripped of all ornamentation, this one still has the old silk wallpaper, remarkably well-preserved: a slightly faded cornflower-blue with vertical stripes of tiny gold flowers. There are also wall chandeliers, but I couldn't switch them on. That was before Taylor explained that they couldn't *be* switched on, because they were connected to the house's old gaslight system that no longer worked. There's a painting on the wall, of Isabella, of course, and an old mirror that also can't be used because it needs re-silvering, black cracks snaking all over the surface below the glass. So I have to do my hair and makeup in the bathroom.

There's a mirror here as well, in slightly better shape. As I lay out my makeup, the tubes and pots look sad on the massive, well-worn marble counter. I imagine Isabella Granger anointing herself with the best cosmetics of her time, dipping her fingertips into pots made of precious metals and enamel—cosmetics that seem, at best, primitive today. They contained arsenic, among other things, which made your face nice and smooth with the teeny-tiny side effect of causing festering sores. Which, then, got slathered in even more arsenic-laden paint to cover them. Or was it gone by then? Did everyone figure out that they were coating their faces and bodies in poison?

I wonder what we're using, today, that will have people a hundred years from now recoil in horror and disgust. I chase the thought away and boldly swipe on concealer.

There are mirrors that are your friends, always showing you in the best possible light—this mirror isn't one of those. Its surface must be uneven, because my face always looks a little bit distorted, and it takes a heartbeat to get used to it each time and realize it's just the crooked mirror's fault. Doing my best to focus on just one detail at a time—eyes, eyebrows, lips—I finish up my makeup as quickly as I can and take a step back to assess the result.

My reflection in the massive mirror with its heavy ornate frame strikes me as pathetic, as if my looks could never live up to its opulence. Even with the gilt coming off the pattern of frolicking nymphs and cupids, it still manages to look magnificent, and I manage to look less-than in comparison.

When Taylor drives me to school, a drive that takes all of five minutes, I spend them all with my face in my phone, trying to puzzle out whatever my friends' feeds are showing behind the web of screen cracks.

As soon as I hop out of the car in front of the imposing iron gates of my new school, a feeling of unease creeps over me, and I start to understand the hapless heroines of the teen movies a little bit better. At first, I nurse a feeble hope that Taylor got the address wrong. This place looks like a jail for children, not a high school. Given the architecture in the rest of this wretched town, I expected some grand structure with turrets, maybe like Hogwarts meets Arkham Asylum. Instead, there's a square, beige building with rows of tiny windows.

The tall fence and sliding gates that mark the entrance onto school grounds compound the impression.

The building is bathed in sunlight, which makes it only a little less grim, and surrounded by a sea of students who seem in no hurry to get to class. My first thought is that they look *preppy*. Not like an actual high school, but the version of one out of a cheesy nineties movie from my parents' vast collection. Pleated skirts abound, and I spy someone wearing an honest-to-god cardigan without a shade of irony. I quickly lose count of guys wearing pastel polo shirts, and the sea of pristine, fitted, un-ripped blue jeans is unsettling. Really, the only thing that places the scene in the present day are the phones. Everyone is so busy staring at them that no one pays any attention to me. This is probably for the best, because I stick out like the proverbial sore thumb. For maybe the first time in my life, I start to second-guess myself. I've never been one to overthink what to wear; the perfect outfits come to me naturally. Eve and I used to spend hours raiding thrift shops for unique finds: oversized jeans from the eighties, a worn leather jacket, a vintage silk blouse the color of acid. But that was in Brooklyn. And my current #OOTD is very Brooklyn: mismatched Converse, one blue and the other pink with silver laces, cropped jeans with holes on the knees, and a crop top with a flower pattern that echoes the pink of my hair. I painted my fingernails navy blue and stacked my silver rings, without which I feel naked. I liked the result enough to take a picture, although it's hard to tell how it came out, with the broken screen and all.

My armpits feel damp, and I wonder, in a moment of panic, if I'd forgotten to put on deodorant. No. Can't be.

My skin crawls, and I mistake it for your average first-day jitters until I catch someone staring at me. Some guy. He's standing by the side of the main path that leads to the school doors, next to a small group of teenagers on bikes, but, at the same time, apart from it. He's dressed preppy, like the others, though there are subtle details that make me think this is more akin to a costume to him—a subtle inside joke. He has dark hair that's a little too long on top and chiseled features that would be a little too Ken-doll perfect if not for the intense, shrewd look in his eyes. His obligatory clean-cut button-down is partially untucked from his jeans, and the worn leather jacket he wears over it clearly comes from another decade. And he's the only one without a phone in his hand. No ubiquitous white AirPods either. Just standing there doing nothing. Like a psychopath.

I pick up my pace just as he starts toward me. Without looking back, I walk to the entrance as fast as I can. Finally, in the narrow hall, I blend in with the crowd—or hope I do. In any event, when I dare check over my shoulder, he's nowhere to be seen.

My first order of business is to find the "campus life organizer"— just the sound of that shows how these people already have one foot in the university down the road. I knock on the door, feeling somewhat reassured. If nothing else, one thing I've always been good at is making a positive impression on adults. At my old school, back in Brooklyn— *back home*—I was on a first-name basis with most of the teachers, who loved me. If I ever needed an extension for a deadline because I'd spent long evenings rehearsing with the theater group, they were always forthcoming, and, if I ever needed to skip out on gym because my legs hurt from dance class the day before, I was always allowed to just hang back and stretch instead.

The campus life organizer is a slim woman in a blue blazer, and everything about her looks dry. Hair, skin, facial expression. Even when she blinks, I swear I hear rustling, like her eyelids are papyrus. Not a good omen.

"Hello," I venture. "I'm Isa Brixton. I'm supposed to—"

"Isabella Brixton, yes. I have a note about you," the woman says ominously. "Why aren't you in class?"

"Because...because I was supposed to stop by here so you could enroll me in my electives," I say, fighting back a stammer. "Because registration is technically over and all."

"And you couldn't do that during first break or lunch hour because..."

"Because I need to get into drama," I fire off.

"Drama will still be there at noon."

"But I was supposed to go see you first thing," I argue, already suspecting I'm wasting my breath.

"Well, if you needed to see me *first thing*, then perhaps you should have arrived earlier. Now please proceed to Homeroom."

I start to say something but stop. "That's...that's unfair," I choke out.

The woman looks at me smugly.

"Miss Brixton, I'm afraid you will find that, at this school, we follow rules. And we also value academic excellence over frivolous popularity contests. So, by all means, go ahead. Twitter away, to all your followers, how unfair we're being in making you comply with the same rules as everybody else. It's not going to change a thing."

I briefly consider just storming out. But that would give this witch satisfaction, which is the last thing I want, so I turn slowly on my heel and walk to the door.

"Oh, and Miss Brixton? We have a dress code at this school. The hem of your shirt must reach the waistband of your trousers. I kindly suggest you keep this in mind for the future."

I manage to make it out of the office and shut the door behind me without committing literal murder.

"You evil hag," I mutter under my breath.

Only when I hear a chuckle do I look up and realize I'm not alone. A girl is waiting on the bench not too far from the door. She glances up from her phone, and our eyes meet.

"Hey," says the girl. "Don't worry, I won't narc on you. If anything, I agree. What did she do this time?"

"I—I just wanted to get enrolled in drama class," I say, measuring the girl with a look. She fits in as poorly as I do. Possibly more so. At least at first glance. Come to think of it, she's also going for a nineties look, but of a different kind.

"Oh, that won't be a problem," the girl says, grinning. "It's not the most popular elective here. Kendra will be glad to have a new face—we never have enough participants to stage anything interesting. You're new, I take it?"

"Yes," I say with some relief. "I'm Isa Brixton. We just moved here…"

"From New York," the girl finishes. "I heard."

I feel a bit miffed. "Brooklyn," I correct softly. It's probably all the same to her anyway.

The girl nods matter-of-factly. If this place does have a dress code, her outfit must violate at least ten different subsections. Her black velvet skirt has a high slit down the side, and, through it, I glimpse fishnets. Her equally black top is flowing and diaphanous, but sheer enough to show a black bra underneath. She has more earrings than I can count and several studs in her lip. I'm actually a bit jealous, although the whole goth thing seems kind of played out.

"Look, how about we just walk down to Kendra's classroom right now and ask her to enroll you? She won't mind."

"I thought you were waiting to see *her.*" I nod at the ominous door.

The girl laughs. "Oh, *she* can very well wait. I'm Alexa, by the way."

The class of the mysterious Kendra turns out to be in the farthest corner of the school's east wing. The older part, not as meticulously renovated and clean as the rest. But I like it better that way—not quite so antiseptic. Paint flakes off aging windowpanes, and the doors are all old, worn-looking solid wood. One of them, the very last one, is open, and, as we approach, I hear voices inside. It doesn't take a genius to recognize Viola's monologue from *Twelfth Night.*

Whoever is doing it could be doing a lot better.

"Hi, Kendra," Alexa says, erupting into the classroom. She doesn't even spare a glance at the girl she just interrupted. "Sorry to bust in, but I brought you someone. A new recruit. You absolutely must meet her; she's a drama prodigy."

"Prodigy, huh?" says a woman, turning around.

I'd mistaken her for one of the students at first glance. She wears flowing pants with an eclectic print and several layered knit tops. Her hair hangs down to her waist freely, swinging along with her beaded chandelier earrings as she advances toward us. "I can use a prodigy around here. Sorry, Ines, can we take five?"

The girl who had been struggling with Viola's speech slinks away to the back of the classroom.

"Sorry if we're interrupting rehearsal," I say.

"No, no. We haven't even started rehearsal yet. I'm Kendra." She holds out her hand, and I shake it. The woman's hand is rough and piled with turquoise rings, which clink against my silver ones.

"Kendra, can you do us a solid? Enroll Isa here in your class. Greer refused to do it."

For a moment, Kendra looks dubious, glancing from Alexa to me and back, and my heart clenches. *She's going to say no!*

But, then, Kendra smiles. "Sure. I have plenty of free spaces. If anything, Isa, bring your friends!"

I'm not sure how to tell her I don't have any because I'm the new girl, and people here don't look all that friendly to begin with. But

Kendra is already tapping away at a tablet, asking me to spell out my full name.

"Lovely," she says. "And Alexa? Ms. Greer was looking for you. You should probably—"

"Yeah, yeah," Alexa waves her hand dismissively. "On my way. See you in class, Isa?"

I say my goodbyes and set off to find Homeroom, even though the time on my phone tells me there's less than twenty minutes of class left.

FIVE

AFTER HOMEROOM, AS SOON AS I FIND MY NEXT CLASS,
I do something I've never done before—I get a desk at the very back
of the classroom. Back home—back in Brooklyn—I always sat in the
middle. That way, you're not kissing up to the teachers outright, but
you're not on the edge like the social rejects and C-students either.
But, here, the desk in the far-right corner seems like the natural place
to sit. From here, I have a vantage point to see everyone who comes
and goes, but no one pays attention to me.

That's why my heart flutters when the creep from earlier strides
through the door. He's ditched the worn leather jacket, and now he's
holding a phone like everyone else—a nice new iPhone, earbuds in his
ears. Yet, somehow, he still doesn't blend in. There's an aura of tension

around him, like a gathering thunderstorm. Invisible no longer, I carefully avoid looking in his direction, but there's no doubt: he's watching me.

Do not sit next to me, I pray. *Don't even think about it.*

When I dare look up, he's not sitting next to me—thank god—but he's at the other end of the same row. He doesn't seem to be looking anymore, but I'm not fooled. My senses remain on high alert. I manage to fidget through the class, and, once the bell rings, I busy myself gathering my things.

When I get up from my chair, he's gone again.

———————

At the end of the day, I exit the school as quickly as I can. I'm tempted to go look for Alexa, but then I spot my mom's SUV waiting beyond the gates. I'm keenly aware I'm one of the few juniors who doesn't drive on my own, so I hurry over and get into the passenger seat, hoping Taylor will drive off before more people can see me being picked up by Mommy like a grade-schooler.

But, instead of hitting the gas pedal and taking me the hell home, Taylor lets the car idle.

"How was your day?" she asks, and I detect caution in her tone.

"Fine," I say, hoping to cut the interview short.

But Taylor's gaze is fixed on my face.

"What is it?" I snap, my patience at an end.

"I got a call from some student life coordinator or someone," Taylor says, and my heart sinks further. "A Ms. Greer?"

"Mom," I say, racking my brain for whatever excuse I could give.

"She said you missed Homeroom…"

"I got lost, okay?"

"…and also something about a dress code. I told her dress codes were sexist, of course." I glance sideways. Taylor looks proud of herself. "And you know what she said? They're not sexist because they apply to everyone. Even theater prodigies from Brooklyn. The nerve of the woman!"

I let myself collapse against the back of the SUV's surprisingly comfortable seat, relieved.

"…but, just in the interest of keeping the peace," Taylor's voice turns supplicating, "could you tone it down just a little bit? For the first little while?"

"Tone it down?" I demand with contempt. "Tell me you're kidding. I'm not bowing to that *prune*. She can—"

"All I ask you is to please not stir the pot. At least for some time. Until you get acclimated there."

I rub my temples, overwhelmed with everything that's wrong in this situation. "I can't believe you'd have me cave to that fascist and her demands. Just to avoid *stirring the pot*."

"Izzy, please…"

"Can we just go home? I'm tired, and my head hurts."

"Honey, I didn't mean it like that." The supplicating tone is back. *She might be a semi-efficient mother*, I find myself thinking, *if only she weren't so obsessed with being liked*. It's a mean thought, I know, and I feel like garbage.

"Here." Taylor opens the glove compartment, and my jaw drops when I see a sleek white box. "This is for you. I figured it was unfair to leave you with no connection to the world."

It's an iPhone. Not just *a* new one—*the* new one, the one that retails for almost a thousand dollars. I never thought I'd see it in my wildest dreams, at least not until two more models were released and it became affordable. Back home—in Brooklyn—I always was the one with the old phone. Although Eve was always too tactful to point it out.

"Mom," I say softly. My face grows warm, and I feel even worse about my outburst. "Thank you."

"Don't thank me. Thank our renovation stipend. It turned out there was an extra thousand dollars."

"Uh, not that I'm not grateful...but isn't that kind of shady?"

"The stipend covers internet improvements. So let's just call it something like a super-modem." Taylor cracks a smile. "I won't tell if you won't."

For the first time in what feels like a while, we share a real laugh. Then, we drive home, deciding to order pizza for dinner. While Taylor calls to order, I tinker with my new phone. Sadly, the newly installed cable is just as spotty as the sorry attempt at a satellite. The Wi-Fi still cuts off randomly just as I try to scroll through Instagram or send a message. My new phone is a beauty, but what good is it when I can't use it for anything, since, apparently, I'm trapped in the Middle Ages?

I look up from the screen when I hear Taylor curse under her breath.

"Bullshit," she fumes.

"What is it?"

"Can you believe it? This place called Pizza Town, supposedly the best around here—they just hung up on me! They thought I was prank-calling."

"Huh?"

"Yeah. When I asked them to deliver to the Granger house, the dude on the other end just said, *yeah right*, and hung up."

"So let's just order through an app."

Taylor shrugs and takes out her phone. But that plan fails too—it seems the app doesn't recognize our address.

"It makes sense, I guess," Taylor muses, looking lost. "I mean, this *wasn't* a real address until we moved in."

Dad isn't home yet, so Taylor decides to drive to the nearest Pizza Hut to bring in takeout. I'm relieved to have some peace and quiet for a change. I need to get my thoughts together.

When my final attempt at Skyping Eve fails, I look around my room forlornly. Sure, the place is as big as our whole apartment back in Brooklyn, but what am I supposed to do with it? It's the walls. They're too thick, so the signal doesn't get through.

Where's a sledgehammer when you need one?

Taylor has warned me off the fourth floor entirely, since the wing beginning at the end of the long hallway is *compromised*. Something about the roof there being in bad shape, which is how humidity got in to ruin the floor in the first place. Well, weakened floorboards or no, maybe I might get a decent signal with a broken roof.

According to that facilities guy, the four floors weren't so much for the house's owners but for all the staff required to maintain a place this size, which seems a little self-defeating. But, then again, turn-of-the-century rich people probably had different worldviews. Hence, we chose our rooms on the second floor: a room for me, my parents' bedroom, a home office for Dad. There's also that beautiful sitting room we don't use yet, because the ceiling is damaged and needs restoring. So, for now, that's where we keep all the antique furniture from the house, wrapped in layers of dusty tarp.

According to Taylor, there's nothing of much interest above the second floor anyway—the servant rooms are small and not very fancy. There's supposedly Samuel Granger's old photography workshop on the third floor, complete with a darkroom, and Taylor is practically salivating at the prospect of getting it for herself. But there's some work to be done there, too, and the door is locked. No one has found the key yet.

I walk up two flights of stairs and peer into the third-floor hallway—half of the rooms here are locked up, too, because of the structural damage. On the fourth floor, in the hallway on the right side, the walls are plain, and wall lamps simple and lacking ornamentation. The left wing, on the other hand, is blocked off with a striped plank that says DANGER as well as a bunch of tape. This is where the roof is broken and the floors are in bad shape. As I crane my neck, it doesn't look all that damaged to me. It looks nicer than the right side, with the same wall chandeliers as on the first floor—bronze art deco renditions of swans. From where I'm standing, I can see a tall door with a dark, lacquered finish.

I duck under the tape and step over the plank without too much trouble. I gingerly put my weight on each foot as I advance, waiting for the telltale snap that means the floor might cave, but there isn't so much as a soft creak. One step. Another, then another—and, before I know it, I'm standing in front of the mystery door. Unlike the simple doors of the servant rooms, it's gorgeously ornate. Like the ones downstairs, where the mistress of the house would receive her guests, this one is made of lacquered walnut the rich color of coffee, with gilt trim that's worn away in places but still regal. The door handle is an intricate art nouveau design shaped like a swan atop a cherry blossom. When I tug on it, though, the door doesn't budge so much as an inch. I'd need the key, which Taylor has…somewhere.

Overcome with curiosity, I lean closer. The delicate whorls of the gilt trim depict more flowers on languid, twisting stems, weirdly sensual. Was this room Isabella's bedroom? No, her *boudoir* was on the second floor. What would she be doing all the way up here?

I press my cheek to the walnut panel that feels unexpectedly warm. Behind the door, I hear something—a faint rustling, like the beat of wings.

Birds, I think. The roof must really be broken if they got in. With reluctance, I pull away. The door beckons to me, the gilt flowers nearly glowing in the deepening sunset light.

And turning to the hall windows, I see the sunset is spectacular. The windows of my room, like those of every room on the upper floors, face the inner courtyard—or what little is left of it. Restoration is ongoing, but, right now, there's not much to see other than some fallen pillars and arches, what used to be a garden hopelessly overgrown with grass and weeds. But the windows in the hall look out front, onto the sprawling field with the imposing towers of the university rising on the horizon like some Scottish castle. Right now, it's all bathed in tender pink light. I glue my nose to the window and watch as the sun's last rays ebb away, the sky turning purple, then indigo, right until it's so dark that the glass ceases to be transparent, reflecting my own face right back at me instead.

I look terrible. Tired. There are circles under my eyes like I haven't slept in a million years, and my hair is a mess. I reach out to touch the glass, but, when my fingertips brush against the smooth surface, I pull my hand away. It's so cold it burns. I stumble back, and, suddenly, my face isn't the only one I'm seeing. I only have time to catch a glimpse: eyes like deep, dark crevices, slits of nostrils, skin like a smeared wax mask.

I back away until I hit the wall behind me. A small decorative table topples, and the antique vase it housed shatters on the floor.

My gaze darts momentarily away from the window, and, when I look up, the other face is gone.

The breath rushes out of my lungs when I understand what I was seeing: it's just a reflection of the portrait on the wall. I hadn't noticed it was there—otherwise, the walls are bare. A trick of the light, or some dirt on the glass, must have distorted it. Isabella Granger's face is serene, her soft gaze directed vaguely toward the window. It's one of the plainer portraits, no lavish costume or artistic devices, just Isabella against a blank wall, dressed simply in a high-collared dress the color of ashes. As I look at it, the expression starts to seem mournful somehow, brimming with sadness.

Thanks a lot, you Edwardian bitch, I think as I survey the mess on the floor. Crouching to pick up the shards, I reach out—and pull my hand away with a shriek. Blood spurts from a deep cut in my index finger like a little fountain. It runs down my palm and into my sleeve.

"Izzy?" comes my mom's voice. I glance over my shoulder to see Taylor racing toward me down the hall. "Sweetheart, what happened? Where have you been?"

"What—what do you mean?" I'm disoriented. I notice abruptly that it's become dark outside—really dark. The night is impenetrable, no stars, no moon. The hallway windows look like a row of coal-black mirrors.

"Where have *you* been?" I ask Taylor. "You went to get pizza and disappeared somewhere."

"Disappeared? I've been back for an hour. I've been calling your name, but— Why are you up here, anyway? Oh my god. Your hand!"

I remember the cut. I look down at my hand, uncomprehending.

The cut is still there, and my index finger is smeared red, but the river of blood is now just a trickle.

"I broke a vase," I say.

"Be more careful, honey. None of this stuff is ours. Come with me. I'll put a bandage on that."

As I follow my mom, I fume. Sure, worry about the *stuff*. Who cares about the stupid vase? I just almost—

Almost what? Nothing really happened. I thought I saw something, but it was just ole Izzy the First over there on the wall.

As Taylor finishes up wrapping my finger, I hear the service door open and shut, which means my dad is home. It's loud, since the high ceiling emphasizes the echo of every step. Then why didn't I hear my mom arrive?

By the time we're ready to eat, the pizza has gotten cold, and everyone is too hungry to properly reheat it or sit down at the table in the vast dining room. We share the tepid pizza at the kitchen counter. I'm not that surprised that conversation doesn't flow. Apparently, no one else had such a great first day either. The university messed up some schedules, so Gordon Brixton's long-awaited first meeting with the fundraising team fell through. And at the photo lab, equipment had been mislaid, so Taylor's first workshop session had to focus on theory. Adrenaline makes me shaky, and the cold pizza sits like a rock in my stomach. I can't get away to my room fast enough.

As a peace offering, my parents agreed to bring my old furniture even though it wasn't necessary since the house is brimming with antiques we could use. In here, it looks small, plain, and out of place. I wish I'd just let them keep the antiques, which had been moved to another, vacant room: a beautiful, massive mahogany dresser, an elegant little desk I now know is called an escritoire, a wardrobe, and, of course, the big canopy bed. They did keep the original artwork where it was, though, because, when they lifted the biggest painting, it turned out to be covering an ugly stain on the wall. Another Isabella, of course, her hair flowing, her eyes downcast, her delicately painted white hand holding an equally white rose.

I often find myself staring at it with a feeling of wistfulness. Sure, the lady lived before lip injections, Tarte highlighter, and camera filters, but, even without all these things, I've got to give her credit: she was kind of beautiful. They say art says as much about the artist as it does about the subject, and, in this case, I think the artist must have had a big crush on her, at the very least.

Nobody ever looks at me this way, that's for sure.

I go to the window and gaze out. There's a lone lamp on the rent-a-fence the workers left, casting its weak light on what used to be the courtyard. I imagine Isabella Granger with that flowing hair, dressed in some elegant gown and gloves, coming downstairs to have dinner with her circle of admirers, basking in their attention, in their admiration, in their love. She wouldn't have had to compete with literally everyone on the planet, who all have social media accounts; she could be secure in the knowledge that, at least as far as her coterie was aware, she was unique.

I have to check myself. It's kind of dumb to be jealous of some woman who died a hundred years ago. But the picture my imagination drew has momentarily became real, and I have a hard time getting rid of it.

Something moves in the corner of my eye.

My heart gives a leap, and I lean toward the window so abruptly that my forehead connects with the glass. Ouch. But, this time, it's not a reflection or a trick of the light. I saw something. Something moved down in the courtyard—a shadow, a silhouette, a wolf?—that darted at the very perimeter of the light to vanish again in the darkness.

SIX

THE NEXT DAY AT SCHOOL, THERE'S NO NEED TO FIND
Alexa because Alexa finds me. Too easily, in my opinion. It's almost
like she's been waiting for me inside the main entrance, because, as
soon as I step over the threshold, there she is.

Still, it's kind of nice to see her. Not just because, for now, she's the
only familiar face in the entire school, but because she's the only one
who seems to be friendly and normal.

"I found you on Instagram," Alexa says. "I'm kind of dabbling in
photography myself. If only I had a better camera—it's just my stupid
phone for now. Can't do much with that."

I nod. Taylor doesn't think phone photography counts as *true art*
and believes phones ruined the whole thing. But I wisely decide not to
say so to my new friend.

"You can see my stuff on my account," Alexa says. "I followed you."

"I'm sorry, I didn't see. There are…some problems with the internet at our new place."

Alexa's eyes light up. "At the house," she says.

I nod. *Well yeah, I live in a house, not in the dumpster out back.*

She's looking at me like a hungry puppy at a bowl of kibble. "I can't believe you get to live there."

So that's why she's following me, I think with a tinge of disappointment. *Not because I'm so appealing and charismatic, but because of the house.*

"It's a very beautiful house," I say airily. "So much more beautiful than the place we used to live in. And it has all these antiques."

"And the artwork. Can you believe it? It's stood like that for, what, half a century, with the doors practically open? And no one has stolen a thing, even though it all just sat there under a tarp."

"Well, that sure wouldn't happen in New York," I say with a laugh that comes out a bit forced.

It turns out we have first period together, history, so we walk to class side by side.

"The woman who lived there was a legend," Alexa says. "This gorgeous socialite and artist's muse. I can't believe the college would just let the house stand empty like that for years."

"They tried to renovate some years back," I reply. "But they ran out of money or something. My mom and the college builder guy told me."

I follow Alexa as we take seats next to each other in the second-to-last row. Finally, someone to sit with.

"I wonder if her clothes are still in that house," Alexa goes on, although she lowers her voice a little. "And her jewelry. Imagine what a photo shoot you could do!"

To be honest, that's the farthest thing from my mind. Working internet would be a nice start. But I can't help but think that, if Isabella's things are really still in the house, they must be in that locked room on the fourth floor.

The teacher arrives, cutting our conversation short. But, when I try to take advantage of the better cell signal to check my notifications, Mr. Delgado notices and confiscates my phone for the duration of the class. Brilliant.

Left to my own devices—or without them, as it were—I let my daydreams float back to Isabella Granger. I rebuild the earlier scene in my mind: a sitting room, soft piano music, Isabella reclining on an antique fainting couch (for some reason, it's specifically a *fainting* couch) making scintillating conversation with a handsome young artist who's dressed like Colin Firth in the *Pride and Prejudice* adaptation but has the face of my middle-school crush. I'm just going over details of her dress and her jewelry when the bell rings.

Looking down, I see the notebook in front of me doesn't contain a single line of notes. Instead, there's a sketch, very rough, like I drew without looking at the paper: the side of a face, eyelashes over a downcast gaze, a hand and a rose. Just like the painting in my room.

And, right below that, an ornate number 6 drawn with a complexity I couldn't imagine coming from my own untrained hand.

I'm not the only one who notices the other Isabella. That evening, taking advantage of a rare moment of five-bar signal, I Skype Eve. Eve takes a while to answer, but, finally, her grinning face splashes across my screen.

"Hey, girl! I thought you'd forgotten about me."

I grin wistfully. Like, what could be so exciting out here that I'd forget my actual life? *They all feel sorry for you,* a thought flits through my mind. Where'd that come from?

"You didn't message me yesterday," Eve says. "I'm a little hurt."

"Shitty signal," I grumble.

"I'm starting to think that's an excuse."

"The new school is nuts," I say, ignoring the comment. "Can you believe it? They confiscated my phone this morning. I mean—hello, 1980 called. Everyone has a phone; they should just cope."

"That sucks," says Eve. "By the way, guess what happened…"

"I miss you guys so much," I rant on. "Everyone here is a weirdo. They dress like extras on *Clueless* and, believe it or not, there's a dress code."

"That's so sexist."

"Totally! And the drama class here still does Shakespeare… straight up unironically. I feel like I've fallen through a time warp, but not the fun kind. The crappy kind that goes right back to sixth grade."

"Well, on our end—"

"The only person who deigns to talk to me is this weird goth chick. Nothing against that. If anything, she's the only one with any sense of style, but she's a little intense. And apparently—"

"Hey," says Eve out of nowhere. "Who's the chick on the wall there?"

"Huh?" I managed to forget where I am. I check over my shoulder and, sure enough, the portrait is right behind me, visible to the webcam. "Oh. Her."

Hang on a second. Wasn't it on the other side of the wall?

"Is this by one of the local pop artists?" Eve inquires with a sly grin.

"Oh god. That's Isabella Granger, to whom we owe this place."

"Okay. But what is she doing in your room?"

"Covering a stain on the wallpaper," I say honestly. I side-eye the painting. If it's really been moved, then the stain should be visible, but the intricate wallpaper is pristine. "Don't be so dismissive. She was this great philanthropist and patron of the arts. Her portraits are all over the house. Some are by well-known artists…" I trail off, picking at the bandage on my finger. The cut underneath begins to smart.

"Must have had quite the ego," Eve points out. "What kind of person hangs pictures of herself all over her house?"

"Uh, every kind of person," I say. "We just post it to Insta instead of hanging it on the wall. But it's essentially the same thing."

Eve shrugs. "I mean, she's all right looking. For a woman of her time."

"She's beautiful," I say, feeling defensive, although unsure why.

"Sure, sure. So how come the place was, like, abandoned for a hundred years before you guys moved in?"

"It wasn't abandoned," I say, simmering with impatience. "She bequeathed it to the university. As a museum of her life."

"Like I said, *ego*," Eve interjects.

"...and, for a while, it was, but then it fell into disrepair. They restored it just for us. All her paintings and things are still here."

"I see that. So where is Isabella herself, then?"

"You're kidding, right? She's been dead for close to a hundred years or something. I guess she didn't have descendants."

"How did she die?"

"I have no idea. It's not on Wikipedia."

Eve laughs. "Don't be silly. Everything's on Wikipedia."

"See for yourself," I huff. "There's nothing. *Cause unknown*. And the same thing for her husband. Who was, if you can believe it, a photographer."

Eve rolls her eyes. "So basically, you're living in the house of a turn-of-the-century Kardashian."

"Hey!"

"Okay, okay. Don't be so touchy. It's a gorgeous house; you should feel lucky."

"Yeah. I would, if only—did I tell you about that creepy guy in half of my classes who keeps staring at me—like, if his eyes were lasers, I'd be dead, you know?"

Eve looks at something off-screen. "Okay. Look, Isa—I kind of have to go. I have a ton of homework, and I really need to improve my grades. My mom is serious this time. So I'm going to—"

"Sure," I say, trying hard not to show my disappointment. As if it's not the first time all week I've gotten to talk to a normal person. "I'll Skype you tomorrow night."

"If your connection can take it."

"Or if the internet craps out again, I'll call."

"Actually, tomorrow night I can't. It's rehearsal, remember?"

"Right," I say, crestfallen. How did I forget already? "The night after?"

"No good. Maybe Saturday afternoon? Anyway, I'll message you. Ciao, bella!"

She signs off. I'm left staring at the blank Skype screen. Stupid old house, stupid backward town. Life would be so much easier with functioning internet.

It's an excuse. She's happy to be rid of you.

My head snaps up. The words felt almost real, like a subtle touch along my spine, leaving goose bumps in its wake. But I get up, and, of course, I'm alone; the room is empty. The only other human in here is painted on canvas.

I make my way over to the wall where the painting is hanging. When I lift it up to see underneath, sure enough, there's the stain on the wallpaper. Looking closer, I find it's a weird shape. Like someone threw something at the wall with great force.

SEVEN

IN THE MORNING, THE HOUSE ISN'T EXACTLY AT ITS BEST.
In all that bright sun, you can see the subtle decrepitude clearly. You
can see that the exquisite wood paneling in the hall could use a coat of
varnish, the mosaic parquet floor is scuffed, what carpets are left are
threadbare, and that rust is slowly setting in on the intricate wrought
iron railings and banisters. Only the frescoes and chandelier are magnificent as ever, crystals sparkling like diamonds in the rays of sunlight,
the colors of the paint bright and clean. But then you look down from
all that beauty and return to the world of dust.

And the dust is pervasive. Even though professional cleaners had
come through, and Taylor spends hours vacuuming and sweeping, more
dust has emerged overnight out of nowhere, swirling in beams of sunlight.

The kitchen, where we're about to have breakfast, is the least impressive room. That's because, as my dad helpfully explains, back in Isabella's heyday the kitchen was the realm of the cook and servants. The mistress of the house never set foot there, so no point in fancy architecture.

When he says that, Taylor giggles like a little girl. "Wouldn't that be nice. Never to set foot in the kitchen while the help does all the cooking. If only somebody around here helped out once in a while, right, Isa?"

"Would you be asking me that if I were a boy?" I fire back.

"Yes, as a matter of fact, if you were a boy, I'd also ask you to help with hauling boxes of equipment up four floors. But I don't suppose you'd volunteer for that either?"

"Mom," I say. "You know I have to go to school."

"Of course."

"And why do you need your boxes on the fourth floor, anyway?"

"I'm storing my stuff up there until I can take over Samuel Granger's workshop. The head of facilities finally found the key. But, for now, it's full of dust and who knows what's in that paint, maybe lead or something worse. I scheduled to have it professionally cleaned."

I shrug and resume eating my cereal. Taylor's right about the dust. It's in everything. Even the cereal tastes gritty.

"I have to make an early start," Mom says. "Your dad will drive you to school."

He does. I'm relieved because, unlike Taylor, Dad never gives me crap when I'm on the phone around him. I have time to catch up on most of my news feed, but my heart gets stuck in my throat when I see the photo Eve has posted. It's of Eve in the costume—my costume; I still think of it this way even though I have no right. But here she is, wearing *my costume*, surrounded by our friends who are all smiling and making faces. And the caption reads, *The show must go on!*

Indeed.

"Isabella?" Dad asks.

"What?"

"We're here."

Right. I look up. The car stands still in front of the school gates.

My shoulders droop. With a sigh, I put my phone away and struggle back into the straps of my backpack.

"Hey, Isabella? Look, I'm so sorry about all of this."

I'm taken aback. "What do you mean?"

"The move and everything. I know you're not exactly in love with the place…"

And here I thought I'd been good about complaining as little as possible.

"It's obvious from how you've been acting. I miss my sunshine girl, and I really want you to be happy. But this is good for the family. And your mom…she needed this. It won't be forever, I promise."

Puzzled, I say bye to him and head off to school. If that speech was meant to cheer me up, it failed.

I feel cowed by it all, and, as I pass a pair of glass sliding doors, I notice that even my outfit reflects the feeling. Without thinking about it, I chose plain leggings and a plain sweater. And I really should have washed my hair, which looks greasy and flat. The color is fading, and it's a bit passé, really. I'll have to dye it myself.

As I take my seat for my first class of the day, my brain keeps buzzing. Having learned from previous experience, I'm a lot more discreet with my phone in class. But scrolling through my social media feeds only makes me feel worse. Here, a picture of Eve—more like Eve's lunch, a bento box from the place where we used to go together. Suddenly, the avocado-rolls-for-eyes schtick seems stupid, like it's mocking me. There, a picture of the whole squad in front of the mirror in dance class. People running around all over Brooklyn. Having fun. Without me.

I realize I'm sulking and throw a glance around to see if anyone noticed. Of course, there's the creep. Looking like he's not looking at me. What's he going to do, rat me out to the teacher for being on my phone, like we're actually in sixth grade?

The whole thing is too infuriating to think about, and so, instead, my mind turns to what my dad said. *Your mom…she needed this.*

And why is that, I wonder.

Taylor, like any creative in the twenty-first century, has a social media presence of her own. But, since Taylor considers herself the coolest mom of all moms, she doesn't follow her daughter on any platforms. I scroll through Taylor's official Instagram, which consists of artsy shots of cool things Taylor snaps throughout the day. The moon that looks like it's balanced on the corner of a roof, things like that. The beauty of everyday objects. When Taylor started the account, I was still in middle school, and I thought it was kind of neat.

But, lately, it's been veering toward the cutesy, not so original—not like my mom at all.

Now, I see that Taylor hasn't posted in a while. Her last few posts are reused images from much earlier, and nothing new has been added in several months. It's hard to determine when exactly she stopped posting. I scroll and scroll.

"Ms. Brixton!" the teacher's voice brings me back into dull reality. "Have you been paying any attention?"

And because, at this school, they still call students Ms. This and Mr. That, I reply, obediently, "Yes, ma'am."

"So what did I just say is the subject of today's lecture?"

I cast a semi-panicked glance around. Back home, someone would have helped me. Someone would have given me a hint. But here, I'm left to fend for myself in enemy territory, kingdom of the blazers.

Then a movement catches my eye, and, before I can check myself, I glance over at its source. The creep is sliding a paper across his desk in my general direction. Before I even read the two words written on it in bold, I notice his hands: he has a musician's long, slender fingers, sinewy, stained with ink—or is it paint? Only his bitten-to-the-quick fingernails ruin the impression.

"Isabella?"

I clear my throat. "The onset of the industrial revolution," I say, feeling my face grow warm.

I give him a nod of thanks without meeting his eye. Sure, it's nice of him. But he's no less a creep.

However, at the end of class, just as I'm done putting my things away and ready to leave, I find him parked in the middle of the aisle. I glance around: there's no other way to leave without moving desks, which would make a bunch of noise and really draw attention to me. And to the fact that I'm moving desks to avoid him. I linger at my seat unnecessarily, observing him out of the corner of my eye, but he's peacefully scrolling through his phone, in no hurry to leave. Today he's wearing a different button-down, which really could stand to be buttoned *up*. Through the carelessly open collar, I can see that he's wearing some kind of weird necklace, a simple black cord with what looks like a mangled paper clip dangling from it. His hair flops over his forehead, but he's so absorbed in his phone that he doesn't seem to notice.

I draw a breath. Suppose I'm going to have to talk to him. I approach at a slow pace, hoping he'll maybe get the hint like a normal human being and get out of the way.

"Excuse me," I say pointedly. He glances up from his phone. As if he really hadn't noticed he'd blocked my exit. Infuriating.

But he moves out of the way without making a fuss. I have to pass right by him. I feel his gaze, curious and observing.

"You're welcome," he says *sotto voce* just as I squeeze by.

My face warms. This is what it's all about? Jeez. Whatever happened to chivalry, huh? He can't even perform the most basic act of human decency without expecting me to profusely thank him.

But, when you think about it, he did save my butt. And any normal person would bother with a real thank you.

"I totally knew the answer, by the way," I murmur. "I would have remembered, anyway."

He chuckles. "Of course. I don't doubt it. But then I wouldn't have had an excuse to talk to you."

This is such a transparent lie—at least the first part is—that I gasp. Inwardly, of course.

"And what makes you think I wanted to talk to you?"

"Nothing. That's a chance I had to take. I'm Nick, by the way."

Good god. His name is as preppy as he is.

"Isabella," I say coolly.

"Is your next class algebra? If so, I'll walk you."

As if you didn't know my next class is algebra. We have it together. Of course.

But, even as I prepare to tell him to get lost, I realize my curiosity is piqued. Seriously, a guy using such a grammar-school ploy to talk to me? It's charming in a way. So, without actually agreeing—let alone showing enthusiasm, heaven forbid—I let him walk by my side on the way to our next class.

"Thank you for saving my butt in history," I say, finally conceding the point.

He half smiles. Smug.

"But the staring, that wasn't cool. I could complain about you to student services, you know."

"I can't be the only person who's looking at you," Nick says.

I'm not sure if he made it better or made it worse. "Yeah, because I stand out or something?"

"Because you're the girl who lives in the Granger mansion."

My spirits sink, although I wouldn't admit it in a million years. The house again. "Is everything here always about that damn house?"

"It has a history," Nick says obliquely. "Or, rather, it *is* history."

"Yeah, well, it's not haunted or anything. I don't believe in that stuff, anyway."

His face clouds over. For just a second. A blink later, his smug expression is back.

"And, okay, so that explains the students. Why are all the teachers here so mean to me?"

"In case you didn't notice, they're like that with everyone."

"Not helping, Nick."

"Wasn't my intention."

"It's like—back home—back in Brooklyn, at my old high school, the teachers were so chill. They were nice. Here it seems like they're always trying to trap me with some assignment I forgot to do or some trick question. Like they *want* me to fail or something."

I catch myself rambling, and my face warms once again. But, if I expected sympathy, all I get from him is a shrug.

"Have you stopped to think that maybe you're just used to free passes?"

That's it. He really is a creep, cute smile notwithstanding.

"Have you ever stopped to think that maybe you're an asshole?"

"Nice. You learn that in Brooklyn too?"

Furious, I storm off, right past the algebra classroom and down the hall. I swear I can feel his stupid, smirky gaze on my back, and so, to escape from it, I turn onto the staircase, which is emptying quickly as people rush to their classes. A moment later, I understand why the hurry: overhead, the bell rings. Literally overhead. When I glance up, it's right there, affixed to the ceiling. By the time it's done, I'm not only late for class, my ears are ringing too. Oops.

I quickly consider my options: if I go to class now, no doubt there'll be some kind of public shaming ritual. Maybe they'll make me stand in the corner for the whole hour like at some British boarding school from the fifties. To hell with that. But getting caught wandering the hallways is probably not a great idea either. I should either get out of the school altogether or find a place to hide out.

"*Psst.*"

I jump, spin around—and, sure enough, as if by some sinister magic, it's Alexa crouching under the staircase like a troll under the bridge. How does she do that? Is she following me around? I'd be mad, if I wasn't kind of happy to see her.

"What are you doing here?" I whisper as I go over to join her.

"The same thing as you, it looks like," Alexa says, nonchalant. "Come on. I know a place we can go."

Following Alexa across the vast field behind the school, I look doubtfully over my shoulder at the hulking school building. I feel a little exposed, like some unseen enemy is watching us from one of those little windows that look black from the outside. But Alexa doesn't seem concerned, so I figure I shouldn't be either. We pass the second gates (at this school, the big sport is soccer, very in keeping with their wannabe-European image), and I understand where we're headed. I've seen the building from afar before and wondered what was inside. Unlike the main building with its brutalist angles, it's beautiful, majestic in a way, tall, with columns by the entrance. It has an abandoned look to it, even though the path leading to the double doors is nice and clean.

"They built the new auditorium years ago," Alexa explains, with nary a glance over her shoulder to make sure I'm keeping up. "Now all the important stuff takes place there, which is just as well, because we have this place to ourselves."

To my surprise—or, really, the opposite—Alexa doesn't head for the front doors. Instead, we circle the building to a side entrance, a door so short I practically have to duck to enter. At first, it's shockingly dark once the door shuts behind us, and I wonder what I let Alexa rope me into. A bunch of B movies I used to watch with Eve flash through my mind. Do they have some demonic-sacrifice ritual going here? But then my eyes get used to the dark, and I realize this is a dressing room. Alexa flips a switch, and the bulbs surrounding a long horizontal mirror hum to life. There are chairs, mismatched and in varying states of disrepair, and a counter littered with discarded articles, a powder puff, a sock, Q-tips. Classic theater posters hang over the mirror, their corners curling from the above-average humidity.

"Oh," I say, and my mood instantly skyrockets.

"Welcome to the theater club," Alexa announces with a flourish. "Come have a look around."

I exit the dressing room and follow Alexa down a narrow hallway filled with echoes, then into a backstage area taken up by clunky mechanisms for raising and lowering decorations. When I look up, I see a catwalk so high it could give me vertigo.

Alexa beams and flips another switch. The gears on either side instantly whir to life, groaning like the bones of an elderly giant. The curtain rises, and I find myself looking out over a huge, empty auditorium. Rows of old-fashioned red velvet seats are waiting for the audience to settle in. Wannabe art deco designs cover the walls.

"Holy shit," I say, and cover my mouth to hold back a giggle. Every sound rockets through the space like thunder.

"The acoustics are great," Alexa says, unnecessarily.

"And only the theater club uses this place?" I ask in a reverent whisper.

Alexa nods.

"Incredible. Back in Brooklyn…"

But I trail off. It seems unnecessary to compare this place to the effective but thoroughly modern auditorium at my old school, which our theater club has to book months and months ahead. Finally. Something is actually better than back home. I take my phone out of my pocket, switch it on, and take a photo from where I'm standing.

"Go on." Alexa chuckles. "Brag. They'll all drop dead of envy."

I turn around just in time to hear the fake shutter click. Alexa has taken my picture with her own phone.

"You look right at home," she says.

For a moment, I *feel* at home. As much as I'm tormented by the idea of my life back in Brooklyn passing by without me, I understand for the first time that this is also a fresh start. This place isn't home, but it could be. Alexa may not be Eve, but she's...Alexa.

"Don't post it," I say. "Everyone will know we're skipping."

Alexa laughs. "Come have a look around."

Backstage, we arrive at a locked door. Looking mysterious, Alexa produces a key out of her pocket and unlocks it.

"Wow," I say.

In front of me are rows and rows (and rows) of dresses. No, not just dresses—costumes. A scent of perfume and mothballs floats in the air, not at all unpleasant. I pick through the dresses closest to me, which are out of order: a baroque gown, a medieval robe, a fifties Marilyn Monroe dress.

"Where does all this come from?" I ask, without tearing my gaze away from the gowns.

"We got a whole bunch of costumes from this old theater in town," Alexa says. "And we make a lot of our own too. Kendra helps design them. And so do I. Although my specialty is sets."

She skips down the row of dresses, and I hear hangers clinking as she searches for something. "Here. Try this on."

I get ready to politely decline, but then Alexa appears from behind the racks and thrusts the dress forward. I forget what I was going to say. The dress is a diaphanous robe made of silky, shimmering white fabric studded with a million tiny crystals. Among the white and silver ones, clusters of red ones are scattered in a seemingly random pattern. The biggest one is on the left side of the chest.

"What play is that for?" I ask.

"The play that never happened," Alexa says cryptically. "Try it on, will you?"

Wasting no time, I pull my sweater over my head and let Alexa help me into the dress. It slithers down my sides like water, settling around my shoulders with a whisper of fabric. To my surprise, that fabric proves unforgiving. Cut to measure, probably for the person who last wore it, it has absolutely no stretch. Yet it fits like it was made just for me.

"Incredible," says Alexa. Without asking for permission, she saunters up to me and pulls the hair tie out of my bun, letting my hair fall around my shoulders. She runs her fingers through it, ignoring my feeble protest. "Almost there," Alexa says, and disappears back into the rows of dresses to re-emerge with a large jewelry box. From it, she produces a rose that I first think is real, but, as I look closer, I realize it's made of fine silk. Alexa gets on tiptoe and pins the rose to my hair. I hold my breath.

"Voilà," says Alexa, and she steps back to admire her creation. Her phone appears in her hand, and she snaps another picture.

"Let me see," I say. Alexa turns the screen to me, and I can't help but be amazed at what I'm seeing. I look like a real theater ingenue from La Belle Époque. The red crystals sparkle, deadly, among the white ones. The rose in my hair looks like it's just been plucked from a dewy garden.

"So are you going to tell me what the costume is?" I ask.

"Guess." Alexa gives another sly grin.

"Uh…Juliet?"

"Close, but no cigar!" Alexa is aiming her phone at me again. Snap, snap, snap.

"Will you just tell me?"

"Sure. When the time comes. But first, you have to let me photograph you."

"Um, didn't you just do that?" I ask. The fleeting feeling of discomfort returns. This is getting a bit intense. My arms start to itch under the silky fabric—oh god, did they spray it with some kind of chemicals? Taylor would flip.

"No, I mean for real. I want you to be my muse."

I stop cold. I never thought of being someone's muse—in my own mind, I'm the creator rather than the inspiration. But I have to admit I don't hate the idea. Especially right here, right now, in this gorgeous dress.

"Okay. Is this, like, a subtle way of asking me out, because, cool, but you know—"

Alexa laughs. "Wow, you're presumptuous. No, I just think you're photogenic, and I'm building my portfolio for Julliard."

"Aiming high, I see."

"Gee, thanks. My point is, do you agree? I have just the perfect setting in mind."

"Which is?"

"Your house. Of course."

EIGHT

IT'S ALWAYS ABOUT THAT STUPID HOUSE. SINCE ALEXA
brought up the photo shoot a couple of days ago, I keep mulling it
over. I have no idea why everyone is so obsessed with it. Sure, it's
old and historic and whatever, but so are half the buildings in this
rundown town.

Thing is, I always thought it was dumb to fixate on the past.
You have to look into the future, not cling to old junk as if it's worth
something just because it's old. And now the earth seems to revolve
around this dusty house. Taylor, too, used to sneer at antiques and the
general obsession with all things vintage, thinking it was classist and a
bunch of other -ists. This house should have been a mockery of everything Taylor Brixton, photographer of the marginalized, voice-giver to

the disenfranchised, stood for. It makes it all the weirder to see Taylor fuss over moth-eaten tapestries and chipped mosaic floorboards.

Speak of the devil—Taylor seems to be in a mood today. As I traipse after her, she's struggling to carry three grocery bags at once to the service entrance. She drops one and curses loudly—something she usually tries not to do in front of me.

"Mom, are you okay?"

"I'm fine," Taylor snaps. "And you could have offered to help."

I suppose that's true. I crouch and start to pick up the groceries. The ice cream has melted, probably in the car while Taylor waited to pick me up after school.

"Sorry, I had a really long day," I say. "I guess I was just in my own head."

"Now there's something new," Taylor mutters.

"What?"

"Nothing. Please take the key from my pocket and unlock the door, will you?"

I do exactly that and carry the third bag of groceries into the kitchen. By the time all the groceries have been put away, I'm sweating.

"Mom?" I ask. "Do you mind if I invite a friend over on the weekend?"

Taylor looks frazzled. Her mascara has smudged above one eye, making her look like that guy from A Clockwork Orange. "What friend?"

"Oh, just this girl from the theater group."

Mom considers this. "Yeah, sure. But please stay out of the condemned wing. It's bad enough that you risked falling through the floor—I don't want to be responsible for someone else's child getting hurt."

"Fine," I say. I already suspect I might not keep the promise, but something about Taylor's tone suggests that it's better to cross that bridge when we get there.

The thing is, apart from Alexa, it doesn't look like I'm becoming Miss Popularity any time soon. I met the others from theater class exactly once and wasn't too impressed with them. They didn't seem all that crazy about me either. We spent the first two-hour session on pointless little improvisation exercises. For all of Kendra's hints at an exciting play of the year, we have yet to hear anything concrete about it. The girls (and it's mostly girls) from theater class seemed to treat Alexa with grudging respect, but also kept their distance, falling back into their own little cliques as soon as class was over. Two or three of the prettier, more talented ones eyed me with open hostility.

So, since the house clearly holds some sort of morbid interest for my only real friend, I have no choice but to give her the house, on a silver platter.

Upstairs, I pause at the door of my room, my hand hovering over the handle. My skin prickles. It's that peculiar feeling again, like on the night I toppled the vase. As if echoing my thoughts, the cut on my finger begins to smart under its bandage.

With a glance over my shoulder to make sure Taylor hasn't come after me, I go back the way I came from, to the staircase. On tiptoe, I go up to the fourth floor, pausing at the entrance of the long hallway of the left wing. I see immediately that the plank blocking the way has been moved aside, although the tape is still there. It looks darker than it should at this time of day. The lamps lining the wall are turned off. Where is the switch? I realize I have no idea what controls all the lamps in the house. They just seem to go on when it's dark. Maybe the workers installed sensors.

The ornate door down the hallway beckons, and I head toward it, maneuvering past the bits of tape. Each footfall raises a small cloud of dust.

Yet, as I get closer, I notice something strange on the shiny lacquered surface of the walnut panel. I have to lean in to see what it is: a handprint, a perfect imprint of a narrow palm level with my face.

I remember pressing my ear against the door, straining to hear that rustling inside. I must have left the print then. Better to wipe it before Taylor notices and asks more questions.

I pull my sleeve over my hand and wipe the door in energetic circles. But, when I stop and look, the print is still there. The lacquer is smooth and undisturbed. Almost as if the print isn't on top of it but…underneath?

How is that possible?

I raise my hand and let it hover over the print, then, gently, place my palm on top of it. I feel a bit like Indiana Jones opening some creepy booby-trapped tomb.

My palm is wider than the print, and my fingers shorter. My mind flashes back to the elegant, narrow, delicate hands in Isabella's portrait.

No freaking way. How cool is this?

Something hits the door from behind with a thump that resonates in my very bones.

I spring back. More dust has risen around the door, swirling around me. My eyes water.

"Hello?" I ask feebly. "Someone there?"

Definitely not birds.

"Taylor?" I take a backward step, another, then another, afraid to turn my back on the door. "Mom? Dad?"

Thump.

My heel catches on something, and I lose my balance, bracing myself against the wall at the last second. Enough. I turn around and run down the corridor, my steps thundering so loudly they drown out even the thrumming of my blood in my ears. I stumble down the stairs, only to stop, breathless, right outside the kitchen doorway.

Although I made a racket coming down, no one seems to have heard or noticed. In the kitchen, my mom and dad are arguing in the kind of forceful, lowered voices that always mean trouble.

I perk up my ears.

"...but what I don't want to do is reward that behavior."

"Did you talk to her about it?" Dad's voice.

"No. I just didn't know how. They called me to tell me she skipped school again, and I don't even know what to do. What am I supposed to, ground her?"

My face flushes. So that explains the weird, spaced-out Taylor from earlier.

"Well, instead, you let her throw a party on the weekend. A-plus parenting, Tay."

"Don't be sarcastic. I already feel like garbage. And it's not a party, it's just one friend."

"Still. She clearly needs some disciplining, and—"

"Maybe making a few friends will help her get adjusted. I know I may have spoiled her a little, but…"

"Too late to think of that," my dad answers.

"You expect too much of her. She's a teenager."

"And when you let her do whatever she wants, you're acting like one too."

"I'm just trying to be a good mom, Gordon, so cut me some slack! We pulled her away from her friends, her school, everything she knows…"

Taylor trails off. For a few moments, there's silence.

"And whose fault is that?" my dad says, softly.

I wait and wait, but neither of them says anything else. I make my way back to my room, not caring anymore whether they noticed. In fact, a part of me wants them to know I've been eavesdropping—that I heard them.

I close the door of my room and lean against it, deep in thought. I can't just storm back to the kitchen and demand they explain. It'll produce the opposite effect. But I can't leave it like that either.

I look up, and my gaze falls on the portrait.

At once, a chain reaction sets off in my mind, and, just like that, I know why the costume I tried on looked so familiar.

———————

The next day is drama class, which I'm starting to look forward to. But, after a sleepless night, I'm loopy and irritable. I power through the first two classes on coffee fumes alone, having drained my thermos within the first fifteen minutes. Then, at the cafeteria at lunch, I remember that I'm out of luck. The smug cafeteria woman behind her counter (even the cafeteria staff here look like snooty Yale PhDs) informs me that coffee is not a suitable choice *for children*, but, if I prefer, there are healthy alternatives such as almond milk, sparkling water, or green tea. The worst part is, normally I would have just gone off-campus for my fix. Except, here, there's nothing for at least a mile, and, without a car, I'm at the mercy of the cafeteria food police.

By the time midday rolls around, I'm fed up and just want to go home to sulk and ponder in the privacy of my room. But, when I walk into the theater classroom with seconds to spare before the bell, I find myself facing another indignity.

As usual, all the desks and chairs have been moved to the back of the classroom and piled on top of each other to free the center space for rehearsal, and all the students sit on the floor, in a semicircle around Kendra like disciples. And, at the very center of the semicircle, with the local drama stars on either side, sits none other than Nick. As soon as I walk in, he gives me the quickest half smile of acknowledgment before turning his attention back to the girl by his side—to add insult to injury, it's Ines, the ungifted Viola. I decide to pay back in kind: without sparing him another glance, I walk over to Alexa and plop down on the floor next to her.

"Did you get the okay?" Alexa asks. She was conspicuously missing from all the other classes we share, and I didn't want to admit I was sort of relieved. I'd secretly hoped that, by the time she came back on Monday or whenever she felt like gracing school with her presence again, she'd have forgotten all that business with the house.

"Yeah," I say, not without reluctance.

"Great!" Alexa chirps. Clearly, she considers this a done deal. "I'll come over on Saturday with all my stuff, and we can get started."

Stuff?

"Class," Kendra speaks up. She waits for the conversations to die down before she speaks, even though it's well after the bell. "I have two very exciting announcements for you. First, we have a new student. Everyone, say hi to Nick. I understand he's new to the theater, so—"

"In a manner of speaking," Nick interjects. He's still not looking at me—*avoiding* looking at me? Not that I'm looking at *him* to see if he's looking at me.

"You'll pick it right up. You'll see, we're a welcoming bunch, and there's no need to be self-conscious. I believe that everyone has a little Sarah Bernhardt in them—or Laurence Olivier, if you prefer."

This is Kendra at her cringiest, but Nick nods in agreement while his two fangirls are fawning by his side. I grimace and exchange a look with Alexa.

"Now, the second thing," Kendra goes on. "I know it's still early in the term, but it's time we start thinking about our play of the year. Now, as you all know, I will have to run the final selection past the committee and the campus life organizer…"

Everyone in class boos, as if on cue.

"...but I'll collect suggestions starting now. If anybody has any ideas, feel free to contribute."

I glance around the semicircle. Several hands shoot up at once, but not Nick's. Alexa is also mysteriously tight-lipped. As Kendra calls on one person or another, the suggestions are super mundane, at least as far as I'm concerned. More old white guys than a stack of dollar bills. I think this might be a good occasion to show off my theater chops by suggesting something avant-garde, exciting, off-the-wall, but, as I try to think of something, I'm surprised to draw a blank. Everything seems to have evaporated from my head. It must be the sleep deprivation and lack of coffee. Plus, something else pops stubbornly into my mind, not at all the stunningly original something I would have liked, but I can't get rid of it. It beckons, coos in my ear, enticing and seductive. Suddenly I'm thinking in scenes and sets and dramatic moments, and the female lead is me, of course, in the best role I've ever taken on. And, the more I let myself dwell on that image, the more it tugs at me, becomes irresistible.

"Isabella?" I hear Kendra's puzzled voice and realize it's not the first time she's called my name.

"Huh?"

"You have your hand up."

I do? Well, that's a surprise. I don't recall raising my hand. But there it is, pointing to the ceiling.

"Uh," I say.

"Go ahead," says Kendra, misinterpreting my awkwardness. "We're just spitballing for now, so all suggestions are equally welcome."

I lick my lips. "We should do," I say, and lick them again. "We should do *The Picture of Dorian Gray*."

The immediate effect this has on the class stuns me. A ripple races through the students. Whispers arise. Even Kendra's face, I could swear, turns a touch red.

"Well," she says. "That's certainly a bold...suggestion."

"There's a version I know of," I say. I have no idea where the sudden ardor is coming from. Yeah, I know about this play, but I know a thousand plays. *What's so special about this one?* "It's a deconstruction. He's haunted by the ghost of Sibyl Vane, who makes him stab the portrait at the end."

"Yes," says Kendra carefully. "I know."

Awkward silence hangs over the class as my gaze bounces from one face to another. Alexa's eyes are like saucers.

"Anyone else?" Kendra says cheerfully, but the cheer is forced. Someone hastily suggests yet another play by Chekhov, but the mood doesn't quite go back to normal until class is over. As soon as Alexa and I are out in the hall, Alexa practically squeals with excitement.

"You figured it out! How?"

"Figured what out?" I feel a bit hollow. I really should sleep.

"The costume I made you try on. That's what it was. You guessed it!"

"There's a painting," I say. "In our house. Of Isabella Granger wearing that same costume. It's Sibyl Vane from *Dorian Gray*."

"Oh my god, I can totally see it!" Alexa shrieks. "You'll be such a perfect Sibyl. And I've seen you do improv—you can out-act those bitches in your sleep," she adds with a disdainful nod at Nick's fangirls, who are walking far ahead of us with their tight little group.

But then, Alexa grows serious in a heartbeat. "I mean, of course it'll never happen. The committee and Greer will kill it. I sort of can't blame them—but it would be so cool! The whole school would talk about it forever..."

"Why?" I ask, puzzled. "Why would the committee kill it?"

Alexa's gaze darts back and forth, checking if anyone can overhear. I instantly get a bad feeling.

"Oh, right! You don't know. I suppose you could have guessed, since you saw the costume and all. The theater club tried to do this play once before. You see, it's kind of like this school's Scottish play. You know what I mean?"

I nod. Anyone who's spent a day at a theater knows about the Scottish play, that one famous Shakespeare play set in Scotland that no one dares name, like it's the Voldemort of drama. Just saying the name out loud will supposedly lead to terrible failure, or worse.

"Yeah, so. The thing is, the last time the school tried to do the play, Sibyl Vane...disappeared."

NINE

"DISAPPEARED?" I HISS. "AND YOU'RE TELLING ME THIS NOW?"

"I was gonna tell you," Alexa says evasively.

"Was that her dress you made me try on? A *dead girl's* dress?"

"Well, technically, she's only *disappeared*, and, technically, the dress belongs to the theater club."

"Technically," I echo. "Have you no shame?"

"It's the play that's cursed," Alexa says. "Not the dress."

"I don't believe in curses. But shouldn't I have heard something about a girl going missing from the school? In a town this size, it should have been all over social media."

Alexa gives me a meaningful look. "This was like the aughts, before social media. I don't know that much about it, truth be told.

Everyone thought she was a runaway in the end. Everything pointed to it, you know? She took some things with her, emptied her bank account. Really, only one thing didn't add up, but the police kind of just dismissed it."

"I'm scared to ask."

Alexa shrugs. "She took off right before the premiere. Of the play of which she was the star. Attended by college recruiters…why would she do that, huh?"

I think about it. To me, it sure as hell doesn't make sense. To throw away such an opportunity… The thought makes my teeth hurt.

"Anyway," says Alexa. "It would be nice if we could do the play regardless. Even better, actually. We could get some real word of mouth."

"That's kind of cold."

"It was like twenty years ago, Isa. Life goes on. And I think Nick Swain would make an amazing Dorian, no?"

I blink. "I'm sorry, what?"

"Nick," Alexa says. "The new guy? He's a bit of a legend around here. Or a legendary asshole—depending on your perspective. First, he lives alone. His parents are in another state somewhere. They rent him a whole house—just so he can live here and go to this school."

I find it questionable that someone would go to such lengths to stay in this awful place. Alexa looks at me like I'm a child. "It means," she says, "that he throws the best parties. Think about it. Whole house, no adults."

"Uh-huh."

Alexa squints. "You seem angry," she says. "Did he already manage to piss you off in the week you've been in town? Oh god. Don't tell me you already—"

"*Hell, no,*" I say, a little too loudly.

"Hey, the world's your oyster; you do what you want," Alexa says. "Just keep in mind, if you want exclusivity or any such thing, that's not really his strong suit. Since sophomore year, he's dated, like, the entire school. And I mean the *entire* school." She wiggles her eyebrows.

Great. And to think I sort of, kind of, found him cute...for half a second. Am I that predictable?

On the way home, my phone dings. It's a message from Eve. An email, of all things. I try to remember the last time we communicated by *email*. Had to be what, third grade?

Hey gurl, looks like you're semi-permanently off-grid so I'm going to try this the old-fashioned way. Hey, if it continues like this, soon I'll be writing you actual letters! On parchment with a quill. Anyway, I thought you'd like to know. Rehearsals are in full swing, and it's really starting to shape up. You HAVE to come and see the final play. It's right before Thanksgiving, so you should be on break.

Anyway, my driver's test is IN TWO WEEKS!!! I think I have a good chance of acing this thing, and then it can be a road trip every weekend. My mom doesn't mind. She knows how much we miss each other (you miss me too, right? You better miss me! LOL).

Oh yeah, and I've been looking up your Isabella Granger. Living history, like you said. Except I can't find all that much. I mean, if she was such a muse, why isn't all the artwork hanging at the Met or something?

I hope you get this okay. Get back to me? Please? I'm starting to feel like I'm talking to myself.

Cheers,

Eve

I immediately start to type up an answer but stop midsentence and lower the phone into my lap. A part of me wants to say that I'll absolutely come see the play, but a part of me is righteously furious. Doesn't she even think about how that makes me feel? All that hard work, and I get to watch someone else take center stage. That's just mean.

To pacify myself, I let my mind wander to the theater, to the gorgeous, sparkling costume of Sybil Vane playing Juliet. *Soon that'll be me*, I think. I conveniently forget that no one has approved the play yet, and that, first, I'd have to outshine all the other wannabes at audition.

Still, something tells me these things will all come through.

I spend Saturday morning on edge. My dad makes a comment about me being moody, to which Taylor snarkily retorts that "Isa is more often moody than not these days," to which I have no choice but to snark back. Then, when I put away the clothes and shoes that are scattered all over my room—to have space for the photo shoot, and for no other reason—Taylor makes a comment about me cleaning up without being asked, *for once*, and it takes me all the patience I can muster not to lob a Converse at her.

The bathroom upstairs is an odd mix of antique and modern: there's an original claw-foot tub, but, above it, a brand-new chrome showerhead that clashes with it furiously. All the other plumbing fixtures also look like they were sitting on the shelf at Home Depot a week ago. The only unspoiled element is the mirror in an ornate baroque frame. While I wait for the water to run hot (which takes forever and a day, thank you for asking), I inspect my reflection. The bathroom has a stained-glass window that's still in pretty good shape, except for a fragment where the tinted blue glass had cracked and was covered with a piece of cardboard. Multicolored light pours in, softening everything it touches.

I lean in closer. The roots of my hair have been growing in, a full inch now. But my face looks softer, like the unflattering mirror decided to take pity on me at last. I look paler than usual. Maybe it's just the tint of the light, but I can't say I hate it. It makes my eyes look like they're a different color, their blue tinged with a sea-green. I pull the elastic out of my hair and arrange it in soft waves around my face.

"'Dorian, Dorian,'" I say to my reflection. "'Before I knew you, acting was the one reality of my life. It was only in the theatre that

I lived. I thought that it was all true. I was Rosalind one night and Portia the other. The joy of Beatrice was my joy, and the sorrows of Cordelia were mine also. I believed in everything.'"

I wince. *Flat, flat, flat. No good.* With an audition like that, I'll be lucky if Kendra casts me as Servant Girl #2, with no spoken lines. So I try again from a different place.

"'I think I shall call you Prince Charming.'"

But, if I've been channeling a Disney princess, it's a fail. Sarcasm bleeds into my words, and even my expression is off. A smirk. As if to say, *I see right through you, bastard, and I know what you're all about.* Nothing like the ingenue Sybil. *My look is all wrong,* I think and lean closer and closer to the mirror until my forehead almost touches the surface. My skin looks different. No—it *is* different: the tiny acne scar on my cheek is gone, and my very pores don't look the same. My skin is finer, somehow, yet sallow, thin and brittle and blue under the eyes, which are—green?

I squint, and the line that appears between my eyebrows belongs on a different face, a much older face. It's deep and dark as if drawn on by a single dash of ink.

What on earth…?

I raise my trembling hands to my face, and they're someone else's hands. My chipped nail polish is gone, and there are rings on my fingers. Not my rings, the thin silver ones, but heavy *gold* rings studded with dulled gems.

Something icy brushes against my foot. The cold shoots up my leg and races up my spine.

With a yelp, I spring back from the mirror, yanking my foot away from the slimy, slithering touch. My ankle wobbles, I lose my balance and go sprawling on my backside.

Right into a puddle of water. I look around, incredulous: water is bubbling over the edge of the tub, creeping across the floor—fast.

Cursing, I get back on my feet and splash toward the tub. I hastily turn off the water, which hasn't grown a single degree warmer. My hands instantly go numb. I grab all the towels off the rack and throw them on the floor. Crap!

"Isa?" My mom is pounding on the door.

I hold my breath, bracing for the icy bite of cold water, reach into the tub, and pull the plug, which has been in place this whole time. Because, obviously, I didn't check before I turned on the shower. The hot water, I realize, is the *other* knob. I'd turned the cold on full blast instead.

"Everything's fine!" I yell out, even though I'm not so sure. "Can I just have an extra towel?"

When I emerge from the bathroom at last, toweling my hair, I feel disoriented for a moment: it's darker than when I went in. A glance at the clock makes me gasp. I've been in there for over three hours. The sun is setting.

Taylor gives me a dubious look as I pass by on the way to my room. She's holding a bunch of albums—the big ones with the heavy covers and parchment paper to separate the photographs. Her portfolio albums.

"So I spilled a little water on the floor," I grumble. "No big deal, right? I toweled it all up."

Taylor shakes her head.

"What is it?"

"Your friend is here."

———————

I dress as quickly as I can and make my way downstairs, hopefully before Taylor can say something to Alexa that will make her never come back. Instead, I come down to an idyllic picture: Alexa is seated at the dining-room table, dressed in a floor-length black tulle skirt and top with flowing lace sleeves. In this getup, she looks right at home in this room with its heavy, dark oak table, aged Louis XV chairs upholstered in threadbare navy satin, and matching blue-and-silver wallpaper. The only thing that spoils the Victorian Gothic wet dream is the cup of espresso she's holding, courtesy of our brand-new machine, and one of Taylor's huge portfolio albums in front of her. She's leafing through it with a slightly exaggerated look of admiration on her face.

"Hey," she says as soon as she sees me.

"Hey yourself." *What on earth is going on down here?*

"You didn't tell me your mom was Taylor Brixton," Alexa says cheerfully, and gives me a wink since Taylor isn't looking. I strongly suspect that, until ten minutes ago, Alexa had never heard of Taylor Brixton.

"Aw, shucks," says Taylor, blushing. "It's just nice that people my daughter's age are still interested in my archaic medium."

This humility is also fake, as I know full well. Yet the two of them play their parts in the skit flawlessly.

"There's something about film," Alexa says without missing a beat. "It doesn't allow for mistakes."

I clear my throat.

Taylor gets the hint. "I'm going to leave you girls to it," she says, gathering up her albums. "Just remember, you promised me you'd be careful!"

The moment she's gone, the Stepford-child look drops from Alexa's face.

"Sorry about my mom," I say. "I know she can be a bit much." In her hunger for approval from the young'uns, that is.

"Never mind. She's cool."

I wince. "You don't have to do that."

"And this *house*!" Alexa exclaims. "It's incredible."

"You can say that again," I murmur.

She jumps right into it. "Let's take some test pictures."

"But I need to do my makeup first," I say. "I guess I sort of—lost track of time."

Which, once again, is a big understatement.

"Nah," says Alexa. "It's just a test run. You can do your makeup after."

"You want to take my picture with no makeup on? Do we know each other?"

But, to my alarm, Alexa picks up her phone and points it right at me. I barely have time to raise my hands and shield my face. "Stop it!"

But I hear the shutter sound, and Alexa exclaims: "Get your hands out of the way. You look great!"

To prove her point, she turns the phone around so I can see. I peer at the screen apprehensively.

My first reaction is to admit Alexa is right. The frizz in my hair and the shadows under my eyes seem to have disappeared in the click of a shutter. I look like I've been photographed with a soft-focus lens, as if my skin and hair glow from within. I never noticed how my fair eyebrows and eyelashes make me look delicate, not washed out like I always thought, and how the subtle pinpoints of freckles sprayed across the bridge of my nose accentuate the fine shade of my skin.

Alexa's chuckle brings me back to earth. "Well, this is going to your head faster than a vodka Red Bull."

I blink. Have I spoken out loud? My heart gives a leap, and heat rises into my face.

Luckily, Alexa shrugs it off. She nods at something behind me, and I follow with my gaze.

"That window," Alexa says. "Can you go stand there?"

"But my outfit," I protest feebly. I'm wearing a plain white off-the-shoulder tee and yesterday's plain leggings, my feet bare.

"It's perfect."

I stand by the window, where the sunset is entering its last phase. At this angle, it looks like the sky is bleeding. I'm so distracted by the incredible view that I give a tiny jolt when Alexa's phone clicks. There's a knot in my stomach that won't loosen. And it's so silly—not like we're shooting for *Vogue* or anything.

"Yes!" Alexa exclaims. "Like this. Don't move."

Click, click, click.

"Gorgeous."

"Can I see?"

"In a second." Alexa squints. "Can you get up on the windowsill over there? I want to get the full arch."

My knees feel soft as I climb obediently onto the sill.

"Good!" Alexa directs. "Now put your hand on the windowpane. Lower. Not that low. Now gaze softly."

"What does that even mean? As opposed to what—gazing hardly?"

"Just do it, Isa. Yes!"

Click, click, click.

"Are you going to show me those photos?"

"Don't rush me, or I won't show you anything at all."

Click, click.

I turn my gaze to the window. The arched windowpane is taller than me, and the only thing that keeps me from falling is the double glass. It's breathtaking, I must admit. Below, I see the semicircle outline of old tiles through the sparse grass—that's where there used to be a gazebo. And, off to the side, another perimeter, now only a low wall marking a ruined foundation. For some reason, it pulls my gaze like a magnet. The air is so still that not a blade of grass moves—like I'm looking at a picture, or an old-school theater backdrop.

"Alexa," I say. Something is scratching in the back of my mind, a realization, or some knowledge I'd forgotten but am now struggling to remember. "This place. It used to be—"

"Stand still." Click, click.

"They're perfect," Alexa says as she swipes through the photos. It's growing darker now, and her face is bathed in the glow of her phone screen. Her eyes are wide in wonderment. "Every single one. Holy shit, Isa, you have to see."

I climb off the windowsill and try to peer at Alexa's phone, but she dodges, tapping busily at the screen. A second later, my own phone, which I'd left on the floor by the window, chimes.

"I sent them to you," Alexa says. I thumb through the photos and have to admit these are some of the best pictures ever taken of me. They make the rest of my Instagram look like a second grader's. They look otherworldly, almost like paintings if not for the sharp definition—and my pink hair and cropped T-shirt that ground them in the present day. In one of the photos, my pose looks uncomfortable, my posture bordering on tortured, my spine bent, my head lolling. But the look on my face is utterly calm, serene. Did I really do this? Wouldn't my neck be hurting like hell right now?

"Can I post them?" I ask, hoping only that the internet connection doesn't let me down.

But Alexa shakes her head. "We can do better."

I don't see how you could improve upon such perfection.

"I don't just want to make some cute Insta shots," Alexa is saying. "I want to make true art."

"Then you better scare up some oil paints," I murmur.

But Alexa is unflappable. "To each era, its own medium!"

Semi-comically, she points one finger into the air, showman-like. "Ours will be photos!"

She's a little too worked up, I think, and, frankly, it's getting a little weird. Like, I can see the whites of her eyes all around the iris. How many espressos did she have?

"We need to go to a higher floor," she says. "I want to capture that view behind you. Quick, while we still have that light."

"There's a terrace on the top floor," I say. "We can go outside."

We head upstairs. But, as I make a right turn, I notice Alexa isn't following me. When I turn around, Alexa is standing at the entrance of the left-wing hallway.

"What's that way?" she asks, her tone light but not fooling anyone.

"We shouldn't go there," I say with an embarrassing stammer. "Something about the floor. Or the ceiling. I—"

"Looks fine to me."

And, before I know it, Alexa is ducking under the remains of the tape and heading down the hall—right toward the locked walnut door.

"What's behind this?" she asks.

And, as if in slow motion, I watch her reach for the ornate handle and jiggle it.

No! I want to yell out that it's not safe, although I can't seem to remember why. But my jaw grows slack, my face numb.

What is happening?

I extend my hand in front of me, but it feels like someone else's hand. I think I see the dull gold glint of old rings.

One blink, and everything goes back to normal, but too late. Alexa is pulling on the door handle, and the door swings open.

But it's supposed to be—why is it unlocked?

I don't run—I fly down the hallway and skid to a halt at Alexa's side. Alexa gives me a look like I'm crazy.

"It's just a room," I start to say. The door opens wider, and the light from the hallway pours in.

"Whoa."

TEN

I STEP THROUGH THE DOORWAY, BREATHING IN THE sweet, musty scent of dust. It's familiar to me by now—the faint whiff of it fills the entire house all the way to the ground floor. But, here, it's the main note and with an undercurrent of something else, something sharper, almost unpleasant. The light that falls through the doors is barely enough to see the enormous room: the ceiling is so high that it's lost in darkness far above our heads.

There's nothing wrong with the roof—at least nothing obvious. This room is unlike anything I've ever seen. This place could be a ballroom, if it weren't on the fourth floor in a distant wing. The ceiling is lost in the dark, but I can tell it's vertiginously high and vaulted. Like a church. Another grand chandelier hangs above our heads, wrapped in many layers of fabric, and more line the walls. The floor beneath my feet is dirty, but I still can make out an elaborate mosaic. I can only imagine what this place was like in its heyday.

Wasting no time, Alexa opens the flashlight on her phone. Its beam roams the walls. Not a single window anywhere but odd rectangles all over the walls. The beam drops lower, and I understand why: matching rectangles wrapped in tarp and plastic stand in rows, stacked against the walls.

"I don't think we should be in here," I say. I don't really think that's true, but it feels like I should say something.

"You're kidding, right?" Alexa says. And, to my dismay, she makes a beeline for the stacked rectangles. She pulls one away from the rest with some effort.

My insides grow cold, but Alexa begins to rip apart the wrappings, ignoring the clouds of dust that rise up. The flowing lace sleeves of her shirt flail, and her black hair whips around her head, falling in her eyes. She quickly pushes it aside, leaving a trail of grime down her cheek and smudging her eye makeup. In the feeble light, she looks slightly demented, or demonic.

"I knew it!" Alexa barely stifles her shriek of joy. "*Look!*"

She turns the painting around.

It's Isabella—this much is clear at first glance. It's done in a pre-Raphaelite style similar to what my googling turned up. And it must have been absolutely scandalous for the day, because Isabella is reclining in a bathtub, her hair flowing down her shoulders and floating on the crystal-clear, perfectly still water just so, to strategically hide her nakedness.

The water, a few seemingly careless strokes of a brush, looks so real I'm sure that, if I reach out and touch the canvas, cold will shoot through my fingertips. Immediately, I think of that story I once heard, of the artist's model who posed for hours in a tub of ice-cold water—the water *so* cold that the woman caught pneumonia and died.

But the painting, the painting lived on forever. And isn't that what she would have wanted? Isn't it the most important thing?

Images conjured up by Alexa and my own imagination invade my mind. I see myself in a diaphanous, flowing gown, my skin glowing like white wax, flowers in my hair.

"Careful," I say in a hushed voice. "This thing must be valuable."

"In that case, why isn't it in a museum?" Alexa parries.

I'm transfixed by the painting. Isabella's profile is sharp, her green gaze fixed on something outside the frame. Her lips are rosy-pink, slightly parted. Is she waiting for her lover, or seeing him off? And something about the scene seems oddly familiar.

Then it hits me. The claw-footed tub. An identical one is in our own bathroom. Unless it's not just identical but—the very same?

A chill travels up my spine.

Alexa is busily unwrapping a second painting. I taste more sweet dust on the tip of my tongue.

"This is it," Alexa is saying. "This is what I want to do. True art."

"I'm not sitting naked in a bathtub," I joke, hoping to defuse the tension. There's a weight in the room; I feel it in my bones. Something about the pressure makes me feel like I have no right to say no. And not just because of Alexa.

"No. We'll make our own images. This is just the inspiration! What I'm asking you is, do you want to go viral or not?"

"Taylor will have a fit, for sure," I say with unease.

"I'm sorry to say this, Isa, but your mother's sense of aesthetics is mired in another decade. And that decade is over. The time of ugliness is gone, and the age of beauty is back!"

The way her voice carries under the high ceiling—I can't help but imagine someone else speaking through her lips.

ELEVEN

"ARE YOU JUST GOING TO STAND THERE, OR ARE YOU going to help?"

I jolt out of my thoughts. Alexa is on tiptoes, her arms straining under the weight of yet another painting, but she can't quite reach the hook on the wall where the painting is supposed to hang.

"I don't know," I say. "Should we be touching all this stuff? These paintings are old and probably have some sort of historical value at least. Maybe we should get someone to help us. My mom, or people from the university…"

I feel cowardly and kind of like a loser. Here it is, the thing I've been waiting for—something fun to keep me busy in my not-so-great new life. But all I want to do is board up the door and go back to my room.

Alexa huffs. "The people from the university left all this beauty to molder under wraps for decades. And your mom is hardly better. No, we're going to do this ourselves."

I look at the painting she's trying to hang up. Isabella is standing near a mirror in an ornate frame, her hair flowing past her waist. She's dressed in a gauzy white Greek-style toga that looks like a bedsheet, her shoulders exposed. Must have been controversial back in the day. She looks beautiful, pure, her skin glowing like the paint is new. Except something is off about it. I can't quite put my finger on it.

"Isabella!" Alexa's voice comes unexpectedly from behind me. Confused, I spin around, just in time for her to take a picture.

"Hey!" I exclaim.

"Hey yourself. It looks amazing. Did you ever notice that the two of you could be sisters?"

I snatch the phone out of her hand. The photo caught me mid-spin, my hair a pale, pink blur. My eyes are the only thing that's in focus, their color surprisingly clear despite the lack of light. I look like one of those ghost sighting photos.

"I'm so going to post that," Alexa says, decisively taking back her phone.

"No!" I exclaim. I'm overcome with a sudden deep, primal fear. "Don't. Everyone will know we went up there."

Alexa gives me a blank look. "And?"

I can't answer.

"Isabella, you disappoint me. We have something unique here.

Something no one else has access to. And you just want to slink away with your tail between your legs? I'm posting it."

My phone dings in my pocket as I get an alert, since she tagged me.

"And it's done," Alexa says. "Now, are you going to help me put up the rest of these paintings or not?"

I bring a small ladder from the third floor, where some workers forgot it in the hallway, and we put up the paintings one by one. It's fairly easy to figure out what goes where, since each one fits its rectangle on the wallpaper.

Finally, only one is left. The biggest one. It's easily as tall as me, leaning against the back wall and shrouded in its tarp. I look at it, and a strange little shiver races up my spine. I'm not sure if it's excitement or fear.

"Looks heavy," I say.

"So don't just stand there. Help me hang it!"

Luckily, it doesn't hang very high. It's meant to be at the center of this whole display, a giant, dark rectangle on the wallpaper, the only empty space on a wall pretty much covered in paintings.

I follow Alexa's lead and take hold of the side of the painting. Dust from the tarp immediately rises up in a cloud, making my eyes itch.

"On three," says Alexa. "One, two, three."

We haul the painting across the room and lean it on the wall against the dark rectangle.

"Ready?" Alexa asks. She doesn't wait for an answer, just yanks away the tarp, which comes away with surprising ease. With a sound like giant wings flapping, it collapses to the floor at the painting's foot, and, in another prodigious storm of dust, Isabella is revealed.

For a moment, I'm breathless. She's wearing a gown of red velvet, far too opulent to be of her era. There's a jeweled bodice and gold embroidery and lavish jewelry to match—another historical costume. Her auburn hair flows down her back, just like in the other pictures. Her eyes are emerald green, a careful blush creeps across her cheeks. So why does she look so different?

It's the look on her face. Not carefully bland, spaced out like the pre-Raphaelites. Not gazing softly, whatever that means, not longing or daydreaming. Not subtly bored like the subjects of real historical portraits always look after hours of sitting without moving. Her expression has the sharpness and presence of a photograph, and her look is unkind. Her lips are pressed tightly together, her jaw sharp and defined like she's clenching her teeth. I swear I can even see shadows of frown lines between her eyebrows and around her mouth.

Is she pretending to be Lady Macbeth? Mary Queen of Scots?

Somehow, this look suits her even more. She's prettier this way than in the paintings where she's clearly trying to appear attractive.

"Hello." Alexa's annoyed voice cuts through my haze of thoughts. I realize she's been calling my name.

"Yeah, sorry," I say, feeling uncomfortable. "I just spaced out."

"I can see that."

"Don't you think it's magnificent?" I ask softly. "Just look at her face."

Alexa shrugs. "Nah. Not my favorite. The dress is incredible, I give her that, but the face is off. Whoever painted that didn't like her very much."

"I like it," I say. I feel vexed for no reason.

"Good, then. Help me hang it up."

So we pick up the painting once again and, after some effort, manage to hang it on its hook.

"Ta-da!" Alexa wipes her dusty hands on her shirt. They leave behind two ghostly gray smears.

I take a step back and look at the wall of paintings. Complete now. There's an odd satisfaction in that. It spills in my chest like a physical warmth. And, as if on cue, the room takes on a different aspect, as though the light has changed. Everything is warmer, coated in a sort of living sepia filter. *Finally, things are back in their place*, I catch myself thinking.

Where did that come from?

I blink, and the room is normal again. Dark and murky.

"If we want to do any more photos, we have to get some normal lights in here," Alexa is grumbling. "Do you think there's a power outlet?"

"I doubt it," I say without really thinking, or even hearing what she said.

Alexa won't be discouraged, though. She inspects the walls like a hound. I follow her with my gaze, which hits the back wall and screeches to an abrupt halt.

"What's that?" I point. Behind the big painting, it turns out, there's a door. How neither of us noticed it when we moved the painting, I have no idea, because it's low but fairly large, covered with the same wallpaper but noticeable.

Alexa whistles. She makes a beeline for the door.

"Be careful!" I yelp, but she ignores me. She turns the handle, and, when the door swings open without resistance, vanishes inside. I see the light of her phone darting back and forth.

"It's a storage room!" she shrieks, hardly able to contain her joy. "Get in here, quick!"

Reluctant, I inch my way to the door and gingerly step over the threshold.

Alexa is already pulling reams of dusty-looking fabric from a trunk. "There're clothes. And probably more. Oh, Isa, oh my god."

"My mom is going to look for us," I say. "We should probably get back downstairs."

"Wow. Way to be a buzzkill."

"If she finds us here, she'll nail the whole room shut. Then who's the buzzkill? And, anyway, we can come back here next week."

I don't know what made me say that. Just as the words escape from my mouth, I realize I don't really want her here again. I don't want to come back here.

Except I do.

Do I?

"Isa, that's incredible. I'm so happy right now, you have no idea."

I'm pensive as we exit the room and close the double doors behind us carefully. It's fully dark outside, and, from downstairs, I detect the scent of dinner cooking. I feel like I accidentally walked through a time portal to find myself in a much more boring era. One glance at Alexa's expression tells me she's feeling the same way.

"Isa," she says, meeting my gaze. "You know what?"

"What?"

"I think this has been, hands-down, the best day of my life."

TWELVE

THAT NIGHT, I GO TO BED LATE. FOR SOME REASON, I'm so hyper that I doubt I'll be able to sleep at all. For the longest time I idle in bed, scrolling through my phone, which chooses this moment to have a crystal-clear signal. And, since it's Saturday night, every feed is like an endless stream of concentrated FOMO designed to torment me. It seems that everyone is doing something cool, everyone is at some amazing house party at a penthouse or a concert or the latest nightclub. Except, as I scroll through it all, I'm not bothered in the slightest. On the contrary: I feel almost smug. Here I am, and I have the coolest thing ever right at my fingertips, separated from me by one floor and some old caution tape. I can't even brag about it, at least not yet, but that only makes it even more special. Hell, I almost feel sorry for all my Brooklyn friends. They don't know what they're missing out on.

The photos that Alexa posted steadily collect likes. Every other second, it seems, my phone is pinging, until I have no choice but to do something I've never done before: turn off the sound. Still, the silent alerts keep popping up. There are names I don't recognize. I think they might be from my new school.

I do keep an eye out for one name in particular, but it never comes up. Eve posted a photo earlier in the evening in which she's wearing my Yvonne costume. I reflexively hearted it before I even realized I should be feeling hurt.

I glance at the time at the top of my screen and notice that it's past midnight. The room and the house are both eerily quiet. It feels almost as if they're wrapped around me, a protective cocoon of silence and darkness and dust. My phone is the only beacon of light in a dark space. It's not spooky at all. I put it on the charger, and, a couple of seconds later, the screen goes dark.

It doesn't make a difference whether I open or close my eyes, so I figure I might as well keep them closed. I don't even notice I drift off to sleep.

In my dream, I find myself in a vast space I can't identify until its edges come into focus: the domed ceiling and wooden floor and the expanse of an empty auditorium are the theater at my new school. I'm on stage, and, when I look down, I'm wearing my Yvonne dress. I spin around, and the skirt flares around my legs. But there are no other actors anywhere, and, when I look behind me, I see that there's no backdrop, no set, no props—nothing. I'm alone in the completely empty theater. With the skirt swishing around my ankles with that particular sound cheap, fake velvet makes, I go backstage. All the lights are on, but there's not a soul anywhere. The door to the wardrobe is half-open, and, when I peer in, it's not the normal costumes that I see but rows of dusty, faded dresses from all different eras. I touch one, then another—not costumes, that's for sure. Not replicas but the real thing. They disintegrate beneath my fingertips, turning to a mass of threads that collapses into dust.

I make my way to the dressing room. Here, everything is dark. I can see the outlines of the makeup tables and the mirrors and the chairs. I feel along the wall for the light switch and find it. I flip it, and, with a faint buzzing sound, the lights flicker on.

My heart does a backflip when I realize that it's not the dressing room I was expecting, the one I remember. It looks antique. The mirrors are all in heavy gilt frames, the chairs are all Art Deco, their once-clean lines blurred with cobwebs and more dust, their brass tarnished to a dull brown. On the makeup table sits an array of ancient pots of creams and cosmetics. Once-elegant little porcelain and glass containers are now grimy and chipped. I give a start when I spot what I first think is a human head in the corner, but, just as soon, I realize it's just a mannequin head holding up an old wig. It, too, hasn't escaped the dust and cobwebs, but I can still clearly see its original color through the gray shroud: a brilliant, deep auburn. *This could only be made out of real human hair*, I think with a shudder.

Next to it on the counter is a brush. I pick it up. The hairs still enmeshed among the broken bristles are long and gray.

A rustle behind me makes me whip my head around. "Is someone here?" I want to say, but, for some reason, no sound comes out of my mouth. Like my throat is locked. I turn back and finally catch my reflection in one of the big mirrors.

Through the web of black cracks that snake across the mercury trapped under the old glass, another face looks back at me. It takes me a beat to recognize the harsh line of the mouth, the hard green eyes, the deep lines etched into skin that's not mine.

With a start, I jolt awake. My head spins. I'm not laying in my bed. I'm not in my bedroom at all. I'm standing in the middle of a small, cramped space, dimly lit by a chandelier's three flickering candles. The air smells like dust.

Panic-stricken, I gulp air like a fish. I'm in the small storage room on the fourth floor, I realize. At my feet is the biggest trunk, wide open, and old dresses spill out over the side like guts from a corpse.

When I look down, my breath catches. I'm wearing the burgundy dress from the big painting. The heavy gold trim tugs at my sleeves. The hard bodice squeezes my ribcage, the built-in whalebones digging into my flesh.

———————

Monday at school, everyone is looking at me strangely. Maybe I just notice more than usual because I'm jumpy, still not over what happened. I didn't tell anyone, not even Taylor—especially not Taylor. Or my dad. I knew that, if I told, they'd board up the room and never let us in there again. Which, when I think about it, isn't such a bad idea, but, somehow, I just knew that I shouldn't say a word.

I practically tore my way out of the burgundy dress before making a beeline back to my room and shutting the door. Once I caught my breath, I propped a chair up against it.

The worst part is, it was impossible. The dress had all these little buttons up the back, from the small of my back all the way to the neck. Every single one of these tiny buttons was done up, threaded through a little woven loop. To get out of the dress, I had to claw at them, twisting my arms out of their sockets. Even then, several buttons came off.

No matter how I think about it, there's no way I could have done it myself, even if I had been awake.

I look around for Alexa, who's nowhere to be seen. Instead, I practically bump into Sara, a girl from theater class, who gives me a big smile that puts me on my guard.

"Beautiful photos!" she says before continuing on her way.

I blink, not sure what she's talking about. Then it hits me. I'd turned off notifications on my Instagram—and, funny thing, actually forgot to look at it for a whole day. I take my phone out of my pocket, turn notifications back on, and watch my screen explode.

I don't think I've ever gotten that many likes. We're talking viral here. My photos where I pose for Alexa got a huge amount, but the one where I'm blurry in front of the Isabella painting is the one that's breaking the internet, it seems.

Here, in broad daylight, in the ugly tiled hall of the school, the photo has lost its eerie quality. It's just a picture on my screen. A good picture. But, the closer I look, the more it feels off. The painting is perfectly framed in the photo—weirdly so. Like Alexa did it on purpose. Isabella is in full focus. You can see every little detail of her face, every little variation of green in her irises and auburn in her hair. As I zoom in, I notice that the hair is painted in extreme detail, something that escaped my attention when I saw it in person. There are many shades in it, ranging from strawberry blond to copper to maroon to auburn so dark it's practically brunette. Like Isabella somehow managed to get a balayage a hundred years before it was a thing.

It also looks vaguely familiar in a way I can't define.

I zoom back out, and I'm stricken by the strange sensation, as though it were Isabella who was the real person, and I, with my blurred silhouette, just an imprint, a picture of a picture.

"Hey!"

Startled, I drop my phone. My insides freeze as I watch it flip over in the air, and I only have time to think, *Oh god, not the new one— Taylor will never replace it now*, when, just as it's about to hit those oh so unforgiving tiles, it flips over again and lands safely screen-side up.

All the breath goes out of me in relief. "Look what you almost did," I say.

"Sorry," a voice says—and it's none other than Alexa. She doesn't sound sorry. "Did you see? It's everywhere! Congratulations!"

"That's hardly viral," I grumble, even though I was literally just thinking the same thing. Crouching, I pick up my phone and inspect it. Not a scratch.

"Are you kidding? The whole school won't shut up about it." Alexa is beaming.

"Not the whole school," I groan. "Everybody saw it?"

Alexa nods meaningfully. And, as I follow her down the hall to our first shared class, I start to realize she's right. Everybody is looking.

And so is Nick. He's standing in a corner nook so I don't notice him until I pass by just inches away, and I feel his gaze, cold as a bucket of icy water down the back of my shirt. I can't help but shiver.

If he did see the photos, then he sure as hell isn't happy about them.

By the time theater workshop rolls around, things are normal again. A little too normal. As I walk into the classroom, everyone is smiling at me and saying, *Hi, Isa*, like I've been going to this school since elementary. Apparently, I'm everyone's new best friend overnight, without any action on my part except posing for a few photos. Even Kendra gazes at me with a sort of serene adoration. Nick is sitting on the floor when I walk in, blithely flirting with Ines. He looks up when he sees me and gives me a crooked grin like nothing happened.

Ines's withering look is lost on everyone but me. I notice that Sara has gravitated across the room, away from her queen bee.

Wasting no time, I go sit on the floor next to Alexa.

"What's their problem?" I whisper.

Alexa shrugs. "Get used to it. You're a star; you're gonna have haters."

"No," I say. "I'm not. Because we're not taking any more pictures in the house."

I had a whole fake story prepared, about being caught by Taylor and forbidden to set foot in the room with the paintings because they're historically valuable and a restoration team from the university is coming over to study and categorize them. But Alexa won't even let me begin.

She scoffs. "I thought we've been over this."

"Yes, but that was then."

"So what changed?"

I'm this close to telling her about my nighttime misadventure, but something stops me. She gives me a look as if to say, *that's what I thought.*

"Besides, you can't back away now. I already started us a new Insta account…"

To my horror, she holds out her phone, and, on the screen, I see the familiar photo I was just looking at. At the top of the screen, I read: @IsabellaResurrected.

"What is this?" I ask in a shaky whisper.

"This," Alexa says, "is five hundred followers overnight. Including half the school and everyone in this class. So, do you still want to back out?"

I'm speechless. I tap at the screen and scroll through the list of names. She's right. The account bio reads: *The Isabella Granger*

Project: Bringing the Art Deco spirit and beauty back to life. Concept by @AlexaTheWolff.

"You could at least have tagged me," I find myself saying.

"Atta girl," Alexa says, grinning.

Kendra claps her hands. "Sorry to interrupt, my lovelies, but we only have an hour, and there's a lot to go over today."

Still, the buzzing doesn't die down for another minute or so, and I can see Kendra getting impatient. It's an interesting sight: she fidgets, knowing she has to call us to order and is clearly uncomfortable with that. The cognitive dissonance is obviously killing her. Cut from the same cloth as my mom, this one.

"Girls," she says at last. She's talking to Sara and another girl, who are scrolling through their phones and talking in low whispers. "Phones on silent, please. Time to work."

Reluctantly, they put the phones away. Kendra gives a shake of her wrists, as if to get rid of the authoritarian persona she finds so distasteful. Her bracelets clink, melodious.

"Welcome, class," Kendra singsongs. "I hope you're all ready to work, because boy do I have a fun announcement for you. We have our school play for this year."

Ironically, now she's got everyone's attention. Including mine. In fact, it's really nice to think about something other than the house and Isabella and my little sleepwalking experience.

Kendra gives us an enigmatic smile. "I've spoken to the committee. We're going ahead with *The Picture of Dorian Gray*."

THIRTEEN

A RIPPLE OF EXCITEMENT COURSES THROUGH THE CLASS.
Alexa whistles under her breath.

"I was afraid there would be pushback," Kendra says, and I understand with a start that she's addressing not the whole class but me directly. "So no one was more surprised than me when it got green-lit. Congratulations, Isa. Looks like your pick won! It was unanimous. Well, almost."

She adds that last part softly, more like an afterthought. But I have a pretty good guess who voted against. Starts with G and ends with "reer."

That should put me right on her favorites list, I think grimly.

"Now, everyone, I know this play has quite the *history* at this school, but I think we should look forward to the future rather than staying mired in the past. Together, we can put on a production that'll make a new history. I know you all can do it!"

"When are the auditions?" Ines speaks up.

"Well, we don't start rehearsals until after Christmas break, and, before then, I'll have plenty of time to decide so that my choice of part can play to your strengths."

Looks like it's not what Ines wanted to hear. "So there *is* no audition?"

"Ines, this is your second year in my drama class—I think you know how I operate. I don't believe in judging someone's ability and merit based on one single, short, high-pressure performance. I prefer to think in the long term." She casts a glance over the quiet room. "And, before any of you get ideas, know that I can see pandering from a mile away. The only thing that'll get you anywhere is consistent effort."

Ines sits down, seemingly satisfied.

Meanwhile, Kendra hands out our exercises for today. Some monologue, photocopied onto grainy paper. I snap out of my thoughts only when Kendra plunks it into my lap.

"This is your chance to shine," she whispers.

But I don't exactly shine. I'm wooden and sluggish and a total zero—especially compared to Ines, who positively sparkles. As I go sit down after my turn, I feel her evil, gleeful stare on my back.

"She totally thinks she's going to get Sibyl," Alexa says on our way out of class. "Well, she's got another think coming."

I gulp. "I am going to play Sibyl," I say softly through clenched teeth. "The whole thing was my idea. She has to give it to me."

Alexa wiggles her eyebrows. "That's the attitude."

I feel momentarily confused, then mortified. Where did that come from? I guess losing the part of Yvonne hit me harder than I thought—and it was totally out of my control too. For a moment, I wonder if I'd lost my touch.

"You are already a star," says Alexa when I share my doubts. "At an art school in Brooklyn, no less."

"Yeah," I say, my mood plummeting the second she utters the word *Brooklyn*. "And they couldn't pack me off across the country fast enough. My best friend Eve seems to have pounced on my role before my moving truck left the city. And I was supposed to go see the play before Christmas break—"

"Wait. The play in which you were supposed to star?"

"Yup. But, honestly, I don't think they want me there."

"First," Alexa says, "it's kind of shitty of them to expect you to go see someone else play your role that you worked on for months only to have it taken away."

It's such a relief to hear someone—especially my new friend—say out loud what I've been secretly thinking since I left. I instantly feel like less of a deluded, envious loser.

"If it were me, I just wouldn't go. That's it. And, second, she's clearly jealous."

"Eve? Jealous of me?" I chuckle feebly, it's so preposterous.

"Of course. She's a small fish in a ginormous pond. And you are here, living in the coolest house in the universe, at an arts college practically rolling out the welcome mat. Stardom is at your fingertips, all you have to do is take it."

"Do you really mean that?"

"Of course! You can out-act these amateurs in your sleep."

That reminds me again of the episode at the house, and my mood sinks even lower.

"One way to make sure you're the star," Alexa says, "is to make sure our Insta account goes viral. If you become the star of Project Isabella, no one will dare stand in your way. You'll get Sibyl; don't you worry."

"Oh, will you stop with that?" I ask. "Besides, I think I already agreed."

Alexa gives a squeal so loud that several people turn around.

"So, you must be feeling pretty good, huh?"

I spent the whole day both waiting for him to talk to me and dreading it. Now that I'm on my way out, here he is, the one and only Nick Swain.

"What's that supposed to mean?"

It wasn't my intention to go on the offensive like that, but I guess I'm feeling pretty jumpy. I crane my neck, searching for my parents' SUV by the gate, but it's nowhere to be seen. And the time on my phone tells me I'm the one who's ten minutes late. Dammit! Nice timing, Mom and Dad.

Nick leans against a fencepost, arms crossed. What's he waiting for? Nobody picks him up—didn't Alexa say he lives alone?

"Well, the play you wanted was picked as the final drama project. And you're blowing up on Instagram. Every girl's dream, right?"

"Sure, if every girl you know is a shallow twit."

"I'm just teasing. The photos are beautiful. And it's not like you're posting vapid selfies all day. I can tell that was a lot of work."

"I just posed in front of some paintings," I grumble.

"I saw. They're just hanging all over your house? Century-old paintings of a famous socialite?"

There's something deliberate about his casual tone, which instantly puts me on my guard. *What do you want from me, Nick Swain?*

"Yes," I say. "They are. Isn't it great? And now I guess you want me to invite you over to see them. If that's what you were going for, well—"

"The truth is, what I was going for was to offer you a ride home, since class ended twenty minutes ago and no one's here to pick you up."

My head whips around, and I realize he's unfortunately right on the money. The car is still nowhere to be seen, and the schoolyard is now practically empty. Everyone else has gone home. In their own cars, presumably.

"I can't just take off," I say, scampering to hide my embarrassment. "What if my mom shows up and I'm not here?"

"You can just call her," he says with an easy smile. My face grows hot. Of course I can just call her. I'm holding the phone in my hand as we speak. So that's what I proceed to do, but the phone rings and rings into emptiness. Not switched off, but no one is picking up. I try my dad, but it goes to voicemail immediately.

Cursing under my breath, I hang up. My only other option is a nice long walk, and I'm not wearing my comfiest shoes today.

"So I take it that's a yes?" he asks.

Shit.

I follow him across the parking lot to one of the few remaining cars. The shiny, new-model Range Rover takes me by surprise, but then he presses a button on the fob, the car beeps, and I realize that this is, indeed, my ride home. I should have seen it coming. Did I really think Nick would be driving a beat-up Tercel?

Doing my best not to look the least bit impressed, I climb into the passenger seat.

Nick starts the engine but lets the car idle. He's looking at me pointedly until I start to fidget. "What?"

"Seatbelt."

"Oh." I hurriedly clip the seatbelt. "So much for the rebel bad boy, huh," I say under my breath.

"Hey, I don't really care if you go flying through the windshield face-first. I just don't want to get a ticket."

He drives out of the parking lot onto the street and takes off with surprising speed. Only after five minutes of awkward silence do I notice that, while he's driving to the house the same way Taylor would, he never asked for directions or even used the map on his phone. It's like he confidently knows the way...to my house.

Fantastic.

"I see you've driven this way before," I say.

He scoffs. "Everyone in town knows the way to the Granger house."

"Sounds ominous."

"People used to sneak in there on a dare, during the full moon or on Halloween," he says with a shrug. "It's a place of legend, no doubt about it."

I feel another stubborn little shiver. "What sort of legend?"

"Do you really want to know? I mean...if the university folks didn't see fit to tell you, maybe it's better if you don't."

I grit my teeth. "Just tell me."

"Oh, there's a bit of a history about dead vagrants turning up on the premises." He must see how my eyes go round because he chuckles. "The investigation concluded that they died of natural causes, though. They were pretty old, it seems. Just wandered in there, probably to find a place to sleep away from the elements, and died in their sleep. So nothing crazy. Except—"

The stop sign pops up on the road ahead at an inopportune moment. He hits the brakes, the car stops, and he cuts himself off. When he hits the gas pedal again, he seems to have forgotten what he was talking about.

Unless he's doing it on purpose. He probably is.

"Come on, Nick. Seriously?"

"It's not creepy or anything. Well—relatively not creepy. Just gross."

"I'm waiting."

Like it or not, I'm now invested in the story. He can tell, so he makes me wait. But his eyes have that spark of mischief.

"You know there's that patched ceiling on the second floor? And the bit that's missing the hardwood floorboards?"

I nod. It occurs to me to wonder how *he* knows all this.

"Well, a few years ago, this one vagrant who died, an old woman, she fell through the floor on the fourth. Crashed through one more floor before going splat on the floorboards, where she…well…decomposed quite a bit before they found her. The mosaic floor rotted beneath her corpse. That's why they took it out."

"Great," I say. "How delightful."

"They never did identify her," Nick says, like the story needed adding to it. "You can see it for yourself if you don't believe me—it's on the town police force's website, under unsolved cases. They just know that it's a woman, very old, probably into her eighties."

"What was a woman probably into her eighties doing out on the street, not to mention all the way out here?"

He shakes his head. "Isa, Isa, you disappoint me. Did you know that elderly women are more likely to live in poverty than any other demographic?"

I did know that because it's one of Taylor's favorite causes. She did a photo story on the subject that caused an uproar back in the day. I remember one shot from it—a gloomy, sepia-colored wide-angle picture of a hoarder's trailer. "I knew that," I say. "It's just odd. If she's from around town, then shouldn't somebody know her?"

"You'd think."

The house floats out of seemingly nowhere, taking me by surprise. Before I know it, he's pulling up to the back entrance. Again, I didn't have to tell him—he just somehow knew the front door was condemned.

"Here you are, Your Majesty. Back at the castle. I'll see you tomorrow at school?"

"Sure," I say. That's it? *I'll see you tomorrow?*

Then again, what did I expect, a porch kiss?

Did I want a porch kiss?

"Are you getting out, or going home with me?"

I jolt a little. But, one look at his face, and I know he's teasing again. "No way," I say. "I'll see you tomorrow."

I get out of the car, make my way up the winding path, and slip into the house. At once, I realize my parents are home: Dad's favorite jazz is playing on the newly installed stereo, and smells of cooking waft from the kitchen.

Wait. They're both home, and no one bothered to pick me up from school? "Mom!" I yell out. "Dad?"

Taylor emerges from the kitchen, wiping her hands on her apron. I hadn't seen her wear that apron in ages. The domestic-goddess thing isn't really her...thing.

"Why do you still have your shoes on?" she harps. "I asked you, no heels on the hardwood floor. And we're going to eat in ten minutes. Tacos. So you might want to change out of your white shirt too."

I feel dizzy and disoriented. "Heels? On the floor? You forgot to pick me up from school today."

Taylor gives me a short look of confusion, then collects herself and rolls her eyes. "Ah. A joke. I see. Well, I'm happy that you're in a joking mood, but you still have to ditch your shoes. Them's the rules."

"Mom," I say. "I'm absolutely serious. You didn't come pick me up! I waited for like twenty minutes…"

"Okay, Isa, ha, ha, ha. Hilarious."

"I had to ask someone in my class for a ride home," I say, "which was embarrassing enough, thank you very much. And I know you feel bad about it, but pretending like it didn't happen doesn't make it better."

"What's gotten into you?" By the look on her face, I can tell that she's not pranking me; she genuinely has no idea what I'm on about. "I got there *early* today. And you were there, and I drove you home, and that was twenty minutes ago. You went up to your room. Are you okay, Isa? Are you drunk?"

"Drunk? I'm not drunk. You're the one who—"

I cut myself off midsentence. There's no point.

"You know what, never mind. I'm going to go change." I kick off my shoes right there, pick them up, and walk past her, barefoot.

All the way up the stairs, I feel her suspicious gaze on the back of my neck.

FOURTEEN

ON SATURDAY MORNING, ALEXA SHOWS UP AT THE
house, and, this time, she came prepared. It takes us close to a half
hour to lug her trunk of equipment up the stairs to the fourth floor.

It helps that my parents are at the university. Dad is preparing
for some sort of fancy event, and my mom is working on her course
materials. We have the house to ourselves.

The week went by without any more weirdness, and I've had time
to calm down and start turning the lights out in my room again. I still
have no idea if Taylor genuinely thought she did pick me up or was
just playing a really good, but really tasteless, prank.

It seems like Alexa also brought the world's longest extension
cord, and now Isabella's portrait room has functioning professional

lights. The first thing Alexa does is haul all the old trunks out of the storage room and onto the center of the floor.

I don't tell her that I spent long minutes inspecting the floorboards with a flashlight, trying to find where they'd been patched. Assuming Nick's story wasn't just something he made up to scare me, because he is, of course, a world-class jerk. But nothing at all seems to be wrong with the floor up here. No matter how hard I stomped over every inch of the surface, everything seemed reliable, every footfall resulted in a heavy thud that only solid flooring makes. No one has fallen through it—this much I can guarantee.

Then how to explain that I did find the old woman on the police website, just like he said? The explanatory text was brief.

The Amory Police Service seeks the public's help in identifying this woman. The subject is a female in her 80s, Caucasian, possibly with some scarring on her face.

And there's the date she was found and one of those robot reconstructions of what she might have looked like. But, like most such portraits, it's a weird composite of traits that barely looks like an actual person.

He probably saw it and made up the rest of the story. Just to mess with me.

"Hey, Isa, check this out," Alexa calls out. I turn around just in time to see something like a giant bird's wing flying at my face. I freeze up instead of reaching out to catch it like she meant me to do, and so it hits me in the face with its feathers and its dust. It's probably another theater costume, a big black velvet cloak trimmed with black feathers that look like they came from a raven.

"Probably a chicken." Alexa chuckles. "Dyed."

I inspect the cloak with apprehension. Sure enough, Isabella is wearing it in a painting. She's decked out like a Disney villain thirty years before Disney was even a thing, glaring from the canvas with that penetrating green stare, her hair up with a diadem studded with black pearls woven in. You gotta give her credit for creativity.

"Isa, look! How cool is this?" Alexa is taking the diadem out of the trunk. The dust and cobwebs dull its shine. Alexa brushes them away.

"This must be worth a fortune," I say.

"It's costume," Alexa says, weighing the diadem in her hand. "Paste. And fake pearls. And, by the way, you know what we're doing today, right?"

I let her do my makeup, which takes forever. She spends a half hour on each eye, I swear, and finally swipes on what seems like way too much lipstick that's way too dark.

"Are you going to let me see myself before we take pictures?"

"Nope," she answers blithely. "Now we just have to find a nice backdrop. There's that beautiful arched entryway downstairs, leading to the living room. Since your parents aren't home anyway…"

We head downstairs. Today, Alexa came equipped with a real camera, the kind of clunky beast that Taylor would appreciate and that probably costs several thousand dollars. Looking at that giant lens that gleams like an oil spill, I feel intimidated.

"Don't think about the camera," Alexa is saying. All the while she's snapping away, the clicks of the shutter like insect wings.

"How should I pose?"

"Just do the same thing Isabella does."

So I position myself in the archway and try to do exactly that.

"No," Alexa says, cringing. "Come on. Stop doing that weird America's Next Top Model thing and try to be real."

"What's that supposed to mean?"

"Your face looks like a mannequin. Goth Barbie. And I want you to look like Isabella Granger, great artist's muse, owner of the coolest damn mansion in the state."

It's easy for her to say. Isabella in that painting looked alluring, seductive, powerful. What the hell do I know about being powerful? Or alluring and seductive, for that matter. I never even had a real boyfriend, for god's sake.

"Pretend Nick Swain is here," Alexa says.

I puff with laughter. "Nick?"

"Well, you like him, don't you?"

Faced with the directness of the question, I'm a little lost. Do I like him, actually? Do I want to seduce Nick Swain?

"Okay, so no. Forget about seducing anyone. Imagine your old theater troupe standing here. They're gazing at you admiringly, and you're thinking, *I'm so much better off without you bitches.*"

"Uh. That's not—"

"Just do it, Isa!"

I try. She clicks the shutter.

"Good. Not great, but good."

"What do you mean, not great? Are you going to let me see or not?"

We both hear the door open and turn toward it at the same time. It would have been too late to try to do anything, anyhow; we've been caught in flagrante. Taylor comes to a stop in the middle of the hallway, right underneath the chandelier.

"I forgot some equipment," she says, looking from me to Alexa and back. "And I see you're keeping busy. Where did all this come from?"

"The costume department at theater club," Alexa lies flawlessly.

At first, I can't tell if my mom buys it or not. She looks doubtful. "And what's up with the setup? Looks sort of familiar. Isa, why are you made up like Marilyn Manson?"

My face flushes. It would be too easy to throw Alexa under the bus and say it was all her idea, because it's technically true. "It's a school project," I say. I just blurt it out. No idea where it came from. School project? But the lies unfurl so easily in my brain that it seems like my mouth suddenly can't keep up. "Extra credit. For history. When our teacher found out we lived in the Granger house, she just couldn't resist. We're doing this whole big photo-essay on Isabella, the person she was and the art she inspired. All the girls in class are participating."

I see Alexa's face on the periphery of my vision. Her eyes pop out of her head—she's at least as surprised by this sudden rush of imagination as I am.

"That's very interesting. Maybe there's stuff in the house you can use?" Taylor looks relieved. Relieved that she won't have to play disciplinarian again, no doubt. What could be more noble than a school project? Only a school project for extra credit. "I know there's that whole room upstairs full of her old things. As long as you're careful…"

"Wow, Ms. Brixton. Thank you!" Alexa gushes. "That would be amazing. It's so hard to find the right props."

"Just be careful, please," Taylor says.

"We will be!"

"Good. Now carry on, girls. I don't want to bother you."

She walks away, and we both stand perfectly still, listening to her fading footsteps in awe, waiting until it's safe to talk out of her earshot.

"Wait," Alexa finally whispers. "Did you just—"

"Got her to give us permission to use the room," I say, still incredulous.

"How did you come up with that?"

I only shake my head. I look in the direction Taylor went, lost in thought. How easy that was. A little lie, and I got what I wanted. Somehow, I forget to doubt and wonder. This *is* what I wanted, right? I now realize that yes, of course it is.

There's nothing I want more.

Click, click.

"There," says Alexa, looking at the screen on the back of the camera with satisfaction. "This. This is the look I wanted. You nailed it. Congrats, Isa."

"Show me!"

"Oh, no. You'll see it tonight. Once I upload it to Instagram."

As soon as I shut the door behind Alexa, I feel like just sitting down on the floor by the exit and not moving. All my energy drains at once, and I find myself without purpose, just floating through time. My skin tingles, and my eyes feel dry. I rub them only to see smears of black all over my knuckles when I pull my hands away. The makeup. I really need to wash my face.

This thought is what gets me back on my feet and in action. I go upstairs, to the bathroom, where I put my phone on the counter next to the sink, turn on the tap, and grab Taylor's new, overpriced facial cleanser that promises clean pores and a burst of freshness. I feel a touch of skepticism. This is something new, something that's not like her at all. When it came to skincare, Taylor believed in coconut oil and Cetaphil. She said she refused to fall for the marketing hype that tricked women into paying bank for tiny tubes of toxic chemicals.

Yet here we are, I guess. I lather up and scrub my face, but, when I look up, I'm in for a shock. My bewildered face stares back at me from the mirror, crisscrossed by streaks of grayish black and red and glitter. Clearly, Alexa used stage makeup on me, heavy and oil-based, and all the cleanser did was smear it around. Makeup-tinted water runs down my neck and onto my shirt collar.

With a sigh, I start the bath. Without waiting for the tub to fill completely, I climb in, scrubbing my face with plain soap. Iridescent oil rings tinted with pigment float on the water's surface before dissolving completely. My pores finally feel clean.

Just as I contemplate staying a little longer to enjoy the spacious tub and pleasantly steaming water, I hear a buzzing noise overhead followed by a loud crackle, and the lone light under the ceiling goes out.

The bathroom plunges into a deep gray half-darkness. I sit up straight.

"Mom?" I call out. My voice is loud, but it seems to bounce off the tiles, trapped within these walls. "Mom? The light bulb is dead!"

There's no answer. Once the last echoes of my voice die down, the silence wraps around me, thick and smothering. Even the soft splash of water is seamlessly absorbed.

A sudden draft ripples through the bathroom, making the semi-sheer curtain my mom hung up around the tub rustle. At the same time, a horrible smell fills my nostrils: a smell of something burning. Not only burning—of something horrible and acrid. A chemical smell mixed with the reek of singed hair.

I should probably get out of the tub. But I sit perfectly still as if frozen in place, paralyzed by a horrible feeling of dread.

On the other side of the curtain, blurry, a dark shadow moves across the room.

My hands grip the edges of the tub so hard it hurts. The smell grows stronger and stronger as the shadow grows closer, looming.

And then I see the clear outline of a hand against the plastic, a narrow hand with long fingers, black as charcoal.

My scream dies in my throat.

Clink-clink-CLINK!

The three-tone chime of my phone notification shreds the silence. The very air seems to shudder. The shadow writhes, and, in a heartbeat, retreats before dissolving seamlessly.

The light flickers back on.

Without wasting another second, I get to my feet and scramble out of the bathtub, not caring that I'm getting water everywhere. I'm trembling as I look around, wild-eyed, but the bathroom is brightly lit and completely empty.

Clink-clink-CLINK!

My phone again. And again and again. My hand still shaking, I pick it up. It's notifications from Instagram. *Sara liked your photo. Emma liked your photo. 100 other people liked your photo.*

I thumb at the screen, and, after a surprisingly short moment, considering the Wi-Fi signal is as poor as ever, the photo that apparently broke the internet appears.

At once I understand what the big deal is.

It's not just the best photo of me ever taken, but probably a contender for the best photo ever, period. Like, Kim-Kardashian's-champagne-bottle, era-defining photo. I hardly look like myself. I look like the painting of Isabella come to life.

I scroll and scroll through all the fawning comments as they roll in. Inside, I'm still numb with incredulity. I'm actually going viral.

Funny, I hadn't even stopped to ask myself if this was what I wanted. But it looks like the internet decided for me.

And so I almost drop the phone when a text message pops up at the top of the screen. It's from Alexa.

> what did I tell you, huh????

All the breath escapes from me in relief. I put the phone down and cast a last glance around the bathroom.

That's when I see it: on the plastic shower curtain, a dark handprint, dark streaks running down from it all the way to the floor.

PART
TWO

FIFTEEN

EVE GOT HOME LATE ON SATURDAY. NOT THAT ANYONE
was at home to notice, but she's used to that. She already had her story
prepared: she and the others from theater club decided to go out for
dinner after the photo shoot and time just flew by. It's not even entirely
untrue—she's just leaving out the after-party at a friend's parents' loft.
What a waste of a perfectly good story.

Eve has every reason to be on top of the world, but something just
doesn't feel right. Maybe it's guilt. Today they did the photo shoot for
the play's poster and promotional graphics on social, with costumes
and all. With Eve wearing the velvet dress that had been Isa's. The
first photos were already up and spreading steadily throughout social
media. No way Isa hasn't seen them at least once.

It's not that Eve isn't grateful for the starring role in the school play, but she didn't want it at the cost of her best friend since grade school. There's no point deluding herself: long-distance relationships don't work, and neither do long-distance friendships. You can't just go from eating lunch together every day to speaking once a week on Skype, if you're so lucky, and expect that nothing will change.

And Isa sure seems to be moving on, anyway, Eve catches herself thinking with spite. *Wait. Am I just thinking that to make myself feel better?* But no. In the last couple of weeks, her Insta was flooded with all these photos of that impossibly cool house. And then the portraits started. Not selfies— someone was obviously there to take the photos. Who? Finally, this girl tagged herself in one of the photos, and Eve couldn't resist the urge to click on her profile. It splashed across the screen of her Mac, and Eve's reaction was immediate and visceral. Isa, friends with this tacky goth chick with the shoe-polish hair and cheesy skull ring with ruby eyes? Really? Eve scrolled down and found a selfie taken at a graveyard. Yes, really.

Eve throws herself on her bed and reluctantly picks up her phone. There's no message from Isa, no notifications, nothing.

Then Eve opens Instagram, and the photo is like a slap in the face. She sits up.

Isa is posing in some kind of black feather boa, her face painted up like a silent movie diva, only in full color. And the look on her face— it's hard to describe. It's that look that reminds Eve exactly why it was Isa, and not her, who was the star of the theater club and a shoo-in for every main part in every play. Isa is a natural chameleon, and here she slips into her character so seamlessly that no one seeing this photo for the first time would ever think this is a Brooklyn high school student. In her gaze there's power and seduction and experience Eve is one hundred percent certain Isa doesn't have.

For some reason, instead of awing her, the transformation makes Eve uncomfortable. *It's like she's possessed*, she thinks.

She taps on the profile tagged in the post—*The Isabella Granger Project*, she reads incredulously. *Bringing the Art Deco spirit and beauty back to life*. She remembers: Isabella Granger, the turn-of-the-century artist's model, muse, and reality-star-before-her-time, the one Isa wouldn't shut up about.

Eve goes back to the photo and looks at it. *I should say something*, she thinks. *Something encouraging. But without coming across as kiss-ass, because I'm sure that's what she'll think once she sees our promo photos.*

Except she thinks, deep down, that Isa probably doesn't care at all about the photos, or about the play, or about Eve taking her place. If she even saw the photos at all.

Eve lets her thumb hover over the photo, then taps once, then twice, as if by accident. The red heart blooms across the photo. Eve's breath catches, and she hurriedly un-likes the photo, unable to help thinking that it's already too late.

She's been noticed.

"Hey, I think you were right," I say as I catch up to Nick before the first class of the day.

He doesn't miss a beat. "Of course I was right," he says. "What was I right about this time?"

I shake my head, but I'm chuckling. "About the dead old lady at my house."

His face changes in a subtle but noticeable way, his expression becoming more serious. "Oh, yeah?"

The casualness of his tone once again feels calculated somehow. I realize it's familiar—it becomes like that every time either of us brings up the house.

"Yeah. I found the listing on the police site. Strange stuff."

"Strange," he echoes.

"And, more than that—I think we might have a legit ghost."

"Really, now?" I can't tell if he believes me or not. His gaze is intent, drinking me in.

"Something weird happened the other day. I was taking a bath when I'm pretty sure I saw a ghost. *Her* ghost." I quickly recap my bathtime ordeal. I try to make it sound like no big deal, but I'm not sure I'm succeeding because his frown deepens with every word.

"Then again, it's probably all in my head," I backtrack with fake cheerfulness. "The streaks were probably from the makeup on my hands. That stuff gets everywhere and is so hard to get out. And, I mean, for all I know I have a brain tumor—everything stank of burnt toast."

I give an awkward laugh that rings hollow, since he doesn't crack a smile.

"Who knows," he says. "Maybe it really was a ghost. How much do you know about the place where you live, anyway?"

"What I googled," I admit. "Plus what you told me. Why? Is there more to know? More creepy old ladies?"

"You probably know the place has quite a history, right?"

History, yes. Quite a history? That sounds menacing. I tell him so.

He shrugs. "Maybe, maybe not. It was all many decades ago. Thing is—"

"Isa! Oh my god."

Alexa's shriek takes me by surprise. I give a start and spin around only to see her and Sara and Ines practically sprinting toward me with several other girls in tow. Before I know it, they've surrounded me, pushing Nick out of the way, intentionally or not. Feeling guilty, I try to catch his eye, but he only tilts his head and saunters off.

"The Instagram is blowing up," Alexa informs me, beaming. "Did you see? Please tell me you saw!"

"I saw."

"You're kidding, right? I spent the whole night refreshing the app. It's official. You're Internet famous!"

She waits for a reaction, and I fail to give her one. She puts her hands on my shoulders. "Isa," she says. "Hello. This is every girl's dream. Can you at least look happy? Or are you mad because I interrupted your flirting?"

"What?" I say, indignant. "I wasn't—"

"You can do better than Nick Swain. You're a star."

My gaze ping-pongs from one grinning face to another, eerie in how alike they look, with stars in their eyes, almost reverent. Even Ines, it seems, forgot that she hates me.

"It's phenomenal, Isa," she gushes.

"I invited everyone over after school," Alexa says matter-of-factly. "I hope you don't mind."

"Sure," I say, distracted. I feel a sudden urge to take out my phone and check the photo for myself.

"To your house," she specifies.

Oh. "You invited people—to my house?"

"Oh, come on. Don't get hung up on details. Besides, it's not just your house. I feel like it belongs to all of us. Don't hoard it. Share it. Spread the beauty around."

I raise my eyebrows, but say nothing. *It is my house*, I think with surprising fierceness.

"I can't wait to see for myself," Sara exclaims.

Overhead, the first bell rings, indicating that classes are about to start. I follow Alexa to our first class of the day, taking a moment when she's not looking to sneak a peek at my phone.

Holy cow. She wasn't kidding. I'd checked it last night before bed and accidentally-on-purpose forgot to look at it this morning, a little overwhelmed. But, since then, the number of likes has literally gone up tenfold.

I stop in the middle of the hallway. For some reason, there's a lump in my throat. Deep unease stirs within me. I wish Nick had had time to tell me whatever he was about to tell me.

Someone bumps into me from behind—some girl I don't know. "Move!" she snaps. Then she sees my face, and her expression does an alarming transformation. "Oh, Isa. I'm so sorry. Great photos!"

With that, she sprints off to class, leaving me standing there even more bewildered.

The only person who seems even more shocked than I am at the sudden intrusion at our house is my mom. She has that look of bewilderment on her face as the girls sashay past her through the service entrance and into the kitchen. She gives me that look, and I know she's thinking *I didn't say you could invite anyone over.* I wonder if I'll have a lecture waiting for me once everybody leaves. *If* they ever decide to leave. From the looks on their faces, they just decided they'll be moving in permanently, and I bristle at the thought.

Alexa leads the way like a seasoned tour guide, and I linger behind as I hear them all exclaiming over the hall and the big staircase. I exchange a glance with my mom.

"I just wish you'd warned me," she says in a purposefully nice voice. "I would have changed out of my dusty sweats."

"They just wanted to see the house," I say. "The photos were a huge hit."

"Well, at least be careful. Don't break anything. And Samuel's old photo room is still off limits."

I decide not to push my luck and follow the others just as they're making their way up the staircase. The light is strange today, probably because of the gloomy weather outside: it's bright but gray at the same time, and everything around me looks cardboard-flat, like the house is just a carefully crafted movie set.

"Wait till you see this," Alexa is saying somewhere far ahead. Her voice echoes, way too loud and obnoxious. The others whisper and giggle. I realize I'm literally being left behind, like they all forgot I even exist.

Momentarily I'm caught up in an unexpected feeling: a deep, visceral anger that's like a dark swarm rising from within, from somewhere deep in my subconscious, maybe. *This is my house. Leave. I want you out of here.*

"Hey, Isa, what's up?"

I blink, and the dark swarm falls away. Alexa is standing just a few steps above, looking at me with curiosity.

"You could have waited for me, you know," I say. "And not left me to deal with Taylor all by myself."

"Why? Is she raising a stink?"

"That's not why!" I struggle to form the words. "Just—I don't want them going into the portrait room without me. I don't want anyone going in there without me!"

Alexa raises her eyebrows. A corner of her lips rises in a smirk. "Wow, territorial much?"

"Sorry," I say. My face warms. That did sound stupid, didn't it? "I don't know what came over me."

"Nobody is going anywhere without you," Alexa says. "Nobody would even be here if it wasn't for you. If they know about this place or about Isabella Granger, it's all thanks to you—you brought it into the world. They worship you."

That might be too strong a word. I look Alexa over skeptically.

"Sara, maybe. Are you sure Ines isn't just looking for an opportunity to put poison in my face cream?"

A sound from above cuts us off. A loud boom, followed by a high-pitched shriek.

As if on cue we both race up the stairs with me gaining on her before finally passing her at the entrance of the fourth-floor hallway. The other girls are up here, standing in front of the ornate door of the portrait room. Ines's eyes are as big as a pair of saucers.

"The door slammed," Sara stammers. "She—we—tried to open it and then it just slipped out and slammed closed."

I advance toward the door. Everything looks normal—just as I left it. I cautiously put my hand on the door handle. It feels weirdly warm. For a fraction of a second, a familiar smell of burnt hair washes over me before dissipating completely.

"Isa?" Alexa's voice over my ear.

I realize I must have spaced out. I pull the handle, and the door opens easily, with no resistance. I let go, and the door stays open without so much as swaying in the breeze.

"There. Nothing." I look over their frightened faces and can't help but feel a smug superiority. I'm the mistress of the house. You're just the guests.

I hold the door open, and they file in.

SIXTEEN

IT'S SUNDAY NIGHT, AND EVERYONE IS GATHERED IN THE
portrait room.

Ever since the project took off, the portrait room has become our
unofficial headquarters: photo studio, editing room, lounge, you name
it, all rolled into one. It's now called the Isabella Project—we decided
to take out the Granger, to keep it from sounding stuffy and too
historical. It's not about the past—it's about the present. And, okay, I
kind of like that, this way, it's named after me.

After all, I'm the star. All the most-liked photos are of me. Me as
Isabella. Isabella as myself. The other girls have their turns, too, but it's
become kind of an indisputable fact: I do it best. I'm the best Isabella
of them all.

"It's this painting that we need to recreate," Alexa is saying. I know which one she means, because we've had this conversation several times already in the past weeks. She means the big painting where Isabella wears the wine-colored velvet gown.

The thing I've never had the heart to tell Alexa is that the dress isn't lost. I have it. That night when I found myself sleepwalking, I couldn't clamber out of it quickly enough, and, since then, it's been hidden in the bottom drawer in my bedroom, beneath an old blanket. It's stupid, I know. It's just a dress. But I'm not in a hurry to put it on just yet.

"Sara, do you think you could sew something like this?"

Sara, who's been going through the contents of an ancient wooden jewelry box, looks up. There's an old feather in her hair that she stuck there. She shrugs, and it makes the feather tremble. "Probably. It would take forever, and the fabric would cost a fortune…and I'm not sure what to do about the gold thread and jewels."

"You could get rhinestones," Alexa says.

"No. It's got to be the real thing or nothing," Sara pipes up. She's taken a pair of lavish earrings out of the jewelry box and is holding them up to her ears. "See? These look just like real gold."

"But they aren't," says Ines. "They'll turn your ears blue after ten minutes."

"They didn't turn Isa's ears blue," Sara argues.

It's true. They didn't. We did a shoot with those earrings on Friday, and the photo already has thousands of likes.

"Can you take my picture, Alexa?" Sara has put on the earrings and turns her head sideways so they're on display. They're long and massive, studded with heavy, rectangular-cut spinel stones that glint like dark eyes, and with those long gilt tassels that brushed my collarbone just so in the photo.

Alexa aims her camera and takes photo after photo.

"Let's go to the window in the hall," she says. "There's not enough light."

I follow them with my gaze. Sara is wearing one of Isabella's dresses, and the hem drags on the floor, collecting dust.

"It's a great shot," Ines is saying. "There's just one thing I don't like."

"What?" I ask. It comes out a little more abrupt than what I was going for. "It'll make a damn great photo."

"Your hair."

"What about my hair?"

Ines shrugs. "Your hair's great. It's just, do you think Isabella would have dyed hers pink?"

I'm ready to snap at her, *well, I'm not Isabella, I'm Isa*. But, instead, I stop, my mouth hanging open. "Who knows what she would have done?" I mutter. "She was the most fashionable woman of her time. So…"

"I'm just saying you could have worn a wig, or…"

"Yeah, right. I don't know about pink hair, but she would never be caught dead in a tacky wig." I nod at the big painting, the one where Isabella's hair is so detailed and resplendent. "And, anyway, my real hair is just about the same color."

A few minutes later, Sara and Alexa come back. Sara is rubbing her ears and wincing. She plunks the earrings back into the wooden box. "Keep them. You were right, Ines." When she takes her hands away, I can see that her earlobes are indeed blue and swollen.

After everyone leaves, it's just Alexa and me. Lately, she's been staying for dinner at our place a lot. I wonder what her parents think of this but don't dare ask. It's a little difficult to imagine Alexa having parents at all—she just always seems to come and go as she pleases, and she's never mentioned them, come to think of it. But Taylor sure seems to love her company. She talks Alexa's ear off about photography, and Alexa pretends to be politely interested.

"How are the pictures?" I ask, seeing that she's scrolling through the shots on her camera.

"Hard to say. I have to see them on the big screen. But, basically... blah."

"Sara doesn't look that good in that dress. It hangs off her like a rag," I say.

"That's kind of mean."

"Well, it's true."

I catch Alexa watching me. "What?"

"She worships you, you know. Don't be mean to her."

"I'm just saying. Hey. Do you think I should change my hair?"

Alexa blinks, startled by the abrupt change of subject.

"I'm not going to chop it all off or anything. I was just thinking—"

"Your hair's great," Alexa says softly. Once again, she has that odd look on her face. "What do you want to shoot next week? I have this idea for a shoot outside. While we still have the yellow leaves and everything—"

"Why outside? There are so many pretty places in the house we haven't used yet."

"I've been thinking—we're going to run out of material inside the house eventually. We should start thinking about that. How to bring in some variety and stay relevant—"

"We're plenty relevant," I say, feeling defensive. "And I don't see why we'd need to go anywhere else when we have this place all to ourselves."

"I'm just saying," Alexa repeats. "Branching out would be a good thing."

At that moment, Taylor yells at us that dinner's ready, and we go eat. Taylor insists this has nothing to do with our relative isolation, but she's been coping by cooking. And, since Taylor doesn't really know how to cook, she's coping with *that* by ordering a ton of cookware straight out of a cooking show and cookbooks that have to delivered to the university, since Amazon Prime doesn't recognize our address either.

The result of all this today is a weird cross between lasagna and casserole, smothered with a thick layer of vegan cheese. One of the drawbacks turns out to be that it's near impossible to plate without making a mess. So, after a long struggle with a knife and spatula, I end up facing a mountain of noodles and sauce and mushy vegetables with no discernible shape or order.

"Taylor, this is delicious," Alexa says blithely, ever the kiss-ass. Mom beams, casting a glance around the table, clearly in search of more praise. My dad has his mouth full, lucky him, and, since the vegan cheese has the same consistency as stress balls, he keeps chewing and chewing until she moves on.

I make a noise that hopefully comes across as appreciative. Thankfully, it's enough, as she moves on to a new subject.

"So, Isa, I snuck a peek at your project today," Taylor says. She's using that tone. That cool mom tone, forcedly casual and cheerful, and I just know that something unpleasant is coming.

"We've reached ten thousand followers today!" Alexa interjects. "Everything is absolutely beautiful. But especially Isa. It's like she's really got that something, doesn't she?"

"In any event. All these photos are amazing," Taylor says carefully.

But? I think. There's always a *but*.

Taylor doesn't make me wait. "It's just—all these filters. Do you really think it's the sort of thing that fosters good self-esteem?"

"Mom," I groan. "It's not like I'm half-naked in them or anything."

Taylor's eyes widen in that familiar way—she's about to get on the defensive. Alexa saves the situation.

"Oh, I never use any filters on Isa," she says between mouthfuls of the lasagna/casserole. "The other girls, sure. But she doesn't need it. She's a natural."

The truth is, even with the filters and editing, they just don't look as good as me. Not one picture of Ines or Sara ever got even half as many likes as even the least popular picture of me.

"All I'm saying is," Taylor goes on, "aren't you kind of drifting away from your original purpose?"

Puzzled, I throw a sideways glance at Alexa.

"I mean, wasn't it supposed to be about Isabella Granger, the house, its history? It's turning into some sort of vanity fest."

Oh. Right.

"But it *is* about Isabella Granger," I say. "If Isabella Granger lived today, I doubt she'd be posing for oil paintings anymore, right?"

My dad chuckles. Taylor gives him a *look*. It only lasts for half a second, but I notice.

"I doubt she'd be refreshing her Instagram a million times a day either," she says. "But, fine. In that case, I have good news for you girls. I heard there are archives at the university, thorough records of Isabella, her life, her paintings. They're valuable historical documents, but maybe I can get you girls a copy for your project."

"Of course!" Alexa says. "That would be great. Thank you so much, Taylor."

"You only said that to get her off our backs," I whisper to her as she's about to leave. Alexa giggles.

"Well, yeah, sure."

"*Yeah, sure?* You don't sound so sure."

"It would be kind of cool. I think."

I roll my eyes. "We don't need a historian. All the history we need is right here!" I gesture at the house around us. In the evening, it becomes timeless. The soft light hides all the scuffs and the jarring modern additions. It looks as if everything is in soft focus. Like in the time of the first Isabella. "I think you're forgetting that the whole project thing was just an excuse."

She looks uneasy. "Yeah," she says at last. "Anyway. I'll see you tomorrow at school. Hopefully I'll come up with something badass for the next shoot."

"See you," I say on autopilot, and close the door.

My parents are in the kitchen, talking in soft voices. I hear the clinking of dishes and the rush of the tap. So, instead of going to my room, I make my way to the fourth floor.

There's still a bit of tape on the floor, even though everyone seems to have forgotten that it was supposedly unsafe. Even Taylor. Isn't that strange? I make my way to the portrait room and gently close the door behind me.

It's so peaceful here when I'm all alone. No other presence or noise to distract me from my thoughts. I can't believe I used to think this place was creepy.

One of the trunks still sits in the middle of the room. Sara left the pair of earrings on top of the lid. I pick them up: they feel heavy in my hand. Were they always this heavy? They don't feel like paste or even gilt, but like the genuine article.

I guess I should put them away. I throw open the trunk's lid and rummage through, looking for the box from which Sara got them. But, when I push aside some folded clothes, my hand hits the bottom of the trunk, and the sound is weirdly hollow.

My heart beats with excitement. I hastily empty the truck and explore the bottom, which is now so obviously false that it's a wonder I'm the first one to notice. More of Isabella's things—and they belong to me alone. Like…like she actually wanted *me* to find this hiding place, not Alexa or the others.

Finally, I hook my fingernails under the edge of the false bottom and ease it out. Underneath is a large jewelry box and, next to it, something large and round, wrapped in layers of dusty cotton cloth. I see the glint of something auburn—

—and recoil. It's a head. A human head with bright, auburn hair.

SEVENTEEN

I STARE AT THE AUBURN CURLS THAT SPILL OUT FROM
under the wrappings in mute horror. Only then it hits me how nonsensical this is. Can you imagine the smell if there was an actual human head in here? None of us could have missed it. And the hair would have been matted and disintegrating.

I reach out—gingerly, still, since my reptile brain is still not fully convinced that there's nothing to be afraid of—and peel away the edge of the wrapping.

And immediately feel like an idiot. A laugh escapes from me, shaky, echoing under the ceiling. The "head" is a blank mannequin's head, made of wood, and the hair is a luxuriant auburn wig.

I ease it out. Dust rises up, but not nearly as much as you'd expect.

I forget to wonder why that is—surely this thing has been hidden for nearly a hundred years.

The wig is magnificent. It doesn't take a genius to recognize it right away—its depiction, frighteningly exact, is right there, in the biggest painting. Of course, there was no way to tell Isabella had been wearing a wig in it. Not just because the artist would have masterfully disguised that fact, but because the wig is of a truly stunning quality. Made of real hair—I don't doubt it for a second. All the shades of red in it catch the feeble light, like fire trapped in strands of fiberglass.

I'm overcome with an urge so sudden and strong that I practically drop the wig in the bottom of the trunk. Hastily, I pull my hair up and tie it with the elastic around my wrist. Then I put the wig on. I've been in theater long enough to know that putting on a wig that doesn't look like a toupee or roadkill atop your head is a whole process, but this one slips on like it was made for me. The hair falls around my face in soft waves. It feels neither dry nor stiff like the wigs we had at theater club.

Oh, if only I had a mirror on hand!

Then it occurs to me that I do. I reach into my pocket and open the selfie camera.

It looks incredible. Even the hairline somehow marries the line of my forehead to perfection. The soft, flattering light probably doesn't hurt.

I can't resist the temptation—not that I'm trying. I take a selfie, then another. A moment later, they're on my Instagram—my personal one, not the Project Isabella one.

Should I change my hair? What do you think? y/n #redhead

The answers roll in immediately at an almost mechanical rhythm.

Y!!!

Yes 😍

Yes yes yes

😙

Definitely!

Queen!!!!! 👑

Goddess 🍒🤍🌸

And then the name I least expected pops up. I didn't even realize until now how much I dreaded seeing it. But I really should have seen it coming, I guess, because I haven't heard from her in ages.

I don't think you should change your hair. I like the pink hair. Answer my messages! Miss u! We all do!

I tap on Eve's profile, which is flooded with photos from theater club. Miss u my ass. It even sounds so fake. *Miss u! We all do!* She never talked, or typed, this way.

Unable to contain my bitterness, I go back to scrolling through my feed. There are all the posts from my Project Isabella friends and Alexa—suddenly they're at the top of my feed, like they're the only people I follow. Those damn algorithms. They really know us better than we know ourselves, because, I have to admit, this is exactly what I wanted to see.

That is, until I scroll down a little bit and see what Ines just posted. It's a selfie. She may have posted it seconds ago, but it was taken earlier today, because, in the background, I clearly see the bathroom. *My* bathroom. There's the arched window with the stained glass and the mosaic tiles and the corner of the antique tub. Ines's face is edited to hell and back—you can hardly recognize her.

"What the hell?" I say loudly.

"Isa?" Taylor's voice gives me a start. "Are you still up here? Don't you think it's time for bed?"

Moments later, she sticks her head through the door. "Jesus!" she exhales. I remember that I'm still wearing the wig, which I hastily pull off.

"Oh, thank god. I thought there was an intruder," Taylor says with a laugh that comes across a tad forced. A thought flashes through my mind: the homeless old woman who supposedly fell through the floor of this very room. Does Taylor know something about that? Something she didn't feel like sharing with me?

"Where did this thing come from?"

"Theater club," I lie. I'm not even trying. But she seems determined to avoid an argument, so she believes me, or acts like she does.

"Anyway. You have school tomorrow. Is your homework done?"

"My homework?" I chuckle. What am I, in second grade? "Uh, yes, it's done."

That's a lie, too, and just as artless. And how am I supposed to think about pointless things like homework in the face of such an intrusion?

"She just posted a selfie," Taylor says when I tell her what happened with Ines. "Don't you post, like, a hundred of them a day?"

"The selfie is not the problem," I seethe. "She took a picture of our house. Without my permission."

"But you're doing a whole project about the house together," Taylor points out. "Of course she's going to—"

"No! It's not part of the project. She had no right to use *my* house for her own personal glory or whatever."

I follow Taylor down the hall and down the stairs, and don't realize how loudly I've spoken until the echo rolls down the stairwell. My dad must hear it, because, seconds later, he appears at the foot of the stairs. "Everything okay?"

"Isa, it's technically not our house," Taylor gently reminds me. "We just live here."

But I didn't say *our*. I said *my* house. Mine.

"She's jealous of me!" I exclaim.

"Who?" Dad pipes up again.

"Ines."

"Ines Mercato, from school?"

Taylor gives him a look. "Oh, just—girl drama."

"It's not *girl drama*, Mom. She should have asked my permission. And, tomorrow at school, you bet that the first thing I'll do is confront her in front of everyone. So they all know."

"Isa, I'd really rather you didn't," Dad says. "Ines's father is a potential donor I'm courting. For the university. So do you think you can do me a favor and play nice with his daughter?"

"Oh, great. Now I have to put up with this—dissent—so that you can kiss up to her dad for money?"

"Isa!"

"What? This is my house, and my project. And it's not like it's my fault that she's not as pretty or as talented—"

"All right. Time out." Taylor crosses her arms. "What's wrong with you? Okay, I see that you're not crazy about this Ines person. And maybe she's been giving you a hard time for being the new girl, but still. Who are you to judge her talent, or her looks, for that matter? And attacking someone because of their looks, anyway? That doesn't sound like the Izzy I know."

"Well, maybe I left the Izzy you know in Brooklyn, where she belongs."

With that, I thunder past her down the stairs, past my dad, and down the hall to my room.

———

At least Alexa agrees with me.

"It's unacceptable," she says, shaking her head. Her outfit today is a bit different from her usual aesthetic, with a distinct 1920s vibe, although everything is, of course, in black.

"Right?" I say in a loud whisper. Class is about to start, although Ines is nowhere to be seen. Alexa posted the remaining photos from yesterday to Project Isabella's Instagram, and we already have thousands of likes. "It's so not okay!"

Sara, who's now sitting next to me on the other side, leans over.

"You know what she said to me the other day?"

"What did she say?" asks Alexa, a little cross at the intrusion. I get the feeling she's not thrilled about how Sara now follows me around like a newly hatched duckling. She totally understands that having the most popular Insta in the whole school comes with its share of fans and admirers, but I think she'd still rather have me all to herself.

"She says she looks better—in the house."

"What's that supposed to mean?" I ask, mildly annoyed.

"I don't know. Haven't you noticed? It's like it comes with its own filters. Everyone looks better."

"I haven't noticed," I say stubbornly, even though I think she might be right. The selfie I took in the car this very morning had nothing on the photos from last night. I mean, it's as nice as any other selfie, but… ordinary somehow. You can see my pores. The photos from inside the house are naturally flawless. Like the glow filter on steroids.

And, when I went through all the pics from the photo shoot, it became even more obvious. Ines isn't ugly—no matter how much I want to believe the opposite, I'm forced to admit that she's as pretty as me, if not more.

Ines doesn't come to class, which is curious, because nobody seems to know anything about it. She even misses theater, which is really not like her.

We don't have an answer until the next day, when she shows up to school wearing oversized sunglasses like a celebrity getting out of rehab and lips that are twice the size they were on Sunday.

"What?" she asks when she catches me staring in history class. I pretend to turn my attention back to my notes. On her Instagram, though, is a slew of selfies of Ines pouting. She got eyelash extensions too. Not subtle ones either. They look like spider legs.

"She's not the only one," Alexa says with a shrug when I bring it up. "Isa, you might not notice, but I think they're all feeling a little bit…overshadowed."

"Overshadowed."

"Yes. Sara got hair extensions put in."

"She did? I didn't even notice."

"Well, not everyone has naturally long and thick hair like you."

For some reason, that makes me think back to the wig I found in the trunk's false bottom. The mannequin head has now taken its place proudly on the dresser in my bedroom, by the mirror. I bet they'll all want to wear it next time we do a shoot…

I catch myself thinking I don't want them to. I feel oddly protective of the wig, just like I do of the velvet dress. Somehow, it no longer creeps me out. It's so beautiful, after all.

So I let Ines and her Kylie Jenner pout be. Everyone is admiring it, and I'm feeling magnanimous. Let her have this.

When I get home that day, I notice the moment I cross the threshold that it's even dustier than usual, and that there's some sort of loud banging overhead. My first reflex is to be filled with worry. I forget to take my shoes off. I drop my backpack in the entrance and race in the direction of the noise.

Even though it's way too early for both of them to be home, my parents are there, along with four or five workers who are carrying some menacing-looking tarp-wrapped objects out of one of the rooms and setting them down in the hall.

I take a look around and recognize one of the rooms that had been boarded up. Taylor told me what it had once been, but it slipped my mind.

"Isa!" my mom shrieks. "Guess what!"

I have no idea, but at least it doesn't look bad.

"You'll never believe what your dad found in Samuel Granger's old photo room."

Right! That's what this room is. Taylor had been wanting to get in there for ages, but she said something about needing experts because of possible asbestos or arsenic or whatever. I guess she finally got around to it. I glance at the objects that now crowd the hall as the workers gently unwrap the tarps.

It's a prodigious collection of ancient cameras. Those that are, like, the size of a TV, and where you had to stand still for five minutes to avoid smudging the image.

Without hesitation, I snap a picture and send it to Alexa before my mom can notice.

A reply arrives within seconds.

!!!!!!!!!

"Wait," my mom is saying, "when your dad went into the room, he found this safe. I had to call the university right away, and they sent people who got it open. There are whole boxes of priceless historical documents. Maybe even Isabella's will, which no one was sure even existed. We're going through it all now—"

I don't wait for her to finish. I walk past her through the door. I've never been in here before, yet it's all somehow soothingly familiar, like I knew what it would look like before I ever set foot across the threshold. Heavy curtains cover the windows—several layers of thick fabric to keep out the light. The walls are lined with built-in shelves piled high with all kinds of accessories. Today all you have to do to take a photo is point your phone, but, in Isabella's time, it was this whole process: there are trays, flasks, beakers, like a prehistoric drug lab or something.

One of the shelves is moved. Not built-in after all, it seems. Behind it is a giant steel door mounted right into the plain wall. It's open, and the vault's contents sit on the floor, on top of one of our blankets that Dad must have put there.

"This thing isn't even on the blueprints!" he exclaims as he paces back and forth. "Extraordinary."

"What do they say?" I ask, nodding at the papers.

"I look forward to finding out."

In that moment, my phone buzzes in my pocket. It's a text from Alexa.

> I know what our next shoot is going to be :))))
> And you better be your best self, because
> you'll never guess who's in!

EIGHTEEN

"IT SAYS HERE THAT, SHOULD THE ESTATE PASS INTO THE ownership of Amory University, an annual gala is to be held in Isabella's name," my dad says. "And that an artist should be featured."

I guess I should be on top of the world, because all this means that Taylor isn't mad at me anymore. She's been giving me the low-key silent treatment since our argument on Sunday night. And, honestly, it would have been better if she'd just gotten really angry and yelled and then got over it completely, like she tends to do. But no. Instead, she's been simmering ever since. Every once in a while, I'd catch her looking at me strangely. Like I'm not her daughter but some impostor.

"That's great," I say. "Is it still—you know—valid? After all this time?"

"I don't see why it wouldn't be. There's even a date. It's right after the holidays."

"And what a great opportunity!" Taylor gushes. "For fundraising. For the college. For us! This is exactly why they brought us in."

"You know what? It would be nice if we could feature you," Dad says. "You're a photographer after all. Isabella would have loved that."

Isabella would not have loved that. She would have hated my mom's kind of photography. But I wisely keep my mouth shut. "Mom?"

"Yeah?"

"Do you think we could use some of the old photo equipment as props? Alexa can't stop talking about it ever since I told her."

I was right to mention Alexa, because my mom obviously has a soft spot for a fellow photographer—especially one of the young people whose approval she craves.

"I really don't see why not," Taylor says. I calculated correctly. "It'll be a great addition to your project."

I can tell she's a million miles away. What's more, there's a look on her face that strikes me, because only now I realize how long it's been since I've seen her like this. She actually looks happy. What do you know?

"Cool," I say carefully, deciding not to push my luck further. "Anyway, I'm going to my room. To let her know."

They both nod distractedly. But, instead of going to my room, I turn around and tiptoe back to the door of Samuel Granger's old studio.

I hear papers rustling, the soft footfalls as my mom paces the room.

Taylor's voice. "It's a little strange, the date she chose for the gala.

Right after the holidays. Everyone is bloated and broke, no one's in the mood for fundraising."

I hear the rustle of my dad's sigh. "Come on, Tay. Are you being a spoilsport again? On the contrary, it'll be great. The whole post-holidays season is dead air. It'll be nice to have a big glitzy event to break up all that monotony."

"I'm not being a spoilsport," my mom answers stubbornly.

"Everything's been going steadily uphill ever since we moved." Dad is energetic; I can practically hear him beaming. "This is just another stroke of luck. Aren't you dying to be the featured artist?"

"Sure," she says.

"That's it? Sure?"

Now it's her turn to sigh. "It's just—do you ever catch yourself thinking how nothing worked out the way you imagined when you were younger?"

"I'm not sure what you mean." His tone is a bit tense, and I suspect that he knows perfectly well what she means, because they've had this conversation before, more than once even.

"Well—you grow up thinking you'll be the next Annie Leibowitz or whatever. Or a war-zone photographer. Winning awards. And, the next thing you know, you're over forty and taking pictures of pretty buildings. Your students are half your age and looking at you with thinly veiled pity, and you realize that's as good as it's ever going to get."

"In that case, this gala is exactly what you need," Dad says. "The spotlight. It'll do you good."

"It's not about the spotlight, Gordon. It's about integrity. I want to go back to the work I used to do before all this."

"Like, photographing homeless people?"

"Don't make fun of me. You know there's more to it than that."

"I'm sure there is. But the donors at the university, they're old-money types who want something impressive they can hang in the family mansion, so that's what we have to give them."

There's a pause. I can hear the tension crackling in the air and wonder if I should retreat before one of them goes storming out and catches me eavesdropping.

"You," my mom says at last. Her voice is soft, but her tone is somber.

"I'm sorry?"

"You. It's what *you* have to give them. It's your job."

My dad groans. "Seriously?"

"No, no. Never mind. I'll do an exhibit of pretty photos of the house—it'll get on your patrons' good side, it'll make money." She sounds so discouraged that I feel bad for her. "I don't mind that I'm a sellout and that no one will ever remember my work. It's just—if only there was a way to keep Isa from the same disappointments that I faced."

"Disappointments," Dad scoffs. "That's some definition of disappointments. Look around you! Sure, I may not have had an Edwardian mansion anywhere in my five-year plan, but, from where I'm standing, things are pretty damn great."

"Gordon—"

"No, I mean it. You want to keep Isa from being disappointed in life? You sure as hell won't accomplish that by taking photos of roadkill and abandoned housing projects. However, getting her a leg up in admissions at a prestigious college, not to mention a well-padded college fund? That might help."

"So, throw money at the problem. That's the solution."

"It may not be *the* solution, but it's *a* solution. Especially since our daughter didn't exactly choose a field known for employment stability, did she?"

Wow. Thanks for the vote of confidence, Dad.

"You know what I think, Taylor? I think your problem is that you're spoiled. Nothing is ever good enough."

"Don't you dare—" Her voice lowers to a hiss, and, even though I strain my hearing, I can't make out any more words. Fear stirs within me. It's unsettling. My parents fighting—this isn't something I'm used to. For the first time it occurs to me that I'm not the only one whose life was affected when we just up and moved here. God, what if they decide to divorce? All my problems will sure seem less serious then.

And that thought prompts another one, much darker: will I have to leave the house?

In that moment, I honestly can't say if I'm hopeful or terrified.

Our photo shoot theme is Samuel and Isabella. With none other than Nick freaking Swain as Samuel Granger, clad in a vaguely Edwardian (really late Victorian) outfit that Alexa rescued from the costume storage room of the theater club. Everybody else is there, too, including Ines with her spider lashes and new lips that look great unless she has to smile or talk or do literally anything other than pout.

Alexa and Sara styled Nick as a sort of dandy, complete with pomade in his hair. He's weirdly game about it. Or, at least, he pretends to be. When I walk into the studio in my dress and makeup, he tips his hat at me. All the girls ooh and aah and with good reason: my dress is a silver Art Deco number that looks closer in style to the 1920s than the '10s, Isabella's heyday. We found it in one of the trunks, packed away in many layers of satin for storage, and perfectly preserved. Like it had barely been worn. It looks great on me, and some heavy jewelry and eye makeup complete the look.

Nick takes his place in front of the antique camera that he's supposedly photographing me with. We're under strict instructions to be extremely careful and not touch anything if we can help it. So the way he cavalierly picks it up makes my hair stand on end.

"Better not drop it," Alexa hisses.

"How can I pretend to take her picture with a camera that I don't know how to use?" Nick asks.

"It doesn't have to look real," Alexa scoffs. "It's art, dummy."

"And I bet none of your Insta followers would even care if I took the picture with the wrong end of it," Nick says with a sneer.

"Yes, because what could us silly girls with our Instagrams know about true art?" Alexa mocks.

But he only shrugs. "There are people who think the Kardashians are art."

"Ignore him," Alexa tells all of us. "He doesn't get it."

I give Nick a sympathetic look. At least I try. Not sure if anyone can tell with the vixen makeup I have on.

While Alexa is testing the light, and the other girls are absorbed in all the photo paraphernalia around us, I come up closer to Nick. "This is how you would take the photo with one of these cameras," I say, pointing. "You turn this thing, then the little lever, and finally press here. But it doesn't work, and there's no film, anyway."

He looks impressed. "How do you know all that?"

"My mom's a photographer," I say, feeling myself blush and happy, for once, for the pancake foundation Sara slathered on my face. But, the truth is, I realize as the words leave my mouth, that I have no idea. Taylor sure as hell didn't show me. In fact, I'm not sure even Taylor knows how. She can be a bit of a snob with her old-school Leica that she treasures, her very first camera from when she was a teenager. But this one isn't from the nineties, unless you mean the 1890s.

"You know," Nick says in a low voice, "I only agreed to this nonsense for your sake."

I'm not sure what to say.

"So you admit you think all this is stupid."

"I didn't say it was stupid. It's just, what's the point? All this energy and time for some photos to put on Instagram for people you've never met to scroll through while on the toilet."

"That doesn't mean it's not art, you know. It's the twenty-first century." For some reason, when I say that, I get an odd feeling like I'm arguing with my mom. "That's how art is nowadays. I mean, better for people to see it than not at all?"

"But art is supposed to have a purpose. A meaning. What's the meaning of dressing up in fancy outfits from a hundred years ago and posing for pretty pictures?"

We both jump a little when Alexa clears her throat. "Okay, lovebirds. Camera's ready. Want to go take your poses, so we can get it over with?"

My face warms once again. Alexa gets into place, camera at the ready. On my way to my spot, I lean closer to Nick. "How about just because? Is beauty for its own sake not enough?"

He grins. "I look at you, and maybe it is."

Alexa circles us, snapping photo after photo. I'm on a dais, posing on one of the antique chairs we brought from downstairs with a swath of dark red satin draped over the back, which clashes pleasantly with my silver dress. Nick is crouching behind the antique camera like he's taking my photo.

"Nice!" says Alexa. "Very nice. Hold still for a little while longer."

"So, Isabella, she was an artist's model?" Nick asks, ignoring her. "All those paintings in the house are by different people?"

"Yeah, in a nutshell," I say. "I think she preferred to be called a muse."

"Old Sammy here must have gotten jealous once or twice," Nick says.

I blink. "I never thought of that. Maybe."

"Maybe? His wife, posing for hours and hours alone with all these famous painters. Scantily clad. I sure would be asking myself some questions."

"Nah. If I were him, I'd be flattered," says Alexa from behind her camera. She's still taking photos. I follow her with my gaze as she circles us. "All these dudes thirsting after my hot wife, and I'm the one she chose."

"I guess," says Nick, looking unconvinced. "But, then again, he kind of ended up the loser in the situation, didn't he?"

"How so?" I ask. I don't want to talk because I could be caught with my mouth open in a photo, but I can't resist. I feel oddly defensive on Isabella's behalf.

"All these thirsty dudes, they painted her and took off. They were only there when she was at her best. But, when she aged and faded, he's the one who stuck around. And now nobody even remembers who he was."

Silence falls over the room. I think back to that Wikipedia page. No one even knows when the poor guy died or where he's buried.

But Alexa scoffs. "How typical. She was the great muse and inspiration, but yeah, let's all worry about the poor obscure guy."

"He's the one who made her popular in the first place, with his photos. Would she have been as great without him?"

"You know what?" I say. "If you think this is so lousy, why don't you go? We're going to do the rest of the shoot without you."

"Isa, come on." He breaks pose and stands up straight.

"You think this is pointless, meaningless, and just Instagram fodder for likes. You made that clear. Why did you even bother? You say it was for me—well, just because you have some kind of weird obsessive crush on me, and I'm not reciprocating, it doesn't give you the right to put down what I do."

I hardly noticed how I got up from my chair and walked over until only a few feet separate us. I'm animated by a strange, visceral anger. Where did it come from? And those words? What on earth possessed me?

Anger flashes through his eyes, and the tendons pop in his jaw. "Me? A crush on you? Seriously, Isabella? Is that what you think this is about?"

"Oh, you think I don't know that you hang around the house after dark? Yeah, well, I do. I saw you on the very first night." What the hell am I saying? The words tumble out as if of their own free will. How did I know it was him? I guess I did, from the beginning. "Creepy, much?"

He looks disgusted. He rips the hat from his head and tosses it into a corner. "You," he says, "are crazy. You're all crazy. You say this is some kind of historical project, but, the truth is, you don't even care. You don't know the history of the place, and, even if you did, it wouldn't matter, because all you care about are pretty pictures and Instagram likes. I'm disappointed, Isa. You're not the person I thought you were."

As he heads to the door, he strips off the costume jacket and throws it on the floor.

"See you tomorrow," he says. "In history class. Just don't count on my help anymore when you daydream through the lecture. And I wonder what would happen if I told your mom there is no assignment."

"Don't you dare!" I shriek, but the door is already swinging closed behind him.

"Do you want me to go talk to him?" Alexa asks, putting an emphasis on *talk* like she's going to break his kneecaps or something.

"No," I say. "To hell with him. We can finish the shoot with just me."

"Are you sure?"

"Yes."

"Was it true?" Sara speaks up. I give a start, having forgotten that my newly acquired mini-me was there. "That he came here to stalk the house?"

I'm overcome with an inexpressible feeling. Like Sara accidentally, without knowing, touched on something that I should definitely know about. "I—think so."

"Of course it's true," Alexa snaps. "Did you see his reaction? Creep. Do you want me to report him to school authorities?"

"No need," I say. "Let's just keep shooting, okay? And forget this even happened."

"That's right," says Alexa. "All that anger—looks great. Use it."

NINETEEN

NICK SWAIN DOESN'T GO DOWN THE STAIRS TO THE EXIT. As soon as the door closes behind him, he takes a decisive turn in the opposite direction. He steps quietly—this isn't his first foray into this territory. But he can't explain it to Isa. He can't explain it to anyone, because they'll all think he's crazy. They'll try to lock him up, and he'll have to go on the run.

Just like Desiree.

So, he climbs the stairs to the fourth floor, silent and swift. The tall double doors beckon at the end of the hallway. His heart starts to beat a little faster. He draws a decisive breath and crosses the distance.

As soon as his hand brushes against the ornate door handle, the door whispers open. *It's all too easy*, he thinks, and the gut feeling that screams *danger* at him grows stronger. Almost too strong to ignore, but ignore it he does.

Inside, there's no light, since the only window, as he knows, has been bricked up. All he can discern are the dark rectangles of paintings on the walls. After a cursory scan with the light from his phone, he finds the professional lamps Alexa brought and switches one on.

With light, the place looks simultaneously more and less spooky. All those faces of Isabella—they seem to be looking at him, their flat, painted eyes riveted on him, following his every move jealously like a spurned lover.

She will never fade. As long as these paintings hang here, in all their glory and beauty, as long as they are seen—she will never fade.

He gives a violent shake of his head to get rid of the unwelcome thoughts. *She's long dead*, he tells himself. These are just pictures. Nothing, and nobody, is watching him.

In the center of the room, just outside the bright circle the photo light makes, sits an array of trunks, big and small, and Isabella's various things are scattered all over the place. He feels a stab of cynicism at how carelessly the girls treat their supposed idol's belongings.

Looking around, he has no trouble spotting the small, discreet door in the corner. But, as he starts to make his way over, his shoe hits something that clatters loudly. He cringes at the sound that rockets like a gunshot, but seconds pass and no one comes looking for the source of the noise.

Only then he looks down. It's a carved wooden box that he tripped over. The fragile latches and lock broke off the lid. He crouches and scoops the contents back into the box: more costume jewelry—at least, he thinks it's costume. Stones that size, if they were real, wouldn't be gathering dust up here for the better part of a hundred years.

It sure looks and feels real, though. One brooch in particular catches his attention: it's a cameo in a heavy gilt frame. He holds it up to the light, and the frame's intricate designs come into focus. Cherry blossoms, swans with impossibly long, curved necks, and, at the top, a calligraphic number 6.

The center of the cameo is some kind of woven design that gleams dully. Silk?

Nick runs the pad of his thumb over it, and understanding races through his nerves and up his spine. Still disbelieving, he stumbles to the spotlight and looks again.

It's not silk. It's hair. Human hair. Light brown, with pale streaks of what might once have been auburn.

He's stricken speechless. Even if he wanted to scream, he doubts he would have been able to. He runs back to where he left the broken jewelry box and rummages through the items: rings, brooches, pendants on what might at first be mistaken for a silk-woven cord. The hair all looks similar but different in subtleties of tone and texture.

Human hair jewelry, he remembers, was a Victorian thing: a mourning ritual, creepy though it was.

Who would Isabella have been mourning?

He upends the box, and its contents spills out onto the floor. At the top of the pile of Victorian relics, something gleams, too new and shiny to belong.

His hand trembles slightly as he picks it up. A necklace adorned with a giant bead in a particular shade of blue, named lapis after the stone the pigment was once made out of.

Recognition races through him as he holds the necklace up to the light.

For the first time, he feels truly terrified.

TWENTY

NICK SWAIN CAN GO STRAIGHT TO HELL. THE PHOTOS were a huge hit on our Instagram. We're quickly approaching fifty thousand followers. Fifty thousand. Chew on that, Nick. Would fifty thousand people follow something purposeless and meaningless?

We already decided what the next shoot is going to be. My mom just reopened the house's library at the other end of the second-floor hallway and said it was safe to use. It's going to be our most ambitious shoot yet.

The day of the photo shoot starts out uneventful. Honestly, I can't wait for it to end, even theater class. I think Kendra might be noticing that I'm not at the top of my game, because, lately, she's been giving me weird looks. I mean, there's been such a major shift in usual dynamics that you'd have to be queen of denial not to notice.

"Isa," Kendra says in that careful voice as soon as the final bell rings. Everyone around me gets to their feet and stampedes out. Nick pushes past me without so much as a backward glance. I might as well be a telephone pole. "Do you have a couple of minutes? I'd like to talk to you."

"Um, to be honest, I kind of have to go," I say. That's not true. Taylor texted me to say she might be a little late to pick me up, so I have time to kill.

"It won't take a moment," Kendra says lightly. And that's when I get it: it's one of those things that's only meant to sound like a request.

"Okay." I cross my arms. It's hard not to get a little defensive.

"I've visited your Instagram account," Kendra says once it's just us. I throw a sideways glance at the door, which is half-open, and spy Alexa's black dress through the crack. She's eavesdropping. "Well—not *your* account, but that project of yours. It's very impressive."

"Thanks."

"But—you know it's not enough to get you the starring role in *Dorian Gray*, right?"

This comes out of nowhere, throwing me off-kilter. "What does that have to do with anything?"

"I just don't want you to confuse popularity and talent, that's all," Kendra says. "It's no secret that you haven't been doing your best in class lately. I know you want to play Sibyl Vane, but, for that to happen, you must step up your game and really bring it."

Um. Hello? What's wrong with this picture?

"I don't *want* to play Sibyl Vane," I say slowly. The dark swarm descends, blanketing my vision. "I'm *going* to play Sibyl Vane."

"Casting hasn't been announced yet, Isa."

"Oh, come on. Who are you going to cast? Ines? She can't act her way out of a paper bag. And you know it. And everybody knows it."

"Isa," her tone grows colder. "We don't talk like this about our classmates in my workshop."

I gulp. The darkness fades a little, and heat creeps over my face. Maybe I blabbed too much. What was I thinking?

Kendra sighs. She must decide to try a different approach, because I can see the shift in her body language and expression, plain as day. Now she's leaning in, conspiratorial, like we're friends and she's not almost thirty and my teacher. "Okay, I'll admit. I had you in mind for Sibyl Vane from the start. Because, no point in denying it, you have oodles of raw talent and the kind of universality that an actor can't do without. Don't tell the others, but, yes, I've been favoring you."

"I think everybody noticed," I say. "I think they've noticed on Mars."

If this rattles her, she gives no indication. "But you can't expect to just show up at the performance and be amazing without any practice or effort. Even the most talented of us have to work at it."

Oh, there's a few things I could say to that. But I stop myself. The clock inches forward, and I have things to do, so I must appease her to get her off my back. "Fine," I say. "But I'm marking your words. You want me as Sibyl in the play."

"Yes," she says, beaming with relief.

"I'll do my absolute best," I say. "Scout's honor."

And with that, I skip out into the hall, where Alexa is waiting. We both collapse in laughter, trying and failing to keep it quiet.

"Do you need a ride home?" Alexa asks. "Or are you going to wait for your mom?"

"I'm not going to wait, that's for sure," I say. "*She* can wait. I'm coming with you. But, before home, can we stop at one place?"

When I do get home, I realize I'm alone in the house. Taylor must still be waiting in front of the school like a loser. Well, so what? Does she think I don't remember how she just forgot me that time?

And, anyway, it's better to have peace and quiet for what I'm about to do. I head upstairs to the bathroom and close the door behind me, even though it's not necessary since I'm home alone, then inspect myself in the mirror.

No point in being modest—I look pretty damn amazing. I forgot the last time I had a blemish or a stray eyebrow hair. And, now that I'm seeing myself from head to toe, reflected in the giant mirror with its ornate frame, I notice that I don't clash with it nearly as much as before. It's hard to explain. Sometime between then and now, I began to look like I belong.

Even my clothes are different. Not sure when it happened but most of my so-called outfits migrated steadily to the back of my closet. I'm wearing a lot of black these days. Maybe it's Alexa's influence rubbing off. Today I'm wearing a sweater with a velvet skirt, and the spinel earrings that tortured Sara's earlobes.

Only one thing isn't right.

But not for much longer.

I grab a towel from the rack and throw it over my shoulders, then get to work.

"Your hair."

Taylor gets home late—she must have been waiting for quite a while. But the first thing she does when she gets home isn't yell at me. She looks at me with big round eyes, and the only thing she seems to manage to choke out is, *Your hair, Isa!*

"What? It's not like I shaved my head. It's my real color."

As close to my real color as I could find at the drugstore's hair dye section, anyway. It turned out even nicer than I thought: a rich, deep auburn with shades and dimension. You'd think I did it at one of the pricey celebrity salons in Brooklyn and not with a $10 box of dye that I shoplifted from Walgreens.

"It's nice," Taylor says. "But—I thought you were super into your pink hair."

"I was," I say with a shrug. "But you can't have pink hair forever."

"It's to look more like *her*, isn't it?"

"Who?"

"Don't play dumb, Isa."

Sure enough, *she* is watching us from the small portrait that hangs in the hall. A simple portrait, where she's wearing a deep indigo dress with a tall collar and a cameo brooch where the hollow of her throat should be. The brooch has almost more detail than her face, which is in soft focus, like an eighties glamour shot.

We should re-create this portrait, I think. I'm sure the brooch is in her things somewhere.

"I'm talking to you!" Taylor explodes. Oh. Right. I almost managed to forget she's there. Happiest five seconds of my day.

"Yeah, it's to look like Isabella. Is something wrong with that?"

"I don't know. You tell me."

"What's that supposed to mean?"

"What it means is that Ines's parents emailed your dad this morning."

I feel like I've been sucker-punched—it's so sudden and so treacherous. Come to think of it, her text this afternoon sounded a little off…but to be scheming with Ines's parents behind my back? That's just—unforgivable.

"Apparently, her classwork has been slipping, and then she got lip injections without asking for permission. And they think it's the influence of you and your project."

"I didn't march Ines to the clinic and force her to shoot a gallon of filler into her lips, Mom."

"But I think you're getting a little too obsessed with appearances."

"Obsessed? Now I'm obsessed with appearances?" an incredulous laugh escapes from me. "Wow, that's really something else. Come on, *Mom*. We both know you hated the pink hair. So, if anything, you should be happy."

"I didn't hate your pink hair!" Just like that, Taylor goes on the defensive. And no wonder—I've attacked one of the cornerstones of her identity, her cool-mom status. "I always let you play around with your appearance, because I know how important it is—"

"—for self-esteem, yeah, yeah. But you hated it. I could tell when I first got it. I wish you'd just yelled at me like a normal person instead of lying and pretending you were, like, totes cool with it. Because nobody believed you, anyway."

"You do whatever you want with your hair." Taylor's voice becomes cold. "As long as it's not the extent of your whole personality."

"And as long it doesn't get Dad's precious donors angry," I say. "Anyway, I was thinking of cutting Ines out of the project. She's starting to be a little too much. Doesn't like sharing the spotlight, this one. So you should be happy."

With that, I turn around and go to my room, ignoring Taylor calling my name.

My hair causes a real furor at school. Okay, not just my hair. For my first day as a redhead again, I decide to go all out. In one of Isabella's trunks, I find a simple, off-white linen dress with a gauzy top layer of lace and a plunging neckline. It takes a couple of minutes of playing around with it and a few safety pins to turn it into this boho off-the-shoulder number. Over it I wear one of her black lace shawls. I skip makeup except for some lip and cheek tint—I don't need anything else because my skin looks great.

I catch incredulous looks as I walk from the gate to the school doors. When I glimpse myself in the glass, all my nascent doubts come apart. I don't look weird or dorky. I look freaking phenomenal.

And I can read the same thought in everyone's looks as I walk into my first class of the day. Alexa is gazing at me with admiration; Sara practically has stars in her eyes.

Only Nick is pretending like he doesn't even see me. Which is really his problem, because he's the one who looks crazy while all the eyes are fixed on me.

Well, at least until our teacher walks in. "Isabella, you can't wear that at school."

"Why not?"

"It's against the dress code."

"What part is against the dress code?" I ask innocently. "My shoulders are covered, and so are my legs. In fact, I'm more covered up than anyone here."

The teacher gives me a venomous look but leaves me alone. The good news is, by lunch, I'm something of a legend. Everyone stops me to ask where I got these clothes. Sorry, guys, but you can't copy me by heading to H&M. My sympathies.

I think I'm always going to dress like this from now on.

"Hey, Isa." On my way to my next class, the voice catches me by surprise. I turn around.

Nick is looking contrite. So contrite that I have to wonder how much of it is an act. "I wanted to talk to you. What I said, I take it back. It was dumb and dismissive." He gives me a once-over. "And you look amazing, by the way."

"Thank you," I say coldly.

"I don't want to fight with you. Especially since"—he throws a quick glance around to make sure no one is listening in and lowers his voice—"it looks like we'll be starring in the school play side by side."

He reacts to my stunned look and goes on: "Kendra pretty much told me so. She already chose you. Congratulations, Sibyl."

I regain my composure. "Not that it was ever in doubt."

"I never doubted it." He reaches out and touches a wavy lock of hair that fell over my shoulder. "I love the new hair, by the way. Are those extensions?"

I snort. "As if I needed extensions!"

"Looks longer than before."

I toss my hair over my shoulder. Is it longer than it was yesterday? Nonsense. It just looks longer because it's not frizzy and fried with chemicals.

"Hair grows, Nicholas. That's what it does."

"So are we good again?" he asks.

"I don't know. Are we?"

"Look, I'm not going to lie, I like you. It sucks that we fought."

I'm at a loss, thrown by his directness. "Well, I—"

"Maybe we can go out sometime. On, like, a real date."

"She's busy." Alexa appears out of nowhere, startling me. "She's too busy to go to some cheesy action movie and a McDonald's drive-through with you. She's got important things she should be doing, and she's not interested. Come on, Isa."

Without waiting, she grabs my arm and pulls me along. Well, she tries to, because I dig in my heels and stay exactly where I am. She turns to me with a quizzical look.

"Actually, I'm not busy," I hear myself say. I feel funny, unmoored—like this is way more important than it seems, especially since she's probably right. I do have more important things to do: choosing photos, brainstorming future shoot ideas, answering comments from my Insta fans. But something within me, deep down, just rebels against the tyranny of it all. For just one evening, I want to be Isa, not Project Isabella. "I'm not busy," I repeat with a little more confidence. "Let's go out."

His grin looks surprisingly sincere. "Cool. Wait for me by the gates after last class."

He walks off, leaving me with Alexa who's giving me a disapproving look.

"Oh, Isa, you know I could give you the whole speech right now about pearls and swine. But I think you already know this."

"Well, maybe I happen to really like him," I say defiantly, although my certainty is a little shaky, to be honest.

Alexa shrugs. "What's there to like? He doesn't accept you for who you are."

"What's that supposed to mean?"

"Oh, that hissy fit he had the other day? If he hates superficiality so much, why doesn't he go date some troll? But no. He's after the prettiest girl at school, as always. Because the non-superficial thing only applies to *you*."

I fall silent, following her to our next class. She's wrong—I can feel it—but I also have no arguments beyond this strange gut feeling that I get when I'm around him. There's something else there. It's not just dumb jealousy or envy.

If only I knew what it was.

TWENTY-ONE

THE REST OF THE DAY KIND OF DRAGS. I COLLECT COMPLI-
ments on my hair and my outfit like glass marbles in my pocket, *clink
clink clink*. I scroll through my phone; the likes and comments and
follows keep pouring in:

> *Beautiful*
>
> *Gorgeous*
>
> *Amazing*
>
> *You. Are. A. Goddess!!!*

And so on and so forth. To think that, just this morning, it made
me so ecstatically happy to see all those notifications, but now I feel
weirdly disconnected from it all.

I get a DM from Eve.

Hey! I really miss you, Isa. So much has been happening and when I get home all I want to do is just tell my best friend about it, and then I remember you're so far away and I just want to cry. We haven't talked in forever and it sucks.

She's typing, but I beat her to it.

Hey,

So sorry—there's been all these problems with the internet. I haven't forgotten! I miss you like crazy too. And I have so much to tell you too!! For one thing I'm going on a date tonight

She replies almost instantly.

Oh la la! With?

Here's the thing about Eve, and about real friends in general. You can always pick up where you left off, no matter how long it's been since you last spoke.

This guy from school. At first I thought he was stuck-up but then he asked me out!

Is he cute?

OMG you know you HAVE to tell me all about it right??

I can't help but crack a smile. Maybe things can be normal between us again, after all.

Call you this evening?

Her reply appears less than a second later.

YES!!!

Finally, the last class of the day is over. I get up from my seat a little too quickly, before anyone else has the chance, which makes the teacher raise her eyebrow.

"In a hurry, Miss Brixton?"

Alexa scoffs next to me. A giggle runs through the class. In spite of myself, my face flushes.

"Eager to get to your hot date?" Alexa murmurs once I sit down and shamefacedly gather my things into my backpack.

"It's not a hot date," I whisper. "We're just—"

"Just so you know, he's taken half the school for a nice scenic drive in that Range Rover. I mean, I'm not here to police you, but, if you're going to anyway, at least put something over those back seats."

"Will you stop that?" I snarl quietly.

"I just think he's bad for you, that's all."

"Bad for me, or bad for the project?"

Her mouth opens slightly but nothing comes out as she looks mildly stunned. Nothing to say to that, I bet.

"Don't worry, Alexa. Nick Swain isn't going to talk me into deleting the whole thing. So you have nothing to fear."

I finally get up and make my way to the exit without looking back. But, when I get to the gate, even though I'm only a couple of minutes late, no one is there. Dread creeps up on me, and I slow down my steps, feeling like a complete idiot. Is he really going to stand me up?

"Hey! Isa!" I turn around and there he is, striding toward me at a nice quick pace but without running. "You're here. Good."

"Where are we going?"

The car fob appears in his hand as if by magic, the logo glinting brightly. "Not much to do in this town, I'm afraid. So I was thinking, start with a nice drive."

There's that dread again. My face warms. Was Alexa right about him? But I guess it's too late, and I follow him to the car. It doesn't take long after he leaves the parking lot to notice that he's going in the opposite direction from where he should be going.

"Um," I say, hiding my nervousness. "Isn't the downtown in the other direction?"

"Yeah. But we don't need it."

"We don't?"

He doesn't answer. I fidget in my seat. It's not just the downtown core and the university that's in the other direction—but so is my house. As I look out the window, it occurs to me I haven't ventured this far away from it since we moved.

Yet, no matter how I search my soul, I don't feel nervous, not in any real way. The opposite is true—I feel relieved. As if, along with the house that fades in the distance, the whole Project Isabella fades, too, as well as all its expectations of me. For the first time it occurs to me that wearing this crazy outfit to school might have been overkill. I play with the hem of the skirt, determined to change out of it as soon as I get home.

Nick pulls to a stop, and I realize we're hardly even in town anymore. The surroundings look almost rural: we're on a lookout with a view of rolling orchards, still beautiful this time of year. I can't lie, it's a nice view.

"Here we are," he says. "What do you think?"

I giggle, not without nervousness. "Hey, I don't know what you think is going to happen, but..."

"Nothing has to happen. I was just hoping I could spend some time with you—away from Amory."

"You make it sound like Alcatraz."

He winces. "It's just that, in a place that size, everyone knows everyone. If we went to one of the three nice places on Main Street, our entire conversation and every gesture will be doing the rounds of the school by tomorrow. And maybe I don't want that."

"Yeah," I chuckle. "And, if we just drive off to Makeout Point all by ourselves—nobody will talk about that, no sir."

He gives a carefree shrug. "Let them talk. No one knows what actually happened, so it's all just speculation and gossip. Which is worthless."

"And now you sound like you're about to murder me and bury me in the woods."

"You sound just like Alexa. And, if I wanted to go on a date with Alexa, I'd have asked her."

"And she would have told you exactly where to go." I'm teasing, but, at the same time, wondering if I'm going too far.

He smirks. "I come here to be away from everyone. I just wanted to share this place with you. Thought you might like it too."

"You know what?" I say. "Maybe you're right. It's nice. To be away from everyone. I feel like—oh, it sounds stupid."

"Try me."

"I feel like I'm constantly being watched. Not, like, in a Big Brother way—but like I'm being scrutinized every moment of every day. Especially since we started that project, I've felt a little…overwhelmed. Like it's taking over everything. And, especially now that it's popular, I feel like everyone's watching my every move unblinkingly. Just waiting for me to screw up so they can say, *Oh, she's not all that.*"

"Those photos are beautiful," he says with a certain careful neutrality that makes me think he's not being entirely honest.

"Yeah. Of course they are. But it's—why did I only become popular now that I'm cosplaying as somebody else? People either like me because of Project Isabella or because they can use me to get into that house. Was Isa from Brooklyn not good enough?"

"I think," he says, "that Isa from Brooklyn is extremely underrated."

I realize I've been staring straight ahead at the view beyond the windshield, and, when I turn, I notice that he's been looking straight at me all along. His eyes are warm. A blush creeps up my neck and across my cheeks. I catch myself wondering if he's going to kiss me, and also whether I want him to.

"I know it must be rough," he says. "To just be dragged away from your whole life and to end up here, of all places."

I find myself nodding along. "You have no idea," I say hoarsely. "I miss my school. I miss my best friend. I miss my theater club—no offence, Kendra's great and so is your amazing auditorium but…"

"It's okay, Isa, you can say it. Kendra's not that great. She just thinks she is, but she has no vision, and her idea of theater is stuck in decades past. And it doesn't help that three-quarters of the theater club can't act to save their lives."

I hold back an incredulous giggle. "Wow. Now I think I know why you wanted no one to overhear."

"Come on, you're one of the good ones. You must have noticed and just been too polite to say so."

I blush, remembering some of the things I've accidentally blurted lately. I still have no idea what came over me.

202 | NINA LAURIN

"And the town sucks, not just compared to Brooklyn, but in general. And I think you noticed that too. Come on, Isa, just say so. You'll see, it's therapeutic." With that, he rolls down the window. Cold air rips through the car. He sticks his head out. "Amory suuuucks!" he yells out at nothing and no one in particular.

"Amory sucks," I say, grinning. "Amory sucks, and I hate it here."

"There. Feel better?"

"Eons better."

He's leaning close again. My pulse picks up speed. Are my lips chapped? Because his look delish. I gulp, trying to be subtle but convinced he can see my throat move.

"Nick Swain," I say.

"That's me."

"I don't mean to be one of those people who overanalyzes everything, but there's something I want to know. I'm getting mixed messages. First, you agree to be a part of the photo shoot even though we barely know each other—and you made it clear that you don't think much of Project Isabella—"

He winces. "I thought we weren't going to talk about the project."

"Why did you agree, then? I mean, really. Not just because you like me. There were other ways to get my attention. And, if Amory sucks—then why are you here? Your family doesn't live here, so I've been told. You're here all alone just so you can go to this high school with its crappy theater club?"

For a few moments, silence fills the car. I wonder if I've accidentally said something tactless—lately it seems to be my specialty. His face seems to cloud over. He runs his hand over his hair.

"Might as well just tell you," he says.

I tense, filled with an ominous feeling.

"Yes," he goes on, "it's correct. I live here alone. My family doesn't live here…anymore."

I don't dare to even blink, mentally willing him to go on and not leave me hanging.

"I grew up here in Amory. That's why they let me stay behind when they moved away," he says. "Growing up, my cousin lived with us. For a long time I thought she was my big sister, but she has a different last name, so that's why some people haven't made the connection."

"What connection? You're being cryptic."

He ignores my comment. "Her name was Desiree. She babysat me a lot when I was a kid. She was super into theater. We'd put on these little plays she starred in. She went to high school here. She was in the theater club. Not just that—she basically was the reason we *have* a theater club. She was no-nonsense and tended to get what she wants. She petitioned the school, collected student signatures—and, voilà. Just like that, we had theater classes. But nobody remembers that now."

He has a distant, glassy-eyed look that puts me on my guard. Clearly, this is not a happy story.

"No, the reason people remember Desiree is because she went missing the night she was supposed to star in the school play."

Slowly, but inevitably, things come together in my head. I draw a breath to exclaim, but he speaks up again.

"She just didn't show up. This part you might have heard of: the play was *Dorian Gray*, the same iteration that we're doing."

I clasp my hand over my mouth. "That must be horrible for you—I can't even imagine—"

He holds up his hand. "Please. No melodrama. Desiree disappeared, and that's it. That's the story. I didn't stay behind because I love our school so much. I stayed behind so I could find out what happened."

"And did you?"

He gives me a somber look. "I'm getting there. Everyone said she ran away, because she'd gotten in all kinds of trouble before. But she would never have run away the night of the play. She loved theater. She gave everything she had to that play. And now—"

He reaches into the car's glove box and comes out with something shiny clutched in his hand. My gaze follows it, uncomprehending. He opens his palm: it's a silver necklace with an opaque dark blue stone with what looks like gold lightning through its center.

"Lapis lazuli," he says. "It belonged to her."

"Are—are you sure?" I stammer. "Where did you find it?"

"At your house, the day of the photo shoot."

I sit there, perfectly still, but my thoughts are racing, a horrible dark swarm of them. They cloud first my mood and then my vision. They devour every shred of romance and excitement and whatever else had been there just moment ago. A familiar dark fury rises within me.

"You snooped around my house? Through my things?"

He recoils out of pure instinct. He's not quick enough to hide it. Even my voice sounds different all of a sudden.

"Do you hear what I'm telling you? My missing cousin's necklace—"

"How do you even know it's hers? It's not exactly one of a kind—they probably sold a million of these cheap baubles."

"It's hers," he says. "I remember it. She always wore it."

But more words are already tumbling out, and I don't have time to even process what he said. "I was right, wasn't I? It's still about the house. You weren't interested in *Isa from Brooklyn*. You just needed an excuse to sneak around my house, behind my back, looking for your bullshit little clues."

"Isa—"

"FYI, Isa is only for friends. For you, it's Isabella. Drive me home. Right now."

"I don't think you're really hearing what I'm telling you," he says slowly. "I'm trying to explain—"

"Home. Now."

———

Once he drops me off, I circle the house to go through the back door. It's completely dark. For some reason, none of the outdoor lights are on, and even the windows look dark. But I know every turn of the path, every rock, and find my way without difficulty. My anger simmers as I enter the house, walk up the stairs, and finally close the door of my room behind me.

I didn't manage to run into either of my parents—oh, the perks of living in a big house—and, to be honest, I don't feel like letting them know I'm home. My mom will barge in and ask all those questions, and I don't feel like talking about it. So I make sure the door shuts as quietly as possible and then block it with a chair.

Then I turn around and find myself face to face with Isabella.

Her green eyes glare at me from the painting as if in accusation. *You let this stupid boy in here. You let him go through my things. You let him place everything in jeopardy—how could you?*

The dark swarm of anger grows and grows until its angry hum drowns out my thoughts. I let myself be buoyed by the anger. I'll get him for this. How dare he?

How *dare* he?

The trill of my phone jolts me. I spin around, disoriented, even though the phone is just in the back pocket of my jeans. Who on earth could be calling me?

Then I take the phone out of my pocket. It buzzes angrily in my hand, Eve's face on the screen.

Right. We were supposed to talk this evening, weren't we?

My relief is shallow, my heart still hammering when I answer.

"Hi! Isa, oh my god. Hi. It's so good to hear your voice."

"Technically you haven't heard it yet," I say. She seems to think I made a joke.

"You have to tell me everything. How are things at the new place? How's the new theater club? How's—"

"You first," I say, a little surprised at the chill in my voice. "I thought *you* had lots to tell me."

I hit my target, because an awkward, static-filled silence follows.

"Go on," I prompt. "You guys shot the promo pics. Tell me all about it. How does my dress fit you? Not too tight in the waist?"

"Isa," she says, her tone muted. "I'm so sorry—I meant to—"

"That's okay. I was going to see it anyway, since everything's online."

"You know I never would have taken your role," she says softly.

"I know," I say. "But I left. So everyone had no choice." *But to cast the second best.* Looks like the dark swarm is still whispering in my ear. At least this time I didn't blurt it out loud.

She breathes a shaky sigh. "I knew you'd understand."

"Perfectly." My own voice is miraculously steady. "Sorry. I just had a really crappy day."

"Didn't you have your big date?"

"Yeah, well, the big date was a big flop. I don't really—I don't want to talk about it."

"Well, it's his loss," Eve says.

"Yeah. He could have dated the most popular girl in school, not to mention a viral influencer. But he chose to be a loser instead. His loss."

Again, that weird pause. "Speaking of which," she says at last. "I saw that's going well. I saw you dyed your hair."

"Do you like it?"

"Isa, you know you look gorgeous no matter what your hair looks like."

"That's a really convoluted way of saying it sucks."

"I didn't mean anything like that!" Eve exclaims. A little too quickly in my opinion.

"Okay, okay. It has people divided, to say the least. Even Taylor thinks I'm nuts. But you know what? *I* like it, which is what matters. That, and I think it'll go a long way for Project Isabella. I can't have pink hair in this setting, and I'm not going to keep wearing itchy wigs, am I?"

But it seems that mentioning Project Isabella only makes things worse.

"I sort of figured it was for the project," Eve says carefully. "And I was wondering. I saw the photos and everything. They're—spectacular. But where do you want to take it from here?"

"What do you mean?"

"I mean, what's the end goal? So you want to be this big influencer—who doesn't? But what do you want to get out of it? Sponsorships?"

A laugh escapes from me. "Sponsorships?"

"I mean free stuff."

"I know what sponsorships are, Eve. But why would I ever want that? What do they have that I could possibly want, when I already have this place?"

"The place is…something. I'm not arguing. But—"

"But it's not really my place. I don't really have it. That's what you were going to say, wasn't it?"

Eve sputters. "If you want to put it that way—"

"Yeah, yeah. What will poor Isa do once Taylor's done fixing it up and the university takes it back? She'll become a nobody again. Which is what you all seem to be waiting for with bated breath."

"Isa, is everything okay? You seem kind of on edge, to be honest."

She means it with sincerity. I can tell. The dark swarm momentarily recedes, leaving guilt behind.

"I think the pressure's just getting to me," I stammer. "There's all this schoolwork, and the project is a ton of work. And then there's theater club. We're doing *Dorian Gray*. Every girl at school is jealous of me, and they're all angling for my role."

"They don't stand a chance," Eve reassures me. Her words sound a bit hollow.

"Hey, Eve? Look, I'm totally wiped out. Can I call you tomorrow after school?"

"Sure," she says. She sounds hesitant but mostly reassured. Good.

We hang up, and, for a few moments, I look at my phone, glassy-eyed, not really seeing all the apps on the screen. Then, out of sheer habit, I open Instagram and scroll through my feed.

As if by magic—or the designs of another evil algorithm—Eve's photo pops up. Eve in the velvet dress. In my costume.

She looks happy.

The dark swarm descends like a black veil over my eyes. And, before I know it, I've muted her. One tap of my fingertip on the screen, and Eve is gone, just like that.

TWENTY-TWO

THE LIBRARY, IT TURNS OUT, ISN'T LIKE INES IMAGINED. She thought of something straight out of Harry Potter: vaulted ceilings, walls covered with shelves groaning under gilded tomes. But it's a small, cozy room filled with rows of dusty bookcases. Any pricey first editions were probably removed and taken to the university's library or storage vault, leaving the airport-reads of the era. While Isa and the others get ready for the photo shoot, setting up the lights and the props, she browses through a cursory selection of turn-of-the century romance novels by famed writers including Marie Corelli, Ouida, and Edith Maude Hull—author of *The Sheik*. Isabella had surprisingly mundane tastes, it seems. There are lots and lots of books on photography and reference books and dictionaries.

But the space itself isn't entirely charmless. There's a fainting couch upholstered in purple satin, an array of coffee and end tables, a pair of big cozy leather armchairs sitting by the bricked-in fireplace. The space by the window is arranged into a reading nook: a bench covered with velvet pillows.

And there's a painting of Isabella, of course.

Ines approaches it, barely noticing that she's walking on tiptoes as if to avoid attracting the attention of the others. Isabella is pictured in a simple white-lace dress, not unlike the one Isa showed up in at school. In her gently folded hands, pressed to her chest, she's holding something: a piece of paper covered in inky hints of letters. Her face is dreamy and tender, simultaneously young and ageless, the way it always is.

Ines isn't sure what exactly drew her here, to this place. Most of her life, she just felt empty, blank, like the first page of a novel that'll never be written. On the surface, she had everything: her parents never refused her a thing. They were well-to-do not only by the standards of the town but in general. But, in a place the size of Amory, everyone knew it, and Ines always suspected that was the real reason she always seemed to have so many friends. Because she grew up in a nice big house and always had the latest video games and gadgets. Not because she, Ines Mercato, was someone interesting.

Isabella was interesting. Isabella wasn't a blank canvas. Isabella the woman, the muse, not Isa, the new girl at school. Ines didn't think much of Isa. *Blows into town, drops into the theater club, steals my place.* Just like that.

And why should Isa get to be the star of Project Isabella? It really isn't fair.

The photo shoot has moved to the window. Isa is perched on the windowsill with its pillows, and Alexa is circling her like a vulture with a camera. Sara is fixing Isa's hair between shots. Sara—Ines knew her since they were little kids. She thought that, if she could call anyone a real friend, it was Sara. But all it took was someone sparklier and cooler.

And now Isa is going to sideline her from the project, Ines is sure. It's so obvious that Isa's been giving her the cold shoulder. Everyone else picks up on it, so now they're all avoiding Ines like the plague.

My god, she thinks as she browses the bookshelves. This place. This house. She doesn't deserve it. Who the hell does she think she is?

The book sits there, beckoning to her.

She reaches out and takes it off the shelf. It's so old it has to be a first edition. Probably rare and worth a lot of money. Someone must have overlooked it and forgotten such a treasure here, in this musty grave of outdated and irrelevant books by forgotten people. Oh, how she can relate.

She opens the cover to the flyleaf. Her breath catches when she sees the inscription in a truly elegant hand, almost calligraphic.

For the beauty that never fades.

Below, the title of the book is printed in surprisingly sharp letters. She barely has time to read it—*The Picture of Dorian Gray*— when, with a loud crack that echoes through her bones, the lights overhead flicker and wink out.

TWENTY-THREE

I BLINK, STARTLED. EVERYONE AROUND ME SHRIEKS IN UNISON.

"Calm down!" I hear myself saying. "It's just a power outage. The thunderstorm must have knocked over a pole somewhere."

Outside the window, rain lashes the landscape. Every few seconds, webby tendrils of lightning lacerate the sky.

"There goes our shoot," Alexa mutters, but she sounds satisfied. We did get a lot of good pics. Gradually, all the girls settle down. Lights of phones dance in the dark, illuminating their faces as they scroll and scroll. It's a beautiful scene, really. And I did all that.

"I guess I'm going to change," I say and step down from the reading nook by the window. "Just as well. This lace is making me itchy."

I undo the brooch that holds the lace shawl together at my throat, a beautiful cameo with some kind of silk-woven pattern in the center. Alexa found it before the shoot in one of the trunks. It's really nice, she says, a great focal point for the photo.

Plus, the colors match my hair to an almost exact degree.

Hey Isa!!

So, as you know (if you haven't forgotten, that is—you haven't forgotten, have you?) the play is this weekend. I guess you'll be staying over at my place? My parents are so stoked to have you for a whole weekend. They miss you, too, I think. (But not as much as I do!!!) Just let me know when your parents are bringing you. Or, if you're taking a bus, let me know when to come pick you up. I have a whole super fun bffs reunion weekend planned! The play, then the afterparty, and the next day we can all have brunch at The Barn, and then there's an indie band playing that night at the usual place. I thought it could be fun. And, on Sunday, we can just hang. (Brooklyn Aquarium, like when we were in 2nd grade?? I think so!)

GURL, I CAN'T FREAKING WAIT TO SEE YOU I MISS YOU SO MUCH!! PLS ANSWER QUICK.

Xoxo,

Eve

Hey Isa,

So I haven't gotten your answer yet. What time are you coming down? I figure we don't have to go to the afterparty. We can just go out to dinner, you and me. Our sushi place? I just really want to catch up. I know I've been super wrapped up in the play and everything, and you have your own thing, too, so maybe we haven't been messaging as much as we meant to. But I really REALLY want to know what you've been up to! And your theater club? Did you get Sibyl? (Ha! Trick question, I know you did. Because how could you not get Sibyl??)

I've seen your Insta photos. They're really something. I know it must all take a lot of time. But I can't wait to see you again! I miss you so much.

Xoxo

Eve

Isa!! The play's next week and you haven't gotten back to me yet. Look, I know (and tooooootally understand) that you're kind of mad. I know you worked so hard and then you just had to change schools. And it wasn't my choice to take your role! It wasn't! I swear! I would trade it for having you back in my life in a heartbeat. So please, please, please don't be angry. You're still my best friend in the whole world, and it just breaks my heart that you've been ghosting. I don't want us to grow apart over some bullshit role.

And, if you don't want to meet up with everyone else from theater, that's totally okay too. It can be just us, like in the old days.

BTW I saw your photos in the old library, they are *chefkiss*!!! is it that alexa girl who takes them cuz im totes jealous.

Haaaaa no, just kidding, I take that back. I know it's Isa and Eve FOREVER

READ

Isa

Isa

Isalsalsalsalsalsalsa!!!

Answer! I know that you've read my messages

Come on

READ

Okay so the play is tomorrow. I haven't heard a single word from you in weeks, and really I might get worried and wonder if you were still alive, except you post photos on here every five seconds so I know you haven't been kidnapped OR locked in a tower with no wifi forever. I guess you don't really give a shit about me or the play or Brooklyn. Good for you I guess??? And I get it, I do. I just wish that instead of disappearing like a COWARD you'd just say it to my face. And at least give me a hint what it was that I did wrong to piss you off so much. I know it's not the play. You

don't seem to give a damn about theater
or anything besides your stupid historical
cosplay. So bye bitch.

READ

I'm so sorry i didn't mean that! I take back
what I said. Just answer me, okay please,
please, please

READ

The play went great. Thought you'd like to
know.

READ

PART
THREE

TWENTY-FOUR

THE MOMENT I OPEN THE APP, THERE IT IS.

The photo is polished, a little too polished. I can tell Ines had a go at editing it. She made her hair longer because, apparently, the extensions are not long enough, and, behind her, I can make out an arched window. This wasn't taken at school, nor at the house—she wouldn't dare. She's posing in a long, white-lace gown, holding a single Black Magic rose to her chest strategically. But it's really the caption that's the cherry on the sundae.

My dear, only days ago I last saw you and already it feels like it's been seven lifetimes. My mind romps as if trying to slip away and run back to you like your loyal hound. I can't read, can't eat, can't sleep; the world is hollow without you in it. And today it's been raining since sunup—my sadness has infected the skies themselves. Everything in my world misses you as much as I do. I think constantly of your eyes—your lips—your hair—your every part, even those that are now consigned to my imagination. My imagination is feverish with you, yet, for the first time, I feel like it is doomed to fall short of reality.

On the bonfire of your beauty, I happily self-immolate.

Yours,

No signature, naturally.

I chew on the inside of my lip, deep in thought.

It's a super sunny winter day, and I have to set the brightness of my phone super high to see. My mom tries to sneak a peek of the screen, her hands on the steering wheel.

"Eyes on the road, Mom," I say. "You're going to wrap the car around a fencepost."

"You seem angry," she says. "Isn't eight a.m. a bit early to be having a bad day?"

"Who said anything about a bad day?"

"Just that you're a bit touchy lately. The only time you seem in a good mood is when you're upstairs in Isabella's portrait room."

"That's not true."

She's not convinced but decides not to argue. At least that allows me to get back to the Instagram post in peace. I reinspect the photo and reread the letter once again. The post is collecting likes by the truckload.

"So, apparently, Ines has a secret admirer. Did you see?" I ask Alexa once I meet up with her and Sara inside the school.

"Who *didn't* see?" Alexa says. This does nothing to improve my mood. Over the last couple of weeks, not only did Ines get hair extensions down to the small of her back, she bought some Victorian outfits off the internet and has been posting nonstop selfies. Copycat. Not that any of it looks anywhere near as good as what I do. But still.

But this is different. This is a shameless foray into my territory.

Ines may not have the house and all the authenticity that comes with it or my acting talent or hair that isn't fused to her head with plastic. But she does have parents who are loaded—as my own not-loaded parents never cease to remind me. So all the things she doesn't have she can just buy. Which is exactly what she's been doing. All the while still being all too happy to keep hanging out with me and Alexa and the others at my house, pretending like nothing is happening. Plotting her stealthy takeover. Hypocrite.

But I don't say any of this out loud. Why would I? It would only make me sound petty and jealous. And I'm not jealous of anyone. I am Isabella. I have close to a hundred thousand followers. People are jealous of *me*.

So, instead, I prefer to focus on brainstorming this weekend's photo shoot. I really have to hit it out of the ballpark. I want to cross that 100K threshold before the holidays. And, as much as I hate to admit it, I'm starting to run low on ideas. We've taken photos all over the house. Every portrait has been recreated. Well—almost every portrait. There's one last one we haven't done yet.

Maybe that's the solution I've been looking for. That dress must still be where I hid it. It seems so pointless to me now. What on earth was I so afraid of—a gown?

"Anyway," I say. The last thing I need right now is Ines trying to steal my thunder. "I bet she wrote that to herself."

Alexa shrugs. "Oh, I bet. It's so overwrought. None of the boys at this school would ever dream of writing a thing like that."

I say nothing. I'm a bit offended that she called it overwrought. It's beautiful, and with that dark sensuality simmering right between the lines. The suggestiveness is only made more brazen by the coyness.

"It's the oldest trick in the book, second only to the boyfriend who goes to another school," Sara speaks up. She obviously thinks she's helping, but that sets my mind on another not-so-pleasant tangent.

Nick's been out of school for the last couple of weeks. Which is annoying, because I really need to get him back under my spell in time to practice *Dorian Gray*. I'm seized with horrible doubt, the dark swarm of anger and envy clouding the edges of my vision. Did Nick write this to her? He's the only one clever enough to come up with such a letter.

To Ines. *Ines*. God, talk about adding insult to injury. No, it can't be. It wasn't him.

"Why are you sulking?" Alexa asks.

"I'm not sulking. I'm thinking."

"Ines can't hold a candle to you, you know."

I give a laugh that comes out super fake and forced. "Ines? I wasn't even thinking about Ines anymore."

"Really? Cause I could've sworn…" She gives me a suspicious look.

"Well, you've sworn wrong."

"We can do our own Dorian Gray shoot," Alexa suggests. "In the real costume. It'll look a million times better than her Photoshop job."

"No way," I snap. "Then she'll know she got to me."

"I thought you just said she didn't."

I ignore her. "And she'll start thinking that I actually consider her something like a threat and not, like, gum stuck to my shoe."

A shadow goes over Alexa's face, but it only lasts a moment. "You seem really stressed out about this, Isa. The project is going great. We're getting a steady increase in followers—"

"Except for that huge drop last Monday. We need new content… like, yesterday."

"Mondays are always a slow day. You can afford to take a break."

I'm instantly horrified.

"Oh, don't I wish I could. I can't afford to let my relevance lapse, especially now that I'm this close to actually being an Insta celeb in my own right."

"I think you're already there," Alexa says carefully.

"If only it were as simple as getting some lip injections or fake hair glued to my head. Isabella is a natural beauty, no filter, no fillers. That's what makes her—me—different from the million wannabe influencers out there. What I have can't be faked."

———————

That Saturday I wake up extra early and head to the kitchen for some coffee and to raid the fridge to see if there are some cucumber slices I can put on my eyes. Can't afford to look puffy in the photos. I fully expect to be alone, with my parents still soundly sleeping, but, when I walk into the kitchen, I give a start. Taylor is sitting at the big table, cup of herbal tea in hand.

"Morning," she says.

"Morning," I answer. She better not start meddling and interfering with the shoot, offering her outdated advice on how to light and frame and this and that. She's tried to do that a couple of times, and Alexa just lets her, which is super annoying.

"Do we have something cold I can put on my eyes? I'm so puffy it's a wonder I can see."

"Oh, Isa," she says. "You? Puffy? You're fresh as a rose. Enjoy it while it lasts."

The fridge is empty. No cucumber, nothing except leftover pizza from last night. I heave a sigh and close the door.

"Isa, I wanted to tell you something," Taylor says. "Are you going to need the portrait room this afternoon?"

Oh god, what now? "Uh, yeah. As usual. Why?"

"Well, you'll have to make it work. Your dad talked to one of the university's donors the other day—"

I brace myself, overcome with a suspicion that it's not going to be good.

"—Ines Mercato's father would like for her to do a photo shoot in the house. With Isabella's things as props."

She might as well have sucker-punched me because all the breath goes out of me at once. The dark swarm of anger pulls over my eyes like a curtain.

"Please tell me Dad told him to go to hell," I say.

"Don't be ridiculous, of course not. Anyway, it's one afternoon. The number of photos you take in this house—you can let a friend share in the glory once in a while."

"She's not my friend."

"Then why do you spend so much time with her?"

I'm furious. "As if you don't know! You told me to play nice so that my dad can kiss up to *her* dad for donations."

For a moment I think I might have gotten to her. Or at least got her to see sense.

"Isa, enough is enough. Ines is coming here with a professional photographer today, and that's final. Plus, I remind you that this isn't your house."

Anger blankets my vision. I clench my fists. I want to scream and break things, but, instead, I just turn on my heel and storm out.

When Alexa shows up, she must notice the look on my face, because she sees me and flinches. "Everything okay?"

"Yeah." I can't bring myself to tell her. I just can't. "Let's just get this show on the road."

But, as she busily hauls bags and bags of accessories over the threshold, I realize I made a colossal mistake.

As it all spills out of the bags—costumes, props, jewelry—I'm taken aback at how cheap and tacky it looks up close.

"We're not really doing this," I say, and it's not a question.

Alexa looks up like she's seeing me for the first time. "What on earth are you wearing?"

I look down, and it's as if I'm noticing it for the first time. Of course. I never changed out of my nightgown. "I found it in Isabella's things."

"You look like a walking lace doily."

"Hey, I'm not giving you *my* opinion of your clothes."

"Since when do you wear a nightgown? Who wears a nightgown in the first place?"

"I think it's classy. Better than my old stretched-out cat pajamas. And you sound just like my mom."

Alexa sighs. "Fine. But how about you change out of this…nightgown…and into something more photogenic?"

"As a matter of fact…no. I know what to do. This is going to be the photo shoot."

She chuckles. "In Isabella's nightgown? You're kidding, right?"

"It's scandalous. It'll be a hit."

"Yeah…scandalous for 1910 maybe. Gasp! What will she do next—dare to flash an ankle?"

We set up the shoot in my bedroom, but not before moving all the modern furniture out of the frame, leaving only the vanity. I sweep all my beauty products into a pile and dump them out of sight. Instead, I set out all the little pots and bottles from Isabella's things. They look so much prettier and classier than the cheapo packaging we have now. Imagine a modern makeup company bothering to hand-paint a porcelain face cream container.

I take my place in front of the mirror as Alexa circles me with her camera. The moment I step into the frame, it's like I'm in a wholly different world—a better world. Why did I bring all the IKEA crap from home? Half of it fell apart in the truck anyway because it's meant to be cheap and disposable. Isabella's things are all custom-made with thought and heart. Meant to last forever.

We've pretty much wrapped up when everyone else arrives, Ines leading. She has the photographer in tow, a tired-looking woman in a pilling sweater. I can tell she revels in her victory. She even looks better than usual. And the infuriating thing is everyone seems to be circling her again, just like before when she was the "it" girl.

As I wash my makeup off in the bathroom, I notice she's putting on hers.

"What a great idea for a shoot, Isa," she coos. "Risqué. I like it."

She's mocking, I can tell.

"But you know what? I have an even better idea."

I watch her in bafflement as she crosses the room to stop next to the antique tub. "I'm going to have my picture taken in the tub. Like the painting."

I carefully watch Alexa's expression. She looks incredulous but also—and I hate to admit it—kind of impressed. "You want to sit in the tub naked."

"That's what I said, isn't it?"

"Uh…is that legal?"

"There won't be any naughty bits. And it's art, no?"

"No way," I hear myself saying. My voice is suddenly kind of… loud. So loud that it carries, echoing under the room's high ceiling.

Everyone grows silent, and their heads pivot all at once to look at me. "No way," I repeat, crossing my arms. "Not going to happen."

Ines gives an annoying silvery laugh. "Wow, what happened, Isa? Suddenly shy? Or just jealous that I dared to do it first?"

"You can't let her do that," Sara murmurs.

"Damn right. And I won't. This is my house and my bathtub and my paintings. And if I say no, it's no. You can take your trashy photos at home with a selfie stick."

"It's not your house," Ines says with a sneer. "It belongs to the university."

"It belongs to Isabella," I say.

"And Isabella is dead."

It feels as though the room gets a little darker. Maybe the sun outside hid behind a cloud, dampening the brilliant light that pours through the stained glass. Anger rises within me, dark and hot. And then, as if by magic, I know exactly what to say.

"Where did that letter really come from, huh, Ines? The one you pasted under your tacky little photo."

"It was in my locker." She raises her chin, nostrils flaring, and I know instantly, on a near-instinctive level, that she's lying her ass off. It's just so obvious. How did I not see it right away? She's such a lousy actress she can't even pretend properly.

"I think everyone here knows it was not. No one would ever write that about you anyway."

The words come out dripping with venom, so mean and evil that they shock even me.

"Isa," Alexa mutters.

"My dear," I quote, and then the whole letter floats effortlessly to the top of my memory. I recite it, and with each line blood drains from Ines's face. She's an ashen shadow of herself. I've never seen her this ugly.

"This was not in your locker, Ines. It's a letter from Samuel to Isabella, November 1904, at the beginning of their courtship. That's right, you're not the only one who has access to university archives."

She looks utterly terrified. Out the corner of my eye, I catch Alexa staring at me in awe. The truth is, I didn't go anywhere near the university archives, yet I was just able to recite the letter from memory—after seeing it on Instagram for half a minute. I don't stop to wonder how this is possible or how I knew when it was written.

"So what if I did!" Ines snarls. "Not like it was written for you either! It's for a dead woman. She doesn't need it anymore."

"That's messed up," Sara says in a timid voice.

"Why would you do something like this? And lie about it?"

"Pathetic," I say.

Ines storms furiously out of the room, slamming the door. For a few seconds we all stand still and listen to the thundering of her steps down the stairs. The photographer woman stops fumbling with her setup and gives me a quizzical look.

"I think your session's canceled," I say bluntly. "You better go catch up with our favorite failed Insta model."

She shrugs and takes off after Ines. She clearly doesn't care either way.

"And, if she thinks she can ever set foot here again, she has another think coming."

"That was a bit harsh, don't you think?" Alexa says softly.

"No, not at all. She stole from me and then made up a story. She has to learn."

"I better go see if she's okay," Sara mutters and starts toward the exit.

"No," I say. "Stop right there. She has to face the consequences of her actions."

Sara looks uncertain but obeys. Of course she obeys.

"From now on, Ines is no longer allowed in our group," I say. "Or in the house. None of you are to ever talk to her again. She's dead to us. Got it?"

"Isabella," Alexa says. "Aren't you overreacting?"

"No, I'm not overreacting. And the rest of you better take heed. I'm Isabella. I'm the star. I won't tolerate impostors and liars."

They exchange a glance. The anger still boils within me, but, for the first time, my resolve is shaken. Did I get carried away just a little bit?

"It's just a stupid Instagram post," Alexa mutters. "You're being really dramatic."

I clench my fists at my sides. The dark swarm descends, only, this time, I don't push it away—I embrace it.

"I don't want her in my house."

My voice carries—carries so well that, for a moment, I think it didn't sound like me at all but like someone else, a deeper, more powerful voice.

A voice that can command.

Hi Eve,

I know this is super weird, but please read this before you delete it. I'm Alexa Horne, I go to high school in Amory, Mass. And I'm friends with Isa. I don't know if you've seen our Instagram account, Project Isabella.

I really don't know how to say this, but I'm just going to go for it. I think you should get in touch with Isa if you aren't already. Isa is acting really strange lately. She always talks so much about you and her old school and theater club back in Brooklyn—well, at least she used to. I think she might be coping badly with the new situation, or...something. To be honest, I don't know. I just think it would do her good if you talked to her.

Hey Alexa,

This is Nick. I know this is kind of weird because we don't really talk much, but it's really important. Isa is probably wondering why I haven't been to school, but please don't tell her I've contacted you. Truth is I can't come to the house anymore. It's not safe. And school's probably been infected too, with everyone walking around dressed like Isabella clones and sharing her photos all over the place. I know Isa is super into Project Isabella—it's her whole life—but please hear me out. You guys HAVE TO DELETE EVERYTHING ASAP. Everything. And, if you can convince Isa to get out of that house, all the better. I think you're all in serious danger.

TWENTY-FIVE

ALEXA HAS TO GRUDGINGLY ADMIT THAT ISA WAS RIGHT. The photo set in the nightgown is a huge hit. It's now been several days since she posted the photos to the Instagram account, and likes and comments are still rolling in.

But, for once, it doesn't make her happy. She's been in a terrible mood ever since the day of the shoot. Not because of the nutty email from Nick, and not because of Ines. Nick has always been, well, Nick, and Alexa was never crazy about Ines in the first place. She always thought Ines was snobby and arrogant, a show-off always boasting about all the nice things her parents bought her. So Ines's downfall won't exactly keep her up at night.

But Isa, on the other hand…

Alexa had liked her right away on the first day of school. She was so different from everyone here. And, sure, it was Alexa's idea to start the Instagram account, so she had something to do with the change that overcame her friend. But, lately, she's been forced to admit that things are getting weird. And not good weird.

It just isn't like the Isa that she knew to be so cruel to Ines. Even if Ines did deserve it.

When Alexa arrives in theater class on Tuesday, Isa isn't there. Which is not like her, to say the least. For once, time in theater class doesn't fly—Alexa finds herself longing for her phone. It's in her bag, and her bag is in the pile in the corner as always, but Alexa feels its pull. If only she could scroll through the Insta account one more time, everything would be right again.

With ten minutes left until the bell, the door clangs. It practically flies open, and Isa strolls in, nonchalant. Like nothing happened. She's wearing another one of Isabella's outfits she and Sara retooled for everyday wear: a cream-colored off-the-shoulder dress with layers of ruffles. Only, today, she threw a leather jacket over it. Her hair is in a long, loose braid that brushes the small of her back, and she's woven flowers into it. *Live flowers, at least,* Alexa thinks, but it's been a whole day and the blooms show no signs of wilting. Must be really good fakes.

She looks phenomenal, Alexa admits. Not without some bitterness. She looks like an otherworldly image in a fashion magazine come to life.

"Hi, everyone," Isa says brightly, as if she doesn't even realize she missed most of the class. Alexa feels a stab of panic as her friend's gaze sweeps the room. "Hi, Kendra. What did I miss?"

Everyone falls silent. It's creepy. Alexa has never seen the theater class so quiet. All the eyes in the room turn to Isa as if on command, but it's not the admiring looks Isa clearly expected. Her easy smile fades a little.

"You missed the audition for Sibyl Vane, Isa," Kendra says in a soft but serious voice.

Isa erupts with peals of laughter. Alexa now knows what the expression means. Her friend's laugh sounds like silver bells, or the inside of a music box. Pretty but cold.

"Good one," she says at last. "Now, seriously. What have you all been up to? And don't look at me like that. It's not a funeral."

"That's what we've been up to," Kendra says, frowning. "We've been auditioning for the role of Sibyl. And I think I've made my decision."

"What decision?" Isa's voice is no longer melodious. "And why would you be holding auditions for *my* role?"

Alexa thinks the silence might burst her eardrums.

"It is not your role," Kendra says levelly.

"You said you wouldn't have an audition! And you said you had me in mind!"

"Sure, but that was before. Lately, you haven't been bringing your best. You daydream in class, and, when it's your time to read, you look like you just want to get it over with. So I decided to hold the audition to give you a chance to prove yourself one last time."

Alexa sees Isa's fists clench at her sides. She can almost smell ozone in the air like a thunderstorm is coming. "This," Isa says in a loud, clear voice that's no longer pretty or pleasant, "is. Such. Bullshit!"

"Please control yourself," Kendra says. But it comes across more like she's pleading. Everyone looks as lost as Alexa feels in the face of such a force of nature.

"This was supposed to be my role. It *should* be my role! Do you seriously think, even for a moment, that I'm replaceable? That any one of you could do what I do? God. You're such a joke." A blush creeps across Isa's delicate skin. Her eyes flash, frightening, their pale blue with a tinge of green in it.

"Well, guess what. I'm the star of Project Isabella. Me! You think you can just put that on like a costume? You're mistaken. A hundred thousand people follow my account to see me. How many will see your stupid play?"

Alexa shoots to her feet, realizing how catastrophically late she is. "Isa, come on. Class is about to end. Let's just go home, okay?"

But Isa turns on her heel and runs out of the classroom. Silence falls over the room again.

Kendra clears her throat. "I suppose that settles that. Why don't you guys go. I'll have the cast list up by the end of the week, okay?"

Everyone files out, still dazed. Alexa pushes past them and out the door. She ignores Sara, who's bleating her name, and races down the hall, but Isa isn't there. She's not on the staircase or down in the lobby. Alexa searches frantically for the flash of bright auburn hair and the swishing, too-long hem of Isabella's dress, but Isa seems to have vanished.

Just like that. She's kicked over all her years of hard work and got booted from the one thing she cares about the most.

Or, at least, used to.

A light bulb goes off inside Alexa's mind. She sprints around the school and all the way to the old chapel. The door opens to let her through, and no sooner do her eyes adjust to the weak light than she sees Isa. She's perched on the edge of the stage, dangling her feet. There's no way she didn't notice Alexa come in, because the echo of her steps rumbles like thunder under the domed ceiling.

"Hey," Alexa says feebly.

Isa finally looks up. She looks tired with deep shadows lurking under her eyes. As Alexa comes closer, she's stricken by the sadness she sees on her friend's face. Not just a normal, bummed-out-because-I-just-freaked-out-at-a-teacher sadness but a profound, existential sorrow.

So Alexa forgets what she was going to say. Instead of *what the hell was that* or, even better, *what the hell is wrong with you*, she just asks, "Are you okay?"

Isa covers her eyes with her hand. "I'm simply wretched, thank you for asking."

Alexa comes closer and climbs onto the stage. Isa gets to her feet.

"Where were you?" Alexa asks. "Why were you so late to class?"

Isa rolls her eyes in an exaggerated, theatrical motion. "Oh, god.

Who caaaaares? It's just more pointless monologues. Kendra thinks she's Stanislavsky."

"You used to care," Alexa replies cautiously.

"And now I don't."

"And why did you say that about Project Isabella? What does it have to do with anything?"

Isa shrugs. "Oh, Alexa. You're so naïve. Why bother with this archaic nonsense when you can get a million fans without all the tedious memorizing of lines and endless improv sketches no one gives a damn about? All we have to do is keep posting photos. We'll have all that and more."

"Don't call me naïve, Isa. The whole thing was my idea, remember?"

"Yeah, I remember. And how far would you get without me, I wonder."

"That's mean."

"It's *true.*"

"You're different, Isa. I don't like it." Alexa crosses her arms. Isa is taller than her, and the long dress makes her look even longer and slimmer. She looms over Alexa and doesn't seem the least bit sorry.

"So why don't you follow Kendra's lead and kick me out of the project? Oh, right. You can't. Because it's my house and my likeness."

"I'm serious. You didn't have to be so cruel to Ines. She's sorry for what she did, and everyone already despises her. You didn't have to kick her while she's down. It's not like you."

"What do you know about it? We've only known each other for, like, a few months."

Alexa is stricken. She's not wrong.

"You know what?" she asks. "You're right. I can't kick you off the project, your house, your image, blah blah blah. But what I can do is quit. You can find yourself another photographer. Someone who won't care that you're being a royal bitch."

The word seems to ricochet off the walls, bouncing between them as Isa freezes. Alexa readies herself for an avalanche of abuse. But, instead, it's like someone invisible had cut Isa's tendons. Her body grows limp, and she sinks to the floor with a sob.

In a heartbeat, Alexa is by her side. Isa lets her head loll prettily against Alexa's shoulder, and Alexa sees the two perfect tears roll out of her eyes and stop midway down her cheeks. A flower falls out of her hair and into Alexa's lap.

"I'm so sorry, Alexa," Isa says in a tiny voice. "I'm so sorry. I didn't mean for any of it to happen."

Alexa is motionless, frozen in awkwardness.

"It's just, everything's been so difficult. I thought this role would be duck soup. But it's so hard! I just can't nail it down no matter how hard I try."

Duck soup? Alexa doesn't dare move a muscle.

"And I know I'm taking it out on you and everyone, but it's been such a torment. And now the boy I was enamored with has left me."

Oh, Alexa thinks. This is about Nick. Strange turns of phrase aside, this is a boy crisis, after all.

"He'll come back," she says, although she couldn't be less convincing if she tried.

"No, he won't. Am I such a beast that even a boy I like won't stick around?"

"You're not a beast," Alexa finds herself saying.

"But I feel perfectly beastly. Oh, Alexa, only you understand. That's why your pictures of me are so beautiful. Because they capture the me that only you see."

Alexa is utterly startled when Isa puts her arm around her and pulls closer. Way closer. Isa's cheek is pressed to the hollow of her throat. "I can hear your heartbeat," Isa says. Her voice sounds different, higher in pitch. "Your loyal, loyal heart. Please don't leave me. Don't back out of the project. Do you promise?"

Alexa is too bemused to say anything except, "I promise."

Isa immediately gets back on her feet. Her face is now aglow with joy. It's whiplash-inducing.

"Dilly!" she exclaims. "Are you going to take me home now?"

Dilly. It's an old word to say excellent, Alexa thinks. She read it in a book.

"Of course," she says. "But, first thing tomorrow, you're going to go apologize to Kendra. She's nice. She'll let you back into the play."

Isa pouts. "Fine," she says in the same voice.

For the first time, Alexa wonders what the hell she got herself into.

Nick,

Sorry I didn't get back to you. TBH I thought you sounded kind of crazy. But Isa's been acting really strange, and I never thought I'd say this but I think you might be on to something.

What exactly do you know about that house????

Alexa

TWENTY-SIX

WHEN I ARRIVE HOME, I NOTICE SOMETHING'S DIFFERENT right away. I ask Alexa to drop me off, and I walk all the way to the front doors.

The plywood is gone. In its place beneath the stone arch are the original doors, solid wood covered in ornate gilt designs.

They're breathtaking. My gaze snakes along the pattern of swans, roses, and cherry blossoms; at the top of each door, I see a beautifully rendered calligraphic number six. It's amazing how well preserved it all is. The gilt is perfect, not worn away, and the varnish looks fresh.

I walk hesitantly up the stairs until I'm close enough to touch the handles. The second my fingertips brush against their polished metal, it's like magic: the doors whisper open, and I step over the threshold.

"Here you are," says Taylor out of nowhere, making me jump. "Incredible, isn't it?"

I can only nod.

"Can you believe I found them in the cellar? Just standing there. I'm one hundred percent sure nothing of the sort was there the last time I went in. Anyway. I called the college right away, and they sent the workers to have them installed. They say these are the original doors."

"Beautiful," I say hoarsely.

"Do you know what all those symbols are?" she asks. "Why the number six?"

"No idea," I say.

"There's so much history," she goes on, but I'm tuning her out.

"Mom, I had a really long and crappy day. Is it okay if I just go to my room?"

"Sure," she says, a little disappointed and not trying to hide it. But I'm already walking past her and up the stairs. Except I don't go to my room. I go all the way to the fourth floor, to the portrait room. This is the place where I really belong, anyway—these days, my room is just the place where I sleep. Once the door is shut and I'm alone, surrounded by the paintings, I finally start to feel at peace.

I face the biggest painting, the one where Isabella is in the burgundy velvet dress, and, before I know it, tears well in my eyes.

Thank god for this place. I was a nobody before I moved here, wrapped up in my boring and pointless little pursuits that kept me from realizing just how generic and replaceable I was. I mean—it took them all of five minutes to give my starring role to Eve after I left. That tells you everything you need to know, doesn't it?

But here—I am not just anyone, not another teenager trying to make herself feel special. Here, I am Isabella.

There's a soft creaking sound behind me, and I spin around. But it's just the door to the storage space that opened a crack. Must be an air current. I walk over there, my steps echoing, but, instead of closing it, I go in.

Isabella's trunks are where I left them, her things folded carefully. I spot the silk cameo brooch sitting on top of a jewelry box. Next to it is a bracelet that I don't remember seeing there before. It's got the same pattern as the cameo brooch, made to match, and the woven silk matches the cameo brooch perfectly. I pick it up, turn it around in my hands, then put it on my left wrist where it looks like it was made for me.

A token of appreciation.

When I look up, I see a door that wasn't there before.

It's crazy—it had to have been there the whole time, and yet I'm only noticing it now. How many times have the girls been in here? But it chose to reveal itself to me. The door opens without resistance. It looked so low, but I don't even have to duck to go through.

Inside, a wall chandelier is alight, and I forget to question it, even though the gas lamps are not supposed to work anymore. But its soft glow illuminates a sight that takes my breath away. Mirrors, mirrors, floor to ceiling, little oval ones, big square ones, larger-than-life rectangular ones.

And all of them reflect my face back at me, endless tunnels of Isabellas as far as the eye can see.

My own face, resplendent in its timeless, ageless beauty.

TWENTY-SEVEN

ALEXA KEEPS TELLING HERSELF THAT SHE'S NOT DOING anything wrong—since when is she forbidden to talk to someone she goes to school with, anyway? Isa doesn't make those rules—but, still, she can't help but feel like she's sneaking around. And, if Isa found out what this was about, she would be furious, this much Alexa knows.

Still, she meets Nick behind the bleachers in the soccer field before school. It's a half hour until classes start, so they have their privacy.

It's a cold day, even for the season, and Alexa gets there first so she has to spend what feels like a small eternity stomping her feet to keep warm, her hands deep in the pockets of her coat. She only has time to wonder if the bastard stood her up or never intended to show up in the first place when he appears. He hurries across the field, dressed in only jeans and a hoodie, his breath billowing in steam from under the hood he pulled over his face. Alexa has to admit she'd kind of been hoping he wouldn't show up, so that she could dismiss the whole issue as a stupid prank and think of it no more.

"Thanks for coming," he says, his voice gruff.

"And are you ever returning to school?" she parries. "People are starting to wonder if you died or something."

Isa sure is, she thinks.

They must be thinking the same thing because his expression darkens. "No. This thing has its claws deep in all of you."

"Then why call me here at all?"

"Because if anyone can put a stop to it, it's you. You see it too. I know it."

"Isa isn't herself," Alexa says in a low voice. Immediately she feels like a traitor. Her face flushes with heat in spite of the icy weather. "At first I wondered if I just didn't know her as well as I thought I did. Or maybe it's just that—"

"Viral fame turned her into a royal bitch overnight?"

Alexa flinches. "I think it's not that. I know how messed up it sounds but, well—"

"Internet fame is one thing, but it's definitely not normal for her to act like an Edwardian mean girl?"

"Don't joke about it," Alexa hisses.

"I wish I were joking. I've been doing a little digging on that house, on Isabella especially. And you know what kind of blows my mind? I didn't even have to look too hard. It's like all this info sits out in the open but everybody brushes it off."

"What do you mean exactly?"

"That this place—the Isabella Granger house—is shady as hell. Sordid. Not only have dead vagrants been turning up in that house for years, but they weren't the first ones to fall through the cracks. Ever notice how there isn't a real death date for Isabella's husband anywhere on record? Or Isabella herself?"

"It was the old times," Alexa says with a shrug.

"It was a hundred years ago. Hardly the Middle Ages. Yet no one knows when they died. I thought it was odd, but I did a little search through the city archives, and I might have an idea why. Isabella wasn't discovered until it'd been years since she died."

Alexa shudders. "So her body just rotted there in the house? Gross."

"Not just gross. Creepy AF. No one thought to check on her because she'd been a recluse in the last years of her life, and...well... when they did, the body they found was so decomposed they identified it as Isabella by her dress and jewelry. There was no trace of Samuel anywhere, but, since no one had heard from him in several years at that point, it was safe to say he died sometime before she did. This is where it gets even weirder. Ever notice there's this old foundation right by the house? There isn't much left, it's just a square of stones in the grass."

"Maybe I noticed it," Alexa says warily.

"I found some old photos where the building is still standing. Samuel took a lot of photos of the house. Anyway. That little shack was a makeshift photo studio where he could experiment with light, exposure, developing techniques, you name it. The guy was a real innovator in the photography field. And, if it wasn't for Isabella, the world might have even heard of him."

"So what happened to the shack?"

"I found reports of a fire on the premises. The place was considered remote at the time, and, by the time the fire team showed up, it was basically a pile of smoldering coals. Isabella refused to let anyone in the house or speak to anyone or offer an explanation. Photo equipment was flammable in those days. My guess is that Sammy went up in flames along with his film and solvents."

Alexa lets that process for a few seconds. "That would have been an agonizing death."

"No kidding. Isa told me she saw a burnt figure that left traces of soot on the walls."

"You think that's—"

"He's trying to warn you away from the place. Away from Isabella. Although, for Isa, it might already be too late."

"So you're saying she's somehow—possessed."

"But it makes no sense. Why her? Why now? Others have gone into the house over the years. I think it's because Isa was…chosen."

"I don't get it." And, to be honest, Alexa doesn't want to get it. It all sounds so ridiculous.

"Ghosts want things. And what does Isabella want more than anything in this world or beyond?"

"She wants to be admired," Alexa breathes. "Seen, and admired, and the center of attention once again."

"Except, now, no one poses for oil paintings anymore. She needed someone young and relevant. Someone with the times."

"So…" Alexa squeezes her eyes shut. Her temples throb with a fierce headache. "What do you want me to do?"

"I don't know. But you could start by trying to get Isa away from the portrait room. From Isabella's things. And then you should try and get her out of that house—by any means necessary."

TWENTY-EIGHT

"WOW."

I've brought Alexa to the mirror room. We stand in the center of it, and, around us, the mirrors reflect each other into infinity.

"Was this here the whole time?" Alexa murmurs. She looks not-so-great, but I've been tactful and haven't said anything. She already thinks I'm a bitch, and I decided to try and stay on her good side, but, today, my efforts seem to be in vain. "Was it on the blueprints?"

"Who cares?" I say with a shrug. "This place is incredible."

"Sure it is," Alexa mutters. Someone's sure determined to be a killjoy today. "Except I don't see how a room this size could just be concealed. It would be visible from outside."

"We have to do a shoot here," I say, to get her out of her funk. "Imagine how badass it'll be."

She gives me a look that I can't seem to read. "Are we sure it's a good idea?"

"Are you serious right now?" I exclaim. "Look at these mirrors. Look. It's like a built-in glow filter."

"I dunno," Alexa murmurs. "Doesn't it give you a kind of uncanny-valley vibe? You look like one of those super-realistic CGI characters. Too perfect to be human."

"Being human is overrated, anyway," I say. "Give me this over being human any day."

Alexa looks me over, doubtful. "What's that?" I notice that she's looking at my wrist.

"Oh, a bracelet I found in Isabella's things," I say. "It matches the cameo brooch." The brooch is right there, pinned to my chest. I'm wearing one of Isabella's gowns today: blue crepe de Chine with a high collar overlaid with cream lace. It sets off my hair to a beautiful effect and makes my skin glow.

"Well, would you mind taking them off? They creep me out."

I blink. "Why?"

"Um. Did you never notice they're made of human hair?"

I chuckle. "Huh?"

"It was a Victorian custom. You take people's hair to weave it into mourning jewelry."

"And? They're beautiful."

"It doesn't bother you that they contain dead people's hair?"

"This whole place belongs to a dead person," I say, shrugging. "Don't be a killjoy, and bring your camera."

Alexa trudges out of the room.

Minutes go by, but Alexa doesn't come back. I venture out into the portrait room, but it's empty. "Alexa?" I call out. There's no answer. I head down the second-floor hall, then down the stairs, and find her in the hall, twisting the lens of her camera.

"What are you doing?"

She jumps a little. Like she didn't expect to see me. In my own house? "Alexa, what's up? You seem odd."

"Odd? I'm not the one who's odd," she mutters.

"What are you doing?"

"What does it look like I'm doing?" She finally succeeds in unscrewing the lens, which she puts away in its case. "I'm going home."

"Home? But you can't." My shock comes across as disingenuous and lukewarm. Inside, I'm angry more than anything else. "What do you mean, going home? Who's going to photograph me in the mirror room? This photo could be the pinnacle—"

"—of Project Isabella, yeah, yeah. Isa, don't you think this has kind of gotten out of hand?"

It's so ridiculous that I start to laugh, but, seeing her serious face, I promptly choke on it. "Alexa, my friend, I believe this is that thing commonly called *success*."

She gives me a heavy look. "If that's success, then I don't want it. Look around you. Try to have some perspective. I know you're really into Project Isabella, but—"

"I'm not *really into* Project Isabella," I interject coldly. "I *am* Project Isabella. And project Isabella is me."

"No!" she explodes. I recoil a little. Her exclamation resonates through the hall. Loudly. Good thing my parents aren't home. "It's not you. It's an Instagram account, for god's sake. And don't you think it's gone kind of far? Weird rooms appearing out of nowhere, where no room should be? Mourning jewelry made of hair, and everyone is acting like it's totes NBD?"

"Maybe because it is NBD," I say. "These are actual traditions, Alexa. Actual culture. Things that stand the test of time. And we're giving them new life on Instagram. Can you think of anything cooler than that? I'll wait."

"Do you even know what happened to the actual Isabella? This whole muse thing, it's not all it's cracked up to be. She died alone and forgotten. No one even found the body until years had passed. As soon as she lost her youth and beauty, everyone just forgot her, like she never existed at all."

It feels as though the room itself momentarily darkens. Fury wells within me, and I struggle to contain it.

"Except she's not forgotten," I say through my teeth. "And she did leave things behind. This house. These paintings. She left more of a mark than any of us ever will."

Alexa seems to hesitate. "I just want you to keep some distance from this whole…thing," she stammers. "It's not you. It's just a project."

"Well, then. If it's just a project, then photograph me in the mirror room." I cross my arms on my chest. But she looks doubtful, and I realize I have to use a different strategy.

"Come on, Alexa, please. After that, we can take a break. Until the end of the month. Until after holiday break, if you want. Let's just take one picture. Please? Just one."

Alexa heaves a sigh and gives the tiniest nod.

"Thank you!" I squeal and encase her in a hug. She has coffee breath. But whatever. I must keep my photographer happy. "Because I already decided exactly what I'm going to wear."

It's still in the bottom drawer of the dresser in my room, where I left it—feels like it was years ago, but I guess it hasn't been that long. Weird how so much has changed in just a couple of months. I retrieve the burgundy velvet dress, which unfurls gently, releasing a wave of that sweet, musty smell of dust and perfume.

It's so gorgeous. How did I not see that from the very beginning? My costume for the school play back in Brooklyn has nothing on it. Eve can keep it.

Even Alexa forgets her cynicism and gasps when I put the dress on. She does up all the little buttons, and I feel her warm breath on the back of my neck.

"How come it was in a drawer this whole time?" she asks. I'm lost in my thoughts, so she has to repeat herself.

"Oh, it's just this stupid thing that happened. I had this little bout of sleepwalking, and I kind of overreacted."

Alexa stops. "Sleepwalking?"

I tell her about the incident that night, so long ago. But she doesn't seem to find it funny. "Hey, at least Sleeping Isa has good taste. This is probably the most beautiful gown in the house."

"Let's just go and take the photos before I get the creeps," she mutters.

It turns out it's really hard to take photos around so many mirrors. The photographer always ends up in some reflection of a reflection of a…well, you get the idea. Alexa circles me this way and that, then lowers the camera, discouraged. "I can see myself from every angle," she says.

I shrug. "So? I don't mind you being in the photo. You're part of the project after all, aren't you?"

"Isa," Alexa says. She's holding the camera aloft but not taking pictures. "Should we be doing this?"

"What's gotten into you?" I ask. "Look around. What do you see?"

"A creepy hidden room with a bunch of old mirrors in it."

Well, I guess she gets points for honesty.

"Isa, creepy stuff aside, do you seriously think this is normal? This chick was clearly self-obsessed. Not just, like, in a healthy high self-esteem way, but *literally* obsessed. And here we are, worshipping her like she's hashtag-goals."

"It *is* goals," I say, noticing a cold note that creeps into my voice.

"For a hundred and six thousand people. Or is it seven? I last checked this morning. For all I know, we got to ten."

"And that's great," Alexa says. Her voice is brittle.

I heave a sigh. "Come here," I say, beckoning her to come closer. She obeys, but not before hesitating for just a moment too long. I can't help but feel vexed. Am I such a monster? Does she not trust me? "Look."

I put my hands on her shoulders and turn her to face the closest mirror.

"I know what I look like," she mutters, nervous. I notice that, in the mirror, her gaze darts this way and that like she's avoiding looking at herself.

"Do you, really? Stop stalling and look. Really *look*."

She does. I see her eyes focus, and then her jaw goes slack with awe.

Because, the fact is, the mirrors—every single one of them—aren't just a built-in filter. It's not simply a matter of blurring the skin and smoothing the frizz out of hair. In them, you only see your best self. You know how you sometimes go around for half a day thinking you look great, only to catch a glimpse of your reflection in some window and realize you have food on your face or your mascara smudged or your hair fell flat? Well, it's the opposite of that. In these mirrors, you see yourself the way you *see* yourself. There's never disappointment. Only beauty, perfection, and happiness.

"Told you," I say, brimming with pride. "This house, this

room—it's not a curse. It's not unhealthy or whatever you called it. It's a gift. Now, are you going to stop being a killjoy and take my photo?"

"Yes," she whispers. "Don't move."

She lifts the camera until it's level with her chest. This is how she wants to take the photo: with me hovering behind her, my hands on her shoulders, a specter of a more-glamorous time. Alexa looks her best, the acne scars on her cheeks erased, her ever-smudgy eye makeup a perfect, smoky haze. But me, my face—I glow.

Alexa shudders. In the mirror, I see her face distort with a grimace of fear—not just fear but a look of naked, primal terror. A shriek escapes from her, earsplitting. And, the next thing I know, her camera hits the floor with a dreadful sound of breaking glass.

Hi Alexa!

This is Eve. I got your message. I don't know if I should come and visit, though. I think Isa made it clear that she doesn't want to see me.

Hey Nick!! Something terrible happened. I'm freaking out. I think you were right—you were right all along. But it's not just Samuel who died in the fire. I think Isabella was in there with him, and she escaped but was burned. Disfigured.

Okay, I'll try to get my thoughts in order. There's a hidden room at the house. It's connected to the portrait room, you have to go through the closet where there's another hidden door. But that's not the strangest part of it. There are mirrors all over the walls, floor to ceiling. I was trying to take a picture of Isa when I saw something in her mirror reflection. Her face changed. It was no longer Isa's face, but a different face. It looked much older. But, before

I could really get a good look, it turned into something out of nightmares. Like all of its hair singed off and the flesh melted off the bones. I'm pretty sure this was Isabella I saw. She hid away because she was disfigured.

Isa brushes me off—I don't think she saw anything. What the hell do I do now??? I was so freaked out that I dropped my camera and shattered a $1,000 lens.

⊙ EMAIL   ⋯ 🗑 🖨

Alexa. Your lens might be the least of our problems. Something really messed up happened. It's on the local news. Here's the link.

TWENTY-NINE

THE NEXT DAY, THE SCHOOL IS ABUZZ. AND NO WONDER. News travels lightning-fast, and gossip even faster, and so, by the time Alexa gets to her first class, everyone has already heard.

Ines is in the hospital. She fell out of the window of her room, crashing right through the glass, and landed two stories below. Had there been pavement under that window, she could have been dead— this way, she's merely very hurt.

Just how hurt—that's a matter of speculation.

"It was the glass," Sara whispers. Alexa sits next to her, and Isa moves her chair to be closer. "The glass cut her up pretty badly. Her face."

"I heard she practically got scalped," adds another girl, Emma, leaning closer. Emma's been circling Isa for weeks, but, then again, who hasn't? All of them waiting for just the right occasion to ingratiate themselves and wheedle their way into their group. Into the house. Into Project Isabella, eager to bask in reflected glory no matter how insignificant. Well, Alexa figures Emma saw the chance and took it.

"Do you think we should go visit her?" Sara whispers. "At the hospital, I mean."

"I think she already left the hospital," Isa says. She looks and sounds bored, like she's barely holding back a yawn.

"It's not a bad idea," Alexa pipes up, carefully watching her friend's face for any reaction. "We could bring a card. Flowers or something. Show our support."

"No," says Isa with a shrug.

"No? Isn't that a bit cold?"

Isa turns to her, her entire attention on Alexa. Her eyes go round like a cat's. "Cold? Oh heavens no. Au contraire! I'm only thinking about poor Ines in all this. I mean, if I were to become tragically disfigured, I definitely wouldn't want anyone to see me in such a state."

Alexa blinks. She throws a quick glance around at the faces of the other girls, wondering if anyone else thought it sounded as utterly insane as it did. But they gaze at Isa with adoration written plain across their faces.

Clearly, Alexa is alone.

Later that day, Kendra asks Alexa to stay a bit after theater class—in that careful tone of hers Alexa knows means trouble, or at least drama, not of the theater kind.

Isa gives Alexa a withering look. She probably thinks this is a new attempt to usurp her stardom or some kind of conspiracy against her.

"I'll be right out," Alexa assures her, even though she can see by Isa's expression that it doesn't convince her.

Once they're alone, Kendra walks over to the teacher's desk, which she moved into the corner so it doesn't take up valuable rehearsal space. Alexa follows her. Incidentally, that way they're far from the door, where, Alexa suspects, Isa is listening in.

"There's a reason I'm worried," Kendra says. She opens one of the desk's drawers and takes something out. A book. "Ines came to see me last Friday. She wanted to audition one last time."

Alexa's heart sinks. Kendra doesn't need to elaborate. Alexa knows what she's talking about. Audition. For the starring role.

"She was kind of off," Kendra goes on. "She seemed agitated. Not herself. And she kept swinging this book around, she really wanted me to see it. She rambled on and on about it being a rare first edition and that it chose her. What on earth does that even mean?"

Alexa glances at the book. It's sitting on the table, cover facing down, and she can read the back blurb. It's a scuffed copy of *Dorian Gray*. Old, maybe, but nowhere near that ancient. Gingerly, she picks up the book: it's one of those generic paperback editions they used to sell in schools before ebooks were standard. The cover is worn, and the corners of the pages dog-eared, the pages themselves yellowed, rippling from moisture.

"This isn't a first edition," Alexa says, stating the obvious.

"No. But she seemed totally convinced that it is. That's what's so strange. And she refused to tell me where she got it."

Alexa has a guess, but she says nothing. She leafs through the book, which smells like old ink and humidity.

"And now Ines is in the hospital," Kendra is saying. "I just hope… I hope she didn't do that to herself."

But Alexa is no longer listening. She has the book opened to the title page, where, at the very top, a name is scrawled in fading pencil.

It's a name Alexa knows, even though she's never met the girl.

Desiree Hale. She was cast as Sibyl Vane in the school play, right before she disappeared without a trace.

hi eve,

   i really think you shld visit anyway. Im forwarding this message I just got.

  —Alexa

From: Nick Swain

FW: The truth about Isabella Granger, just FYI.

THE AMORY HERALD

FEBRUARY 12, 1983

THE DARK SIDE OF BEAUTY

ISABELLA GRANGER IS PART OF AMORY'S HISTORY.

BUT NOT THE PRETTIEST PART.

BY , CHAIRWOMAN, AMORY UNIVERSITY HISTORICAL SOCIETY

It has recently been announced that Amory University is undertaking another attempt to restore the Isabella Granger house, with the city pledging to cover at least a part of the considerable bill. And it's hardly surprising to anyone who's ever driven past the house. A massive structure once dazzling with beauty and architectural innovation—part of the Venetian Gothic Revival movement, a brief but significant current in architectural design of the late nineteenth century—it has been standing in a state of quasi-ruin for decades. Previous restoration attempts failed for various reasons. Yet here we are again.

Some say Isabella Granger contributed so much to local history— put the town on the map, even. But is this really history we want to dredge up? Who was Isabella Granger, really?

Most people only know Isabella from the paintings she posed for and the art she inspired. As a result, her image has not only survived and outlived the woman, it has completely eclipsed her. It is almost as if there never was an Isabella outside the paintings and the photographs. Perhaps this is what she wanted. In that case, she paid a hefty price.

Isabella was born in 1886 into relative wealth. She received the best education money could buy and was introduced into high society where she immediately made a splash because of her startling beauty and lively spirit. She dabbled in art herself, but, eventually, she flouted social convention and became an artist's model and muse, which led to her meeting Samuel Granger. Not a moment too soon, because, shortly after, her family lost all its money. Luckily, Samuel had a vast inheritance of his own, and he was only too happy to lavish it on his wife. He built her the house, and soon it became a sort of artistic haven in what was then still a somewhat conservative society. Isabella single-handedly launched many an artistic career. She paid, generously, to arrange exhibits for the artists she favored—meaning those who painted beautiful portraits of her and added to her fame. She commissioned artwork, too, and spent a fortune on the most controversial and scandalous works of the time. Sure, she may have been vain, but no one could ever have called her shallow. She had vitality and the kind of hunger for life that drew people to her, especially artists.

But, as time marches on, so does fashion, and, by the time Isabella was in her thirties, even her more risqué stunts began to seem tame against the backdrop of the Roaring Twenties. She threw herself headfirst into photography instead of painting—her husband convinced her it was the future, and he wasn't wrong. Isabella always liked to think of herself as someone who had her finger on the pulse. But, by then, she was starting to show her age. And it was a lot harder to disguise in a photo than in a painting. As time went by, fewer and fewer artists came to the house to have her pose for them. Her stardom began to fade.

She didn't take that well.

Old accounting books show that she bought heaps of creams and ointments, getting them delivered to the house every month. But, since many contained lead and arsenic and other ingredients we now know to be noxious, we can guess that they did more harm than good. Every single day, the reflection in the mirror that Isabella had come to love and rely on aged a little bit more. Skin wrinkled, and that fantastic auburn hair that she was so proud of turned dull and then gray.

It must be said that Samuel Granger still loved her every bit as much as before. He went out of his way to cater to all her whims, even as they got increasingly out of hand. For one thing, he traveled all over the state buying hair from the most beautiful redheads he could find to mix it all together into a wig that could rival the mane she had once boasted. She wore it a handful of times, namely in one last portrait where she went all-out with a lavish gown and jewelry. But, still, it did nothing to fix things, because the portrait only highlighted the decay she saw in the mirror.

Samuel realized that what his wife needed the most was to look beautiful. He used colored glass, tricks of light, and retouching to make her look young and flawless once again. But Isabella was aware of all these tricks, and so it only made her feel worse even as she demanded more and more.

It's not known when exactly Isabella died. Debt collectors ventured into the house in the late 1930s to find decay everywhere and Isabella's remains barricaded in a room on the top floor, surrounded by gilt mirrors. No one knows where she and Samuel are buried. And, since, in the 1940s, the world had other things to worry about, everyone forgot about her.

Eventually the house passed into the ownership of the university. Since then, there have been two attempts to restore it and reopen it: the first time, as a university building, and, the second, as a museum. The first attempt ground to a halt when two workers died after some scaffolding collapsed, prompting a lawsuit by the labor union. The second attempt floundered after the university ran out of money. Perhaps the third time is the charm, but we, citizens of Amory, should ask ourselves if there isn't a better way to spend public funds. The Granger house, like Isabella Granger herself, sits there, festering, in the middle of prime real estate, a testament to the futile nature of vanity. Maybe it's time to let it go.

THE AMORY HERALD

NOVEMBER 1, 1991

FIRE ON THE GROUNDS OF THE GRANGER HOUSE LEAVES 3 BADLY INJURED

An illegal Halloween party on the grounds of the historic Granger House turned to tragedy on the night of October 31 when three Amory University students were admitted to Memorial Hospital after a bonfire blazed out of control.

An anonymous source told the Herald that the students snuck onto the grounds for a Halloween celebration shortly after 9 p.m. on October 31. The house and the grounds are currently blocked off from public access, as the house's decrepit state makes it dangerous to trespass. According to the source, the students started a bonfire in the middle of an old foundation that remains from a demolished service building. Despite the windless and humid weather, the fire blazed out of control, igniting the clothes and hair of three of the female students. The fourth one ran across campus to get help.

The three students are currently at the intensive care ward. Even though their overall condition is reported to be stable, they've suffered disfiguring burns of up to 50 percent of their faces and bodies.

THE AMORY HERALD

NOVEMBER 28, 2010

UNIDENTIFIED BODY DISCOVERED AT GRANGER HOUSE

In the afternoon of November 28, the body of an unidentified female was discovered inside the abandoned Granger House. The grisly discovery was made after an anonymous call was placed at the Amory police station. The police believe a student of the nearby Amory University trespassed on the grounds and didn't wish to come forward.

The body was determined to belong to a Caucasian female of at least 80 years of age. It is likely that she wasn't a resident of the town of Amory. The body had been at the house for some time, which makes identification difficult, but it's possible that she was suffering from some kind of facial disfigurement.

If you have any relevant information, please reach out to Amory Police.

THE AMORY HERALD

MAY 23, 2010

MISSING: DESIREE HALE

Amory High School junior Desiree Hale, 17, disappeared yesterday, May 22, 2010, after failing to show up for a school play in which she had a role. Desiree is 5′6″, brown hair, blue eyes. She was last seen wearing a dark-blue hoodie and jeans, walking across the campus of Amory University toward the north gate.

If you have any relevant information, contact

THIRTY

WHEN ALEXA ARRIVES AT THE HOUSE, SHE FIGURES SHE'S the first, because there are no other cars in front of the house. To her surprise—and alarm—even the Brixtons' new SUV is nowhere to be seen. Are they gone? Would Isa have left and not let anyone know?

It doesn't sound like her. Then again, these days…

With a heavy heart, Alexa trudges up the stairs. The new doors are in place, their magnificence on full display. Alexa had stayed up late into the night googling, and now she has an idea what all these designs mean. Six is the number of Venus. Cherry blossoms, swans, peacock feathers, all the things she assumed were there just to look pretty actually symbolize youth, beauty, and, of course, eternal life.

She hesitates before lifting the heavy knocker. She doesn't want to touch the smooth metal, or go anywhere near these doors at all. It's a feeling she can't explain, almost like an intuition. And maybe it's just the early winter leeching the color out of things, but the house doesn't look beautiful today. It looks grim and foreboding. *Uninhabited*, she thinks as she finally overcomes her reluctance and knocks.

To her surprise, the doors open almost immediately. It's still early, but Isa looks fresh as a rose, fully dressed in another crazy-elaborate mishmash of Isabella's historic gowns and modern elements that she and Sara put together. Her dress is the color Alexa thinks is called puce, which really looks like old, dried blood. It has super-long, extravagant cream lace sleeves, and more of that same lace covers the plunging neckline in a gauzy layer. Then there's the heavy-looking fur cloak she's wearing on top of it, with an ash-gray marabou boa around her neck. Her heavy earrings clink when she tilts her head. Long, pointy ostrich feathers stick out of her elaborate hairdo. *Does she even know what she looks like?* Alexa thinks.

"Hey," Isa says in an unusually friendly tone. "It's you."

"Yeah, it's me." *We used to be friends, remember?*

"Come on in," Isa says. Alexa steps reluctantly over the threshold, and the house greets her with its sweet, dusty smell. It's overcast today, so some of the lights are on, creating a pleasant penumbra.

Isa spins, which makes the skirt of her dress flare and reveal frothing petticoats underneath. "I'm wearing this for the shoot today," she says. "What do you think?"

Alexa opens her mouth to answer, but the lie refuses to come out.

Isa seems to have forgotten she asked her opinion at all. "Maybe it needs more jewelry," she says decisively. "Come on. I've taken all the jewelry boxes and clothes to my room. That's where they belong. Let's go and choose."

Without waiting, she starts up the stairs. Alexa watches her with a tinge of worry. Isa holds up her skirts expertly, like the motion is second nature, ingrained over many, many years. And her shoes have ridiculously high heels. Alexa had never seen her wear anything but kitten heels day-to-day and, whenever she had to for photos, she always kind of stumbled. But now she's flitting up a steep staircase in those pointy shoes without a care in the world.

"Isa," she calls out. "Hang on."

Isa stops and casts an impatient look over her shoulder. "What is it? Come on, everyone will show up soon."

"We need to talk."

Isa rolls her eyes. Huffing, Alexa races up the stairs to catch up with her.

"We're not going to take photos today," she says.

Isa blinks. Her eyes look like cold, blue marbles. "What do you mean?"

"We're not taking any more photos. Not today, not ever."

"Alexa." Her tone is different now. The lightness in it is gone. "What do you mean by that?"

"I mean that we're shutting down Project Isabella."

"Why?" Isa blurts. In that moment, the incomprehension on her face is so complete and so earnest that, for just a split second, Alexa thinks she got through to her. That she's speaking to Isa and not Isabella. Gripped with a sense of urgency, she grabs Isa's shoulders. Dust rises out of the ancient fur cloak. Alexa doesn't know how long she has before Isabella takes over again, and there's so much to say.

"Isa, I don't think Isabella is gone."

"That's crazy. Isabella died a hundred years ago."

"But don't you get it? It all makes sense!" Alexa hisses. Spittle flies from her lips, and Isa recoils in disgust, which cuts Alexa deeper than she expected. "All the weird things that have been happening. It's Isabella."

"That makes no sense at all," Isa says. "My parents and I have been living here for months now. And absolutely nothing bad happened. I mean, you're here right now." She gestures widely around them—at the grand staircase, at the chandelier, at the house itself.

"That's because I think Isabella spared you. Because she—well, I think she chose you."

"Chose me? A dead woman?"

"Yes. She chose you to be her vessel. To bring her into the twenty-first century, where she'll never run out of admiration ever again."

For a few seconds, Isa stays silent, tilting her head as if deep in thought.

Then she bursts out laughing.

"Oh my god. Do you realize how crazy you sound?" Isa's laugh carries, which makes it all distorted and sinister. "These have been the happiest months of my life. I was nobody back in Brooklyn. I was lost. I hated coming here at first, but it turned out to be the best thing that ever happened. Here, I finally found myself."

"Maybe that's the problem," Alexa says hoarsely.

"Well, if that's what you think," Isa says, her eyes glinting with something cold and hard, "maybe you should leave. Like, right now."

"I'm not leaving," Alexa says. "Not until I've deleted Project Isabella for good."

The color drains from Isa's face. "You wouldn't dare."

"Oh, yes, I would. Just watch me."

She grabs the phone out of her pocket, but, before she can unlock it, Isa grabs her wrist and twists. Alexa gasps at her sheer strength. Her fingers unclench, and the phone falls down the stairs, hitting one stair, then another, and then landing at the bottom of the stairwell with the typical sharp sound of something breaking.

"I'd like to see you delete it now," Isa—Isabella?—sneers.

"Don't be an idiot," Alexa snaps. "You know I'll just go home and delete it from my laptop. That, or we can do this together, right now. End it for good."

Isa looks at her, incredulous, shaking her head so the earrings clink softly. "You can't be serious. You can't mean that."

"You bet I mean it."

"Then I won't let you."

Alexa feels a momentary panic, then disorientation. Her gaze remains riveted on Isa, who stands still and doesn't move a muscle.

Not a single marabou feather in that ugly boa stirs, like time itself has come to a halt for everyone except for Alexa.

An unseen force crashes into her from behind with such strength that even her feet come off the floor. For a split second, she's suspended in midair, between the unknown and the unknowable.

Then she comes hurtling down the steep staircase.

The whole world spins. She feels the impacts of the steps on her ribs, her spine, her shins. Bones crack, splinter, break. Vertebrae disconnect.

The last thing she sees is herself, hurtling at her with terrifying speed. Her eyes are wide, her face distorted and bloodied. It's a mirror, she realizes a millisecond before collision.

It's a mirror.

Then her head connects with the hard, shiny surface, and the world explodes into a million shards like diamonds.

Isabella looks down at the wreckage of broken pieces of mirror and the broken body at the foot of the stairs. Her face hardly twitches—what little emotion she feels stays safely locked up inside. One should never show one's feelings too eagerly; they give ammunition to your enemies, not to mention cause wrinkles.

What a mess, she thinks. What a waste. She had grown used to this girl. She did, after all, make her beautiful again. In the eye of her lens, Isabella was once again her true, full, best self.

But—oh well.

"A pity," she says softly. "Perhaps another photographer will keep up with the times better."

PART
FOUR

Hey Alexa! It's Eve. I read everything you sent me. Normally I'd say that's crazy, but then again, Isa has been acting so weird that I don't know what to think. I sent her a message that she's seen, but she's ignoring me. I'm starting to think that maybe I really should come over there. At least for, like, a weekend.

Hey Alexa, you haven't seen this yet. What's up? Is everything okay? The Project Isabella account is still being updated so I guess you're busy with that. Anyway, please write back...

Hey! I saw the photos that Isa just uploaded. You still haven't answered and I'm freaking out. These photos were really weird. Especially the one where she's posing in front of the broken mirror frame with that creepy makeup that makes her look older. She hardly looks like herself at all. And that creepy jewelry she's wearing—the pitch-black pendant? Is that Victorian human hair jewelry? Please tell me it's fake??

Then again, those photos don't look anything like yours. The composition and framing is off. They're selfies, aren't they? She took them herself. Alexa, I'm really starting to worry. Please answer.

Hey Taylor! I think you may have forgotten me by now, but I sure hope not! It's Eve, Isa's friend from back home. Isa's been ignoring me, and I know we've grown apart with everything she's doing in her new school, but I'd really like for us to reconnect. My parents are okay with it. Can I come spend a couple of days?

Hi Eve! What a wonderful idea. I think it will be GREAT for EVERYONE to get in touch with our normal selves. YES I would love it if you came. In fact Gordon and I are throwing a gala at the university this weekend. Maybe you and Isa could spend some time and reconnect.

Cheers,

Taylor

THIRTY-ONE

JUST AS ISABELLA IS ABOUT TO LEAVE THE HOUSE, SHE hears timid steps behind her in the hall. She has every intention to ignore them, but then she hears the woman call her name. Well, not *her* name, presumably—that of the other one. *She* would never go by Isa. How silly.

So, with a discreet sigh, she stops and turns around. Taylor is standing a good distance away, like she's afraid to come close.

"Is this what you're wearing to school?"

"Yes." Isabella knows she must be patient and bide her time.

Taylor heaves a sigh, twisting her hands. "Look, Isa, I know the last few weeks have been stressful. I'm sorry I was absent so much, but you know how it was—we had to pull out all the stops to get the university to fund the gala."

"Oh, yes," Isabella says. "The gala. Of course."

The gala was this close to not happening at all. Someone contested the old documents Gordon found in the safe. But that only seemed to spur Gordon on. He became determined to stand his ground and make the gala happen before another department made a grab for the funding.

"Well, the gala is on, isn't it?" Isabella says. "And you're the featured artist. You should be over the moon."

Taylor's face twitches. Isabella knows why: if she had provided those awful photos she'd be cringing too.

All the photos Taylor took of the house she made into large-scale prints in old-fashioned black and white. The grainy quality of the prints brings out the cracks and the scuffs.

Isabella finds it perfectly ghastly. "Can I go now?"

"Isa," Taylor says. "Hold it right there."

"What?"

Isa measures her with a look of annoyance.

"How's school going?"

"Fine," she says mechanically.

"Oh. Really?"

Taylor steps closer.

"I suppose you're still working on your historical project."

"Yes." Obviously.

"Isa, knock it off. Enough with the weird costumes and weird accents. I got a call from the school. I talked to your teachers. I know there never was an extra-credit project on Isabella Granger."

Isa covers her eyes with her hand and heaves a sigh. "Can we not do this now?"

"I can't think of a better time than now, actually." Taylor crosses her arms. "Your behavior's been unacceptable—"

Isa laughs. "Wow, what language. You're really not that good at the whole mothering thing, are you?"

Taylor's face drains of blood. "You shut your mouth."

"And what are you going to do if I don't? Your lack of practice is showing. Mom." Isabella chuckles. Taylor opens her mouth and draws a breath for another angry tirade, but Isabella beats her to it.

"Go to your room!" she snaps. Taylor springs back: Isabella's lips are moving, but the words and the voice that comes out of her mouth is Taylor's own, with that little Valley girl inflection she has. "Did I get it right?" Isabella asks, in Isa's normal, sweet voice once again.

"Why did you lie to me, Isa?"

"It's not Isa," she snaps. "It's Isabella, once and for all. And I *lied* to get you off my back."

"All your grades have slipped. Imagine my shock when I was told that, at this rate, you'll have to repeat the year."

"So what?"

"I just don't understand. You...you were always such a good student! And, you and I, we've always trusted each other. So I just want to know why!"

"Trusted each other?" Isabella exclaims. "Taylor, we didn't trust each other. You patted yourself on the back for being one of the cool parents, and I told you just enough to make you feel like one."

Taylor slaps her.

It's a shock to both of them. Isabella doubles over, gasping for breath. This really happened. She just did that. Who does she think she is?

"How dare you?"

Taylor gulps. "We're going to deal with this," she says hoarsely. "It's your luck that I have the gala tomorrow. After it's over, we're going to have a talk. A serious talk."

And Taylor turns around and runs down the hall, leaving Isabella with her hand pressed to her burning cheek, gasping, all alone.

Isabella wonders how much longer she can keep up the charade. Everyone at school wants to know where Alexa is. First Nick stopped showing up, then Ines fell out of the window, and now another one from the theater club who's nowhere to be found.

And now she's been called into Greer's office. She swans past the door, the hem of her dress sweeping the floor. Greer is sitting behind her desk, thin and pale greenish like a human string bean. To think she used to find this witch intimidating.

"Isa," Greer says, wasting no time.

"Is my outfit inappropriate again?" Isabella asks, batting her lashes with fake innocence.

"This is not about your outfit." Her voice drops to a hiss. "I called you here to ask about your classmate."

"Which one?" Isa picks up a random sheet of paper that sits on the desk in front of Greer and fans herself.

"You must have noticed that Alexa stopped attending school."

"There's nothing wrong with Alexa. She's at my house."

"Why hasn't she called her family?"

"Oh, she said to tell everyone she's just really upset and doesn't want to see anyone. She's broken up because the school play got canceled. Which you helped do, so…"

Some of these things are technically not a lie. Especially the last part. Greer did cancel the school play, with two cast members unaccounted for.

"If it were up to me, I'd have that whole theater department shut down," Greer says coldly.

"But it's not up to you," Isabella sums up. "So, if that's all, I'm going to go."

As she walks down the hall, Isabella can feel everyone looking. It's probably her favorite sensation—like taking a champagne bath. All those gazes riveted on her in fascination, wonderment, adoration, and even a smidgen of fear that makes it all the more delicious, like that final dash of spice in a dish. She doesn't care that the play was canceled. She doesn't need the play, or the theater club, or Kendra, or Alexa, or Nick, or anyone. She has waited for so long for this, and her patience paid off. Now she doesn't have to do anything. All she has to do is just exist.

And she can be sure that everybody is looking.

THIRTY-TWO

EVE ARRIVES IN TOWN ON A POSTCARD-PRETTY, NORMAN Rockwell—esque Saturday morning. Last night it snowed, and the town of Amory looks like the inside of a snow globe with that historic charm that the tourism website boasted about. But Eve, clutching the steering wheel of her car, barely notices it. She's jittery like she had too many energy drinks before rehearsal.

It really doesn't help that she's only been driving for a month or so. The road is slippery, and the snowbanks everywhere are huge. Which probably explains why most of the cars she encounters are SUVs, hulking over her compact little rental. What's worse, the GPS on Eve's phone seems to have lost the plot. She only realizes she missed her turn when the slightly annoyed voice of the GPS announces *rerouting*.

When she chances looking away from the road to glance at the map, the GPS can't seem to find her at all: the blue dot that represents Eve's car darts like mad all over the screen.

Oh, well. Hopefully the town's too small to get lost in. She drives up to the university, which looks like some romantic castle shrouded in snow, a sight straight out of a Disney movie. She circles the campus over and over but can't for the life of her figure out which way to go. As she passes in front of the gates yet again, she sees someone, probably a student, idling by the fence.

"Excuse me," Eve yells, rolling down the window. Her breath immediately billows in a puff of steam, and ice-cold air rushes into the car's toasty interior, making her shiver. "I'm looking for the Granger House."

Even before she speaks, she realizes something's not right. The knot of foreboding in her stomach tightens. First of all, the girl's dressed way too lightly for the weather. She stumbles through the snow in high-heeled stilettos, huddling in a sweatshirt that she wears over a ridiculous dress. Theater costume? It must be. She turns around slowly, and Eve recoils at the sight of her face. It's streaked with tears that freeze in the cold air. The eyelash extensions on her right eye are coming off, which makes it look like her eyelid is drooping. Her lips are obviously fake, swollen from injections, with a ring of bruises around her mouth. Her hair is matted, but it's her skin that makes Eve instinctively recoil. It looks like some sort of Halloween costume a few months too late: her face is crisscrossed with a web of badly healing cuts.

"Are you okay?" Eve asks, feeling like a complete idiot because she's obviously not okay.

The girl doesn't answer. She raises her arm and points to somewhere behind Eve.

Eve shudders.

"What you're looking for," the girl rasps. "There it is."

Eve whips her head around and gives a start. How could she not have seen it? It's right there, across the expanse of snow-covered lawn. It stands tall and proud, less like a palace and more like a fortress. She recognizes the Venetian arched windows right away.

The Isabella Granger house.

"Thank you," Eve chokes out. But, when she turns around, the strange girl is nowhere to be seen.

Not a great start.

The road leading to the entrance of the house is snowed in. Eve's car manages only a couple hundred feet before getting hopelessly stuck. She supposes she really should have gone for a model with all-wheel drive when she had the chance. But, as it stands, the wheels spin pointlessly in nothingness with a loud whine, and the car refuses to budge another inch.

With a groan, Eve opens the door and climbs out. Her winter boots are barely a match for the deep snow, and so she begins the slow, painful trudge to the front doors of the Granger house. The cold creeps inside her coat and under her scarf. She wishes she'd worn a hat.

When she reaches the steps that lead to the majestic double doors, she's had just about enough. Snow has gotten into her boots but also behind her collar and under her sleeves, and her teeth are chattering. Still, she momentarily forgets about everything when she finds herself face-to-face with these doors. They loom over her, majestic yet ominous. The gilt number 6 at the top glints painfully bright in the cold sunlight.

Eve picks up the heavy knocker and knocks. The sound is deep and powerful, resonating in her very bones. But, if anyone inside hears it, there's no way to tell, because the doors stay closed.

"Isa?" Eve yells out. All that gorgeous snow seems to absorb all sound, and her voice, which carries so well in a theater, fizzles out, weak and powerless. "Isa! Open the door!"

She reaches for the phone in her coat pocket. Her hands are freezing, and her fingers are stiff and barely move. The screen, too, seems slowed down by the cold, shimmering weakly under her touch. She tries to dial Isa's number, but, just as she finally manages to hit the call button, the one bar of signal she has out here disappears, and the call disconnects.

Cursing, she tries to stick the phone back in her pocket, but her cold hands fumble. The phone slips out, goes flying, bounces off the stairs, and vanishes in the snowbank.

Eve curses and dives after it. She feels around in the snow with her hands until she loses all sensation.

"Who are you?"

The voice comes from above her, and she shoots to her feet. But in the doorway isn't Isa. It's some girl Eve doesn't know but who looks vaguely familiar. She's dressed in a strange period costume—or more like someone's idea of a period costume. The result is an anachronistic mishmash of Jazz Age, art nouveau, and frilly Edwardian fashion. Her dress is short and tasseled, with Victorian low-heeled boots, a lace shawl over her shoulders and a giant brimmed hat garnished generously with feathers. With all that, plus saucer eyes in dark kohl and so many strings of (fake?) pearls it's a wonder how she holds her head up.

"I'm Eve," Eve says. "Isa's friend? I was supposed to come visit. I don't know if Isa told you—"

"Isabella didn't tell me anything," the girl says coldly.

"Well, if you tell her it's Eve, she'll let me in."

"Why should I?"

Eve takes a small step back, baffled. It finally clicks who this girl is. She saw her on the Project Isabella account.

"Out of my way," Eve says, and pushes past her. The girl's indignant yelp follows on her heels.

Eve bursts through the doors and can't help but stop cold. She's both amazed and overwhelmed. The photos and Isa's stories can't hold a candle to the real thing. It's enormous. Dust and echoes swirl under the high ceiling. The chandelier is lit, but the cobwebs that shroud it mute the light, tinging it dull yellow like an old photograph. The staircase looms at the far end of the room. From upstairs, soft music wafts down, mellow jazz full of the scritch-scratch of an old record. Eve hears voices and laughter, and, without thinking, races up that giant staircase.

Once she reaches the second floor, she stops, trying to get her bearings. She peers into the hallway, but it's empty. Only one or two wall lights are on, projecting a cold, otherworldly sort of light onto the walls. She goes up another flight of stairs—how many floors does this place have? Who needs that many rooms?—but the third floor is another disappointment. When she gets to the fourth, the music grows louder. Eve understands right away that she found what she was looking for: the tall double doors at the end of the hall are wide open, and that's where the music is coming from. The same cold light falls through the doorway in long beams onto the parquet floor.

Eve takes step after step toward those double doors. Her heart hammers. Finally she can see inside: another oversized room, one that used to be a ballroom. The walls are covered in paintings from floor to ceiling. All paintings of Isabella.

At the center of the room is a long fainting couch surrounded by mismatched end tables, armchairs, and ottomans. Like someone raided an antique shop. An honest-to-god ancient gramophone sits on the floor, and that's where the scratchy music is coming from. With all the voices and laughter she heard, Eve expected to find a whole party, so she's a little shocked to see the room empty except for Isa, who lounges on the couch. In one hand, she's holding a tall glass, and in the other, her phone. Eve stands there awkwardly, wondering if she should say something, because Isa is wholly absorbed in the screen. She scrolls, her face bathed in the light, the screen reflecting in her eyes, which makes her look unnerving and robotic but also weirdly angelic. She smiles at something she sees, then scrolls on without wasting a second.

Eve looks her over. She's a little shocked to see in person just how much her friend changed. Sure, photoshopped pictures are one thing—everything on Insta is fake, anyway, everyone knows that—but to see it with her own eyes is overwhelming. Isa's hair is down past her waist and auburn again, and her face looks different. Like Eve is looking at her through a filter. Her features are sharper and more angular, and her skin tone is perfectly even but flat, like she's wearing three coats of full-coverage foundation. For all Eve knows, she is, but it didn't used to be her thing.

And that crazy outfit. It reminds Eve of a late Edwardian tea-gown with its excess of satiny fabric, lace, and ruffles and its loose lines. Except Isa is wearing sneakers with it. Pale-blue Converse high-tops that peek out from under the skirt. Eve remembers buying them with her back home.

Eve is so taken aback that she doesn't notice that Isa has looked up from her phone and is now staring right at her. When their eyes meet, the knot in Eve's stomach tightens.

"It's you," Isa says in mild surprise. "I didn't invite you."

THIRTY-THREE

"TAYLOR INVITED ME," EVE SAYS. "SO HERE I AM. SO SORRY you're not happy to see me."

Isa shrugs. "Taylor can't invite anyone. It's not her house to invite people to."

"Then whose house is it? Yours?"

Isa rolls her eyes and giggles. "The university's. Duh. I know it's not my house. What am I, crazy?"

"Then maybe you can stop pouting and say hello to your best friend since first grade, Isa."

"Isabella," she corrects, almost mindlessly. "And, fine, if people seem to think it's okay to just pop in unannounced, I'll play along." She gets up and stretches languorously. "Hello, Eve dear."

In that moment, Eve hears hurried steps behind her, and spins around. It's the girl from the entrance. She's panting from racing all the way up here, and she looks lost. "Isabella, I'm so sorry," she exhales. She crosses the room and stops cold in front of Isa, a few respectful feet away, and lowers her head. *Like she's Isa's actual maid*, Eve thinks incredulously.

"I didn't want to let her in! She just—"

"That's all right, Sara," Isa says in a honeyed voice. "Don't you see, this is my old friend Eve. How kind of her to spare some time from her fabulous life in Brooklyn to come down and visit little old me, out here in the sticks."

That stings. "I know I should have come sooner," Eve mutters.

"No matter, no matter. Call the others, Sara. Let's have a little celebration in my friend's honor. After all, the rest of the world may have descended into chaos, but I still have my manners."

Who the hell talks this way? Eve thinks. Sara takes out her phone and starts texting, the only element in this strange picture that reminds Eve that she is, in fact, still in the current year.

Isa sashays over to the gramophone—if that's what it is—and turns up the volume. The music grows louder and, if it was at all possible, scratchier. "Drinks!" Isa exclaims. She swans over to a vanity that looks a little out of place—*How did they manage to drag it up here?* Eve wonders—and pulls open drawer after drawer. Glasses appear, followed by dusty bottles. *They look like nothing from this century*, Eve thinks in alarm.

"Isa, you don't drink," she finds herself saying. "At least, you didn't used to."

"Exactly. And now I do. I'm a big girl, Eve. Now, do you want a cocktail? Aviation, White Plush? I'd make you a gin fizz, but I don't have any eggs."

"I've never heard of any of those." *And neither have you.*

But Isa ignores her. She busily mixes the contents of those scary bottles in two highball glasses and stirs with a long spoon. "Here," she says, holding one glass out to Eve. Its contents look alarmingly green. Eve takes the glass.

"Santé, santé," Isa is saying, clinking her glass aggressively with Eve's. Then she drinks. Not a ladylike sip either. She gulps from the glass, emptying half of it in seconds. Eve pretends to drink, dipping her lips in the liquid while keeping an eye on Isa. She doesn't want to leave her out of sight for a second. Whatever is in that glass has a smell so eye-watering it might as well be gasoline. "Eve," Isa says, and claps her hand on Eve's shoulder. "You know what? You're just in time."

"In time for what?"

"I might be in the market for a new photographer," Isa says in a loud stage whisper as she leans closer.

Eve decides to tread carefully, not to give away how much she guesses. "Why? Isn't Alexa your photographer?"

Isa shrugs. "Alexa, I'm afraid, can't keep up anymore. For the future of the project, I need someone new."

"I don't see what I can do," Eve says coolly. "I'm not a photographer."

Isa's silvery laugh rolls under the high ceiling, sending goose bumps down Eve's back. "Oh, darling. You don't have to be. You just have to point and click. The house will do the rest."

Eve nods like she understands what the hell this means.

"Alexa has let me down," Isa says. Suddenly, she's the very image of sorrow, her chin drooping, her lips pressed together in a mournful grimace. "Everyone lets me down. Desiree, Ines, Nick, Alexa…everyone."

Nick—the name faintly rings a bell. That guy Isa had a crush on. Finally, a normal subject. Maybe the Isa she knows is in there somewhere after all. "What happened with Nick?" she asks.

"With him?" Isa echoes. "He's gone. Who knows. But, then again, aren't we all authors of our own downfall?"

"Isa," Eve says, her mouth dry. "You're seriously freaking me out."

"A shame," Isa says. "What a shame. And for the last time, it's Isabella."

Eve takes a small step back. Isa's gaze is riveted on her.

"I notice you're not drinking your cocktail, Eve."

"What? I totally was." But Eve's acting abilities, such as they were, seem to have gone into hiding. The lie is unconvincing. To make it worse, she brings the glass to her lips again, without drinking.

"Drink. Your. Cocktail." Isa advances toward her. Something about her eyes isn't right. The color. *It's not her eye color*, Eve realizes.

"I'm not drinking that," Eve snaps. "I have no idea what you put in it. Smells like roadkill."

"I've been nothing but a great hostess to you," Isa says, "and look how you repay me. Drink it. Now."

In that moment, another girl bursts through the door behind Eve. The icy look on Isa's face evaporates. Now she's beaming. "My friends! Welcome!"

There's a flurry of air-kisses and weird mannerisms. The other girl is dressed just like Isa and Sara, in a historically inaccurate turn-of-the-century outfit. "Eve, meet Emma," Isa says matter-of-factly. "My dear friend and, not to mention, a friend of Project Isabella."

Eve's gaze darts from one heavily made-up face to another, but all she feels is revulsion. They look like dolls brought to life, their faces frozen in those same expressions she saw in the paintings. That pre-Raphaelite stupor of someone on too much laudanum. Off the canvas, it doesn't look nearly as appealing. Everyone is wearing gobs of foundation to get that signature pallor and way too much eyeshadow and mascara.

Before Eve knows it, drinks are being passed around. They drink the same nauseating stuff without flinching.

Okay. Time to get out of here. Eve carefully sets her glass down on one of the end tables and begins to back away toward the door.

"And where do you think you're going?"

Isa's voice cuts through the music and the noise. Eve doesn't know why, but she stops cold. *I should just keep going—what's she going to do?*

But the girls close ranks with surprising speed and coordination. *Like they're controlled by one and the same mind,* Eve thinks. Her exit is subtly but effectively cut off.

"I just wanted to look around," she stammers. "You're the hostess—aren't you supposed to give me the tour?"

Isa's face breaks into a smile. She's the only one of all of them who smiles for real, showing teeth. All the others' grins are close-lipped. "Why, of course. Where are my manners?" She strides past Emma and Sara, who part as if on cue to let her through. Eve follows on her heels, but the girls don't look at her at all, like she's not there.

"The house has four floors," Isa is saying. "But you know that already."

At some point, Eve thinks, *I can just slip away. Hopefully get my phone out of the snowbank and call somebody.*

Just who she plans to call, she doesn't know yet.

"On the third floor," Isa is saying, "that's where Samuel's old studio is. God rest his soul."

Eve peers into the room. Ancient photo equipment is scattered on the floor among heaps of dust. The wall with its uncovered safe door draws her gaze.

"That's the safe Gordon found," Isa says matter-of-factly. "Well— for now it is. It's a door, and a door can be many things."

Eve remembers the email Alexa forwarded her and shivers. Where's Alexa? By now, the rotten feeling in her gut is more than just a feeling. She's almost certain that something terrible happened. She just doesn't know what. Would Isa have seriously hurt her friend? Could she hurt Eve too?

"…the library, my old bedroom," Isa drones on. "I hardly ever use that anymore, though. I just live in the portrait room."

"Where do your parents live?" Eve asks carefully.

Isa gives her a sideways glance, and, in her gaze, Eve reads confusion. A moment later, it's gone, like she finally remembered that she does have parents.

Or like she's pretending to.

"Oh, right. Taylor and Gordon live in the other wing of the second floor. Separate bedrooms." She chuckles.

"What are you talking about?" Eve asks. She doesn't really expect Isa to answer, and she turns out to be correct. Isa just brushes her off.

"They're off at the university, throwing a gala. In my honor, if you can believe it. Or, at least, they think it is. Gordon found those papers, but, the thing is, I never wanted any such thing. And especially not with Taylor as featured artist!" Her face twists in a grimace of disgust.

"Why not?"

"Taylor is not an artist," Isa says with conviction that sends shivers down Eve's spine. She'd never heard the old Isa—the real Isa—talk about her mom that way. Not even when she was angry. "Taylor is vile. She's a poseur. At first I thought she was all right because she's a photographer, but I made a mistake. She only sees the ugliness in everything. That's why all her photos are ugly. Even those of beautiful things. She made my house look like some sort of dusty relic. Taylor Brixton can go to hell."

"Where did the papers come from?" Eve prompts.

Isa shrugs. "The house. It's a wonderful house. It knows exactly what's in your heart. Gordon wanted an occasion to attract glitzy patrons for the university, to secure his new job. So he could provide for his family." She giggles again. The sound is unnerving. It's not laughter—it's the idea of laughter by someone who's never heard the real thing. "Isa wanted to be unique, to leave her mark in a world that has the attention span of a gnat. And I wanted to be young and beautiful and admired and seen again. And here we are." She smiles. "And you, Eve? What is it that you want?"

To get the hell out of here, Eve thinks. She wraps her arms around herself. Despite her coat, she's freezing.

"Look here," Isa is saying cheerfully. "The first floor."

On the wall just opposite the staircase, Eve notices an ornate frame as tall as she is, maybe taller. It's empty. When she comes closer, she sees the patterns of the frame: cherry blossoms, swans, peacock feathers, all rendered with a strange fluidity, not at all like your typical baroque frills. They all melt into each other—when you look for too long, it seems like they're moving.

"Don't get hung up on broken old junk," Isa's annoyed voice rings out behind her. "You're just like Taylor. Look around you! This place is a jewel of history and architecture. Do notice the original carved doors. And the frescoes! Don't forget to look at the frescoes."

Eve wants to remind her that she's seen the frescoes. Isa had taken pictures and posted them to Instagram in her first days here. Eve found the frescoes kind of dull, to be honest. Pretty in a saccharine way. But, as she looks up now, she realizes with a sinking feeling that the frescoes look nothing like what she remembers. They've become darker—not just in color and tone. The Aphrodite is no longer Aphrodite. She looks more like Persephone, a malignant demon lurking overhead among billowing cloth and the wild waves of her own auburn hair. Even the Cupids look vaguely evil, their angelic faces contorted in smirks.

Then, right in front of her eyes, the frescoes start to move. The peaceful blue sky in the background covers with bruise-colored storm clouds. Aphrodite's eyes move, fixating on Eve, and her nostrils flare in fury.

Something crashes into Eve from behind, and she goes flying, sprawling on the floor.

"Don't you dare come into my house with ill thoughts!" Isa's voice is unrecognizable, and the only way Eve knows it's Isa at all is because there's no one else there. "Is this how you repay my hospitality?"

Eve rolls over onto her side, struggling to catch her breath and wondering if she'd broken a rib. "Isa, this isn't you," she gasps. "I don't know what's going on, but—we have to get out of here!"

"Get out of here? This is my house. This is my home. I'm never going to leave."

Eve manages to get on her hands and knees. Her side hurts, and her vision is swimming. "What have you done with real Isa?" she rasps.

The only answer is Isabella's tinny laughter.

Eve scrambles to her feet. Isabella is advancing toward her. Her face is calm, not a single line on her forehead or around her mouth, but her eyes—

Eve starts to run.

THIRTY-FOUR

EVE RACES ACROSS THE VAST LOBBY AND DIVES THROUGH
the door into the kitchen. At first she's surprised at how drab the kitchen
is, even though, like every other room, it's about five hundred square
feet bigger than it needs to be. Then the light bulb goes off: in Isabella's
times, the mistress of the house rarely even set foot here. And, for the
servants, the plain walls and little slits of windows are good enough.

Eve spins around. There's a modern fridge, a shiny new faucet and
sink, a fancy gas stove with six burners. It all looks out of place here,
like an alien spaceship on the set of Downton Abbey. Why bother? As
far as Eve remembers, Taylor was never big on home cooking. Could've
done with an induction cooktop and called it a day.

Then she remembers the old gas lamps she spotted throughout

the house. Electric ones were added hastily right on top of them, but she bets the original piping is still there. They probably just connected the stove to that.

She thinks she hears steps down the hall and jolts into action. She circles the room. There's a door in the back, but, as Eve tugs on the handle, she sees the huge padlock that holds it locked.

So much for that.

She makes a beeline for the cabinets, but the ones that contain anything sharp are conveniently locked up too.

In that moment, the door shakes. The chair with which Eve propped it up creaks alarmingly. Someone—Isabella—pounds on it with her fists. There's nowhere to go, Eve realizes in a panic. Then she sees the solution— she's standing on it. A huge trapdoor with one of those built-in rings.

"Open the door, Eve," Isa's voice. At least now it sounds like Isa. "Come on. Please. I think we got off on the wrong foot. I just want to make things right."

Moments ago she was freezing, but now sweat runs down Eve's back and pearls on her forehead. She tugs at the ring, and the heavy trapdoor begins to budge.

"Don't be silly, darling," Isa's silvery voice, muffled by the door, takes on a threatening note. "Let's work this out. Open the door."

Eve finally throws the trapdoor open. Sweat rolls into her eyes. *I'd have to be crazy to go in there*, she thinks.

The door shakes. "Open," growls the voice, no longer Isa. "Open, or I'll—"

Wooden steps lead into darkness. Eve decides not to think about it too much. With a sharp intake of breath, she dives into the space.

At first, the weak light from above isn't enough, and she doesn't see the light bulb on the ceiling until its string hits her in the face. She yelps, then, realizing what it is, pulls on it.

There's a strange smell down here, overwhelmingly cloying, like perfume gone bad or something. Eve looks around. There's a bunch of construction materials, some boards, some broken tiles. She almost steps on a pile of rusted, bent nails.

The cellar is bigger than she thought. Maybe there's a way out. A tunnel or another trapdoor leading outside. She advances cautiously, boards creaking softly beneath her feet.

The pale face takes her by surprise. With a shriek, she stumbles back and nearly goes sprawling, which, with all the rusted nails and sharp bits of tile underfoot, isn't a good idea. She regains her balance and finally sees that the face, which looks like it's floating in darkness, disembodied, isn't a real face. It's just a canvas propped up on an easel. Another painting of Isabella.

Eve comes closer and inspects it. There are Isabella's familiar features, the pale, foxlike face, the green eyes. But the rest of it dissolves into sfumato. When she leans closer, she sees that the edges of the canvas are blank, untouched by brush or paint.

Eve is both fascinated and repulsed. That's not how paintings are made. Who would paint the center with such detail and leave the rest for later?

Eve reaches out gingerly and her fingertips brush the surface of the paint.

Still soft.

She pulls her hand away like she touched acid.

"What the hell is going on?" she yelps, and her voice echoes nightmarishly, bouncing off the walls. She stumbles forward, and that's when she sees the body.

Eve freezes, unable to force herself to move. The dark figure is lying on a piece of cloth on the floor, wearing what she at first thinks is a long, black Victorian mourning gown. She can see the glint of her gray hair. The hands are veiny and claw-like, folded on her chest, and Eve can tell that they belong to someone in her eighties. There's a ring on the right hand, which is an oversized skull with red rhinestones for eyes. The ring, too, looks like she's seen it somewhere before.

Then she remembers. She's seen it in Alexa's selfies on Insta.

This is her ring.

This is…Alexa.

The only clear thought in Eve's mind is, *I have to get the hell out of here.*

Isabella on the other side of that door suddenly seems like something she can handle. She spins around with the intention to run as fast as she can.

Right in front of her, the shadows move.

THIRTY-FIVE

"HOW DID YOU GET IN HERE?" EVE HISSES.

"Keep your voice down. You're Eve, right?" Once he throws off the hoodie of his black sweatshirt, the guy looks familiar. It's not hard to guess that this is Nick Swain, the heartthrob.

"And you know that how?"

"The same way anyone knows anything. Instagram."

"Oh." That doesn't explain what he's doing here, though.

"Listen, Eve—"

"Does Isa know you're here?"

He looks bitter. "I'm not sure Isa is aware of much of anything right now. The house sure is, though. I think I'm trapped too. I can't get past the first couple of stairs no matter how I try."

What is he on about? Eve briefly wonders if he, too, has gone bonkers. Then again, with everything she's already seen—

"And I'm starting to think that only you can save her," Nick says.

"Me?"

"You're the only one this house hasn't yet sunk its claws into. And that's why you're here, aren't you?"

Eve gives a weak nod. "How long have you been hiding here?"

He shrugs. "I think—it must be days. And I think I might have figured out how to undo all this."

Eve gulps. He continues:

"What you have to do is get upstairs, to the fourth floor. Concealed behind the portrait room is another room. It's where Isabella stashed away all her many mirrors after she was disfigured. That room—it's the epicenter of everything. The heart of the house, where Isabella is the most powerful. She's never been able to let go of her faded glory, not even in death, and she lives in the house, in the mirrors and the portraits. She feeds on any girls who wander in here, consuming their youth and vitality. That's what happened to Desiree. My cousin. The house lured her in and destroyed her."

"But not Isa?"

"It's different with Isa. Eventually Isabella won't be able to sustain herself anymore—and now she's found a way to leave the house altogether, to go out into the real world again, by using her new host."

Eve is filled with panic.

"But how do I find the mirror room?"

"There might be a way. Come on."

He advances toward the stairs that lead back up into the kitchen. Hesitant, Eve waits a beat too long to follow.

"Are you just going to stay there until you get repurposed into another painting? Like Alexa?" he snarls over his shoulder. Eve starts after him without another word.

When they make it up the stairs and through the trapdoor, the kitchen is empty. A cold draft sweeps through the vast space. The door stands ajar.

Nick curses under his breath.

A voice startles them both, seemingly out of nowhere. "Oh, wow. Do forgive me, I didn't realize a gentleman was in attendance, or I would've worn something less drab."

Eve can't help it—she shrieks when the silhouette of one of the girls appears in the doorway, seemingly out of thin air. This isn't Isa, just one of the imitators. What was her name again?

"Get out of the way, Emma," Nick says. Well, that answers her question. Emma looks indifferent.

"Oh, Nicky. You've never been good at dealing with rejection. Isabella doesn't want you. Take a hint."

"If anyone here has to take a hint, it's you," Nick says with a sneer. "You're only here because Ines screwed up. But, as soon as you displease Isabella, you'll end up just like Ines, if not worse. Get out while you still can."

Emma raises her chin. The glint in her eyes is frightening.

"Isabella rewards loyalty," she says. Her voice crackles, notes of an almost animal-like growl breaking through. "Not exactly your biggest strength, Nick Swain."

"At least I'm not a brainwashed bootlicker like you."

Emma screams. Before Eve can react or even close her eyes, the girl lunges at them and wraps her hands around Nick's throat. She's much smaller than him, and skinny, but, somehow, she manages to knock him off his feet. They roll across the floor as she claws at his face and he frantically tries to throw her off.

Eve blinks out of her stupor. In a few bounds she crosses the kitchen to the ancient, unused hearth at the other end. It's boarded up, but, next to it, a few heavy-looking metal pokers still hang on the wall. Without thinking too much, she grabs one. It's covered in many years' worth of dust, but it feels slick in her sweaty hand, and so heavy she can barely lift it.

Nick screams. Eve swings the poker and hits Emma square on the side of the head, the impact so much more powerful than Eve intended that she squeezes her eyes shut, horrified. The poker slips from her grasp and clatters to the floor.

When she opens her eyes, Nick is struggling to get back on his feet, still grasping at his throat. Crimson scratches crisscross his face. "Damn," he chokes out.

Emma is sprawled on the kitchen floor, motionless. Eve doesn't dare look at her face.

"Is she—dead?" she stammers.

Nick spits on the floor. "I can only hope."

"Nick, this isn't just a mindless drone of Isabella's. This is a girl, just like me, and—and Isa. And I might have killed her."

"Look, if we don't get you to that mirror room soon enough, it won't matter," he says. "So let's go."

Eve quickly scans the kitchen and picks up a marble rolling pin, which she tucks under her armpit.

She follows him out into the hall.

The fresco overhead is static once again, Isabella's face frozen in a smirk.

"Where do I go?" she asks Nick. "I bet they're waiting for me at the top of the staircase."

He shrugs, his expression grim. "We'll just have to fight our way through."

Eve draws a shuddering breath.

"Thank you," he says suddenly, out of nowhere. "For saving my life. And for coming here to save Isa. You're a real friend."

To her shock, she manages a small giggle. "You know what, Nick Swain? I'm starting to understand why Isa had such a crush on you."

He breaks into a grin, and, for a moment, Eve has time to wonder if she's spilled a secret.

Something moves behind him. Eve only has time to see a shadowy blur and to shout out a warning.

A moment later, the chimney poker slices through the air inches from Nick's face. He spins around and barely has time to block it with his forearm. There's a sickening crunch, and he cries out in pain, nearly losing his balance.

Behind him, Eve recognizes the skinny silhouette of Emma. Half her face is crushed inward like a broken doll, but, somehow, she's grinning with broken, bloodied teeth.

"You didn't think it was that easy, did you? Isabella rewards loyalty."

Her words are as mangled as her face, but Eve understands everything.

"And now it's your turn."

Nick takes a swing at her with his good arm and hits her in the stomach. Eve can see that this doesn't really hurt her, but still, she stumbles back, loses her focus for a crucial second.

"Eve!" Nick yells. "Run! I'll hold her off. Save Isa."

With a low growl, Emma charges him, poker aloft.

Eve turns around and runs. She pauses for only a fraction of a moment, turning around just long enough to see Nick on the floor, Emma standing over him. She raises the poker, its pointed end aimed into the dead center of his chest.

She darts behind the door frame just as Emma brings it down.

THIRTY-SIX

IF SHE WANTS TO SAVE ISA, EVE NEEDS TO GET TO THE
heart of the house, to destroy whatever it is that allows Isabella to
control everyone.

The mirror room.

As if on cue, the scratchy music starts up again. Only now it's not
jazz, it's a pompous, overwrought classical piece.

Eve darts into the next room, away from Emma. She finds herself
in the living room, and it's immediately clear the Brixtons didn't use it
much. The floor is covered with an undisturbed coating of gray dust,
and some of the furniture is still covered in tarp. And no wonder: it's
hard to feel at home in a room like this. At least for a normal person
who doesn't think she's a turn-of-the-century socialite. It's enormous,

and way too ornate for anyone's taste in the current year. There's just too much of everything: too many moldings, too much gilt, the wallpaper is too busy with its pattern of flowers and peacocks and swans. It's obvious to Eve she won't find anything useful here, so she moves on.

The next room is a dining room, even less used than the previous one. Eve supposes everyone's been eating in the kitchen lately. The table is big enough for at least thirty people. It's uncovered, and the little place mats Taylor must have bought, with a pattern of fruit on them, look silly and out of place at the farthest end. Three of the chairs are also uncovered, the rest sitting under tarps. They're upholstered in velvet, Louis XV–style, and tacky as hell. There are more gas lamps on the wall. Eve approaches one. It's a pretty, Art Deco-style design: the lamp itself must have been made to look like a flower. But, since the glass lampshade is gone, all that's left is the stem. Eve turns the switch, but nothing happens—at least at first. A moment later, she gets a strong whiff of gas that makes her eyes water, and she quickly turns off the switch. These would probably have needed to be individually ignited by servants. Not too convenient.

She circles the room. There are no paintings here. A couple of rectangles on the walls, but the paintings that once occupied the spot are nowhere to be seen. Up in the portrait room, Eve guesses.

As she looks closer at the squares of wainscoting, the last panel catches her eye. She knocks tentatively, and the sound is hollow. She presses gently on the door, and an unseen spring opens it with a creak.

Eve peers inside with a feeling of dread. But all she sees is a flight of stairs going up. No ornaments, for once. Just plain wooden stairs and blank walls.

It's the servants' staircase, she realizes. The one they'd use when called by the mistress of the house, to keep themselves discreet. Because god forbid a lowly servant tread on those beautiful marble stairs the guests can see.

This means that Isabella probably had little idea it even existed.

Eve races up the stairs. They're so steep that, by the time she reaches the first landing, she's breathless. But, when she peers out the door, she sees the second-floor hallway stretching out into semidarkness.

Her heart beats excitedly. For the first time, she feels something like hope. She jumps over two stairs at a time to get to the last floor and peers out into the fourth-floor hallway.

The music is loud. She slips out and shuts the door behind her. The portrait room is open, but she can't see Isabella anywhere.

Eve advances toward the open double doors, then peers in. The room looks empty. Except for the portraits that smirk at her from the walls.

"There you are," says a cheerful voice. Eve turns around to find herself face-to-face with the other girl, Sara.

The best I can do is play dumb, she thinks. She gives Sara her best theater smile. "Hi!" she says brightly. "I'm looking for Isa. This place is so huge I have no idea where I am."

"Good," says Sara. Eve can't tell if she's buying it or not. "Because Isabella's been looking for you."

Well, that bodes well.

Sara hands her a glass. Damn, Eve had forgotten about it. The green beverage still looks nauseating, a rainbow-colored film floating on top. "Drink," she says.

"I kind of don't want to. I already had too much." Eve tries to make it sound lighthearted, but Sara's soulless eyes stare right into her soul.

"Drink."

Eve knocks the glass out of her hand. It flies across the room, the liquid making a wide green arch in the air, and crashes to the floor, shattering.

Sara lunges for her with an angry shriek. Eve struggles, gives her a powerful shove, and sends her flying backward.

As Eve watches, Sara crashes right into the largest painting, the one of Isabella in the burgundy dress. The frame falls from the wall and shatters when it hits the floor. Eve hears a sickening tearing sound as the canvas rips down the center, severing Isabella's hand from her body and stopping halfway up the side of her face.

Sara collapses to the floor and doesn't get up. A horrible shrieking fills the room. It's not coming from the painting or Sara but from everywhere at once. Sara begins to convulse on the floor like she's having a seizure.

There might not be another chance, Eve thinks. She crosses the room in a few leaps, ducks into the storage room, and throws open the door into the mirror room.

Except these are no mirrors. In every reflective surface, Isabella is screaming. It's the young Isabella, from the portraits, but her beautiful face is distorted in a grimace of all-consuming rage and hatred. Darkness ripples through the mirrors like billows of ink in water.

Eve raises the rolling pin, which feels alarmingly loose in her sweat-slicked hands, and smashes the nearest mirror.

Shards go flying in all directions, and she barely has time to shield her eyes. They shred the back of her hands, blood running into her sleeves. She raises the rolling pin again and smashes another mirror.

Isabella's face changes. It's a deterioration so quick it all happens within seconds: the skin sags and turns crepey, the hair thins and grays, the hands turn skeletal.

And then it accelerates.

Half her skin melts off, leaving two holes where her nose should be, and her hair is gone on the burnt side, only tufts of gray and pale red sticking out haphazardly from the deformed flesh. Overcoming her terror, Eve smashes another mirror, then another.

The screaming becomes deafening. Eve can no longer tell the difference between the inhuman screech and the sound of breaking glass. When she's done, only a few pieces of mirror cling to some of the frames. She's panting. She can feel the cuts on her face, which sting like hell.

Time to get out of here.

But, first, she has to find Isa.

As she exits what used to be the mirror room, Isa is nowhere to be seen. Sara is still convulsing on the floor underneath the ruined painting. When Eve dares look, all she has time to glimpse is a flash of grayed hair and Sara's face, withering away in front of Eve's eyes, the flesh collapsing in on itself. The painting flaps around grotesquely, thin, ghostly threads of paint desperately trying to stitch themselves together.

Too little, too late.

Eve leaves Sara there and runs down the hall, stopping only at the gas lamps. She flips one switch, then another, and the soft hiss of escaping gas fills the air.

"Isa!" Eve yells out. No answer. "Isa, where are you?"

She makes it as far as the stairs when she sees a familiar silhouette and grinds to a halt. Emma has her back to Eve but Eve has no trouble recognizing her. At this angle, you almost can't see the mangled half of her face. She turns around slowly, and Eve realizes she's holding a large piece of a broken mirror in her hands. She holds it up, tilting her head as she examines her reflection.

Eve doesn't dare draw a breath, but Emma hardly seems to notice she's there.

"It's all over," she says, her voice perfectly normal and brimming with deep sadness. "It's all gone."

Under Eve's horrified gaze, she raises the piece of silvered glass and plunges it into her throat, grinding it in deeper and deeper.

Eve snaps back to reality and races down the stairs, trips, and rolls all the way down to the third-floor landing where she collapses in a heap, panting, dazed by the pain in her sides. When her vision stops swimming, she looks up to see no trace of Emma except for a giant bloodstain at the top of the stairs.

"Looking for me?"

The voice comes from the hallway. Eve scrambles to her feet. She's lost the rolling pin and has nothing to defend herself with. Isabella is standing in the middle of the hall, and one look tells Eve that it's very much still Isabella. It's Isa, yet it isn't. She looks older, meaner, and her eyes are still that dazzling shade of green.

"You're wasting your time, Eve," Isabella says smoothly. "You really thought you could hurt my house and get out alive? You won't make it."

"But at least you'll be dead too."

Isabella laughs. It's no longer silvery but demented and demonic. "This is where you're mistaken."

She raises her hand, and something glints in her clenched fist. A blade? Eve backs away as Isabella swings it at her head.

"Isa!" she screams. "I know you're in there. Stop her!"

"Isa is gone," Isabella snaps. Her voice warbles, distorted like a bad record. "She was weak. I'm something much better now."

She takes another swing at Eve's face, but Eve grabs her wrist in midair. She twists with all her might, sinking her fingernails into Isabella's skin.

"You're not worthy of doing Isa's laundry," Eve hisses. "You hideous bitch."

Isabella cries out, and her grip on the blade loosens. Eve wrestles it away from her—it's not a knife but a silver letter opener with an ornate handle. Isabella snarls and tries to make a grab for it. Eve swings her arm and the blade connects with skin.

It slices neatly right across Isabella's cheek. The cut is shallow, Eve can see, but big droplets of blood well up immediately.

A gasp escapes from Isabella, a truly horrifying sound like the last breath leaving a body. She clasps her hand over the injury, blood seeping through her fingers. Her knees buckle, and she sinks to the floor, her expression empty and blank. The green in her eyes falters and flickers, giving way to the normal pale blue.

"Isa!" Eve dives to the floor and threads her arm around her friend. "Isa, can you hear me?"

Isabella—Isa?—blinks slowly. "We have to hurry," she says, and her voice is once again normal Isa's voice. "The injury to her face—it only stunned her. She's still traumatized by being burned in the fire. But she'll be back."

"What do we do?" Eve asks.

"You have to leave me and go."

She helps Isa get back on her feet. "Absolutely not."

"I—I think it's the only way." Isa's voice is terribly small and full of sorrow.

"No. I've released the gas from the stove and the lamps. The place is about to catch fire. We're getting out."

"All the doors are locked," Isa says.

"But we have to try."

Eve drags Isa down the hall, back toward the stairs. Three floors down, and then she has to find a way to get the doors open and to haul them both out before the house explodes.

Isa trembles. Eve glances at her, and, panicked, sees her eyes flicker to green once again. Isa gives a violent shake of her head.

There's a whiff of natural gas in the air.

There's no time.

Eve drags her to the nearest room—Samuel's studio—and shuts the door behind them. The safe door is half-closed.

It's a door, and a door can be many things.

Eve lets Isa sink to the floor and throws her entire weight against the safe door. With a groan, it opens all the way.

Inside, there's no safe. There's only a passage, dark and empty and seemingly endless.

"Isa!" Eve yells. "Come on!"

But Isa is shaking violently. Her face blurs, then regains focus, then blurs again.

Isabella, Isa, Isabella.

Eve's fresh out of options. She grabs Isa and pulls her along into the safe that never was. The tunnel angles down, steep, and, within moments, Eve loses her balance. She and Isa tumble down, into the darkness—

—and then there's a rush of cold and fresh air. Eve collapses into a pristine expanse of glittering snow, headfirst, gasping. At first she's disoriented, flailing around in the waist-deep snowbank as she struggles to regain her footing.

Isa is in the snowbank next to her. She seems to be unconscious.

"Isa!" Eve cries out, but all that gorgeous, fresh snow muffles her voice. "Isa! We did it!"

Isa's eyes open. She's looking up, and at first, Eve isn't sure if the blue is the color of her irises, or just the reflection of the dark sky.

And, a moment later, the house goes up in flames.

FIRE, EXPLOSION IN HISTORIC MANSION NEAR AMORY UNIVERSITY

A series of truly baffling, not-yet-explained events near Amory University culminated in an even more bizarre fire and explosion last week. The tragic event claimed the lives of several students from the local high school as well as several others who have not yet been identified.

The house, the historic mansion that once belonged to socialite Isabella Granger, has been university property for decades and represented an important part of the city's cultural heritage.

The investigation concluded that the fire was a result of a faulty gas duct.

It was occupied at the time by the family of one of Amory's professors. The professor as well as her husband were away at the time of the fire, and their daughter made it out safely. The family asks for privacy at this difficult time.

TURN-OF-THE-CENTURY ARTIST MUSE HOUSE DESTROYED

The Isabella Granger House in Amory, Mass., became the site of a life-and-death drama last week when firefighters received a call about an explosion and a fire. The house burned to the ground, and all the priceless artworks within it have presumably been destroyed and are lost to us for good.

Or are they?

Don't you fret, my darlings! Luckily, we live in the internet age when nothing truly disappears. Dozens, maybe hundreds of photos and paintings of Isabella Granger survive online. The great artist's model can live on forever and ever on the internet and social media.

But don't take our word for it! One of our staff found an incredible Instagram account supposedly belonging to the girl who used to live in the house. (She's fine, by the way, although neither she nor her family responded to our requests for comment.) Project Isabella brings the enigmatic socialite—about whom so little is known, to shame!—back to life, along with her era. The pics are truly incredible. They capture the spirit of a time lost with an impeccable sense of beauty and aesthetic.

Here's our selection of the best of Project Isabella. This Edwardian diva was the inspiration to so many great minds— who knows what she'll inspire in you!

ACKNOWLEDGMENTS

First, thank you to my agent Rachel Ekstrom Courage and everyone at Folio Literary Management. Also huge thanks to Adam Wilson and Ruth Pomerance.

Thank you to the team at Sourcebooks for your enthusiasm, excitement, and hard work on this project! Heartfelt thanks especially to Molly Cusick, Wendy McClure, Meaghan Summers, Cassie Gutman, Danielle McNaughton, and Casey Moses.

And finally, thank you to my lovely family for always being there for me.

ABOUT THE AUTHOR

Nina Laurin studied creative writing at Concordia University in Montreal, where she currently lives. She arrived there when she was just twelve years old, and she speaks and reads in Russian, French, and English. She is the bestselling author of the adult suspense novels *Girl Last Seen*, *What My Sister Knew*, and *The Starter Wife*. Nina is fascinated by the darker side of mundane things, and she's always on the lookout for her next twisted book idea.

FIREreads

#getbooklit

Your hub for the hottest young adult books!

Visit us online and sign up for our
newsletter at FIREreads.com

 @sourcebooksfire

 sourcebooksfire

 firereads.tumblr.com